THIEF OF DESTINY

THIEF OF DESTINY

The Saga of the Panther

JAY REQUARD

Falstaff Books

ACKNOWLEDGEMENTS

Thanks to Melissa Gilbert of Clicking Keys for all her help in bringing this project to life.

Thanks to James R. Tuck for his awesome covers.

THIEF OF SHADOWS

THE GEM OF ACITUS

MANWE LEAPT FOR THE UPPER BALCONY, HIS HAND OUTSTRETCHED TO CATCH
the small length of rope he had tied to the platform's façade the previous night.
No longer than a foot, the hemp cord dug splinters into his palm, drawing a
hiss of pain.

He dangled in the air. Muscles screamed in agony, braced on the point
between snapped tendons and dislocated joints. Forcing himself not to let go,
Manwe checked the gardens below him. Guards decked in iron breastplates
and horsehair-crested helms roamed the edges of the hedgerows, unaware of
the intruder to their master's home. Their spears glinted in the light of the
braziers set on a red clay patio, the only light save for the stars in a pitch sky.

Manwe slowly pulled himself up, one hand at a time until he found purchase
on the balcony rail. He vaulted to the other side, his body beaded in sweat.

Through the arched doorway a lavish bedroom waited, its cool shadows
calling him to leave the balmy warmth of the summer night. He slipped inside
the house, crouched, and allowed his eyes to adjust to the deeper darkness.

A young woman slept naked on the wide bed, her white body swaddled in
thin sheets of silk. Ringlets of black hair framed her supple breasts.

He paid her little attention as he passed by, drawing a small pick from the
linen cloth tied around his wrist. Manwe squatted in front of a chest on the
far wall, prodding the lock near its hinge. Two tumblers clicked in unison.
Taking a small file, he inserted it into the key slot and slowly turned it. The lock
opened with a sharp pop.

Manwe lifted the lid, and there it sat: The Gem of Acitus. An emerald worn
by some of history's greatest conquerors, its green facets sparkled with promise
of wealth. Cushioned upon a large pillow of red satin, it was the only thing in
the chest, the immediate sign of a trap.

He eyed a line of sharp iron running along the inside of the lid to a wire
near the chest's hinge that stretched down the side and underneath the pillow.
If he lifted the gem, the lid would snap and take his hand.

"Is it worth it?"

Manwe spun to one of the room's corners, where the darkness was the deepest.

The girl had sat up in her bed. A slight grin curved her pouty lips.

He slowly rose, taking his hand off the knife stuck in the rear band of his loincloth. "Why aren't you calling the guard?"

"I'm curious." She crawled forward on her feather mattress, the outline of her body revealed in the low light of the nighttime ambiance. "It's not every day I meet a burglar."

"Aren't you frightened?"

"No." She rolled onto her back, on full display. "So how are you going to do it? How do you get past the trap?"

"How indeed…" Manwe looked around the room and spotted a strange wooden pole near the door. Three pieces of ivory tusk stuck out from the top like a crown, and on one of these horns hung a delicate cloak of green silk. "What's that?"

"That? Some odd ornament some tribal elder gave my father in tribute. We didn't know what to do with it until I hung a cloak on it one day. They're now the craze in Gypus."

"A waste of good tusks." He retrieved the strange piece of furniture. Rolling its heavy weight in both hands, he walked back to the chest. "A waste of good ebony, too."

"Why is that?" she asked.

"You'll see." Manwe propped the stand on the edge of the chest. The girl gasped as he thrust his right hand into the box and lifted the gem from the pillow. The wire warped as it broke, the lid snapping down. The sharp edge chopped into the dark wood of the stand, levering its entire length off the floor.

Manwe slipped his hand out. He held the gem up to show her, his smile wide.

She giggled, clapping her hands. "So you must be The Panther. Tolivius' best thief has come to my home."

"Correction. The greatest thief has come to your house. And you've been a wonderful audience." He dipped for a slight bow and headed for the balcony.

"Wait," she called after him.

Manwe stopped in the doorway.

The tip of her tongue probed the edge of her lips, and dark eyes gleamed in lust. "Is that all you're going to take?" she asked. "There are still treasures in this room."

"And yet I only came for this one." He laughed at her wounded expression as he left.

MANWE SAT ON THE WIDE BRANCH OF THE JACKALBERRY TREE, HIS BACK PRESSED against its massive gray trunk. He swung his feet as the morning sun emerged on the horizon. Orange light bled into the sky to banish darkness from the earth's face, revealing the endless grassland dotted with forests of scrub trees. Umbrella-thorns waved at the sunrise as the wind moved their bright green boughs.

The way the trees swayed, the brush of the air against his bare chest, the song of the birds—the savannah was his piece of the goddess, a treasure beyond anything he could ever steal. The outline of Tolivius, the city the Gypians had built long ago when they conquered his people, also sat on that same horizon. The only piece of civilization for miles, the sight of the metropolis was the lone damper of his joy.

He looked down at the gem in his lap. One day, one bauble at a time, that city wouldn't be there.

Out of the corner of his eye rose a line of dust in the distance, a rider charging through on route to Manwe's tree. Tall and handsome, his linen tunic buffeted against his wiry frame as he dug his heels into the sides of his dappled mare. Drawing up to the jackalberry, he slid off the saddle and let the beast carry off into the grass.

"Do you have it?" the man called from the ground, his eyes brown and bright.

"What's the passphrase?"

"Oh come, Manwe," the rider said, hands on his hips. "You know me."

"And you know we are supposed to say a passphrase before the start of all business."

"Fine, fine. 'Hippo'."

Manwe gave him a wink. "Get up here, Toba. I have it."

"You have actually Acitus' emerald?" Toba scurried up the tree, finding the natural handholds in the ridges and bark. He climbed onto the same branch as Manwe and sat in front of him. "Let me see!"

Manwe held up the gem to let the sunlight glitter in its facets, refracting verdant beams that dappled the space between them.

Toba gaped in amazement. "May I?"

"Of course." Manwe placed it in the center of his palm. "You're going to fence it, after all."

"And the gold I shall get," he said, mesmerized. He closed his fingers around the gem. "Did you run into any trouble?"

"Nothing worth mentioning."

"And there were no other problems?"

"Nothing." Manwe eyed him warily. "Why? What have you heard?"

Toba shook his head and tucked the gem into his shirt. "Nothing at all. I just imagined this job would be harder than it was."

"So how much gold do you think you can get?"

"For the Gem of Acitus?" Toba grinned and glanced toward Tolivius, now gleaming white as the morning struck its high walls and thin towers. "I can probably get five thousand drachi for it. I'm sure that the Gypian you stole it from will have his men out looking for it, but the buyer was adamant."

"Make sure three-quarters go to your brother first. We'll split the rest."

"Are you sure you don't want a bigger cut?"

Manwe sniffed and leaned forward. "No. Spears and shields for the people, pleasures second."

"You know he wants to meet you," Toba said. "Kosey tells his men and women about 'The Panther.' He's building a legend."

"Then it is better that we don't meet at all. The less he knows, the safer I am, and the less I know, the safer the cause."

"Fine, fine. Keep your secrets."

The two sat in silence. The wind roared as it swept over the savannah. A herd of blue wildebeests emerged from the grove below and ambled off slowly in the direction of a nearby pond. The smaller ones charged ahead of the adults while the older ones, their heads hung low under the weight of their large black horns, sauntered behind.

"I should go," said Toba. He held up a hand to Manwe, the fingers spread apart.

Manwe took hold, his fingers laced with his lover's.

TOBA NEVER RETURNED WITH THEIR PAYMENT.

Manwe left his tree three days later, taking the dirt highway north instead of slinking his way through the wilds of the plain. The sun was high in the noon sky when he made it to Tolivius' iron gates, its stone frame carved in the reliefs of great elephants. He hid his sneer as he passed by the guards posted in the long tunnel to the city's proper, drawing his beet-red cloak around his shoulders to conceal the knife tucked in the twisted band of his loincloth.

The streets were stained with the ruin of the "civilized." The poor huddled in the mouths of alleys, their bowls and cups held out for any alms a passerby might give them. A few were lepers, their skin spotted and crusted with lesions, who lay crumpled against the corners of buildings as they struggled to beg through the pain. A few were even children, orphans left to wander alleys where they were hunted by those larger and more lecherous.

In Tolivius' temple district was a brothel run by the priestesses of Hertathia, the Gypian goddess of the night and lovers. A small set of stone steps behind the main temple led down to the establishment, a place frequented by many of the thieving world's fences when they had the coin to spare.

He knocked four times on the olive-wood door.

A viewing slot slid open, and a pair of dark blue eyes lined in black gazed out at him. "What is the goddess' secret?"

"The goddess has no secrets," Manwe answered.

The slot shut and the door cracked open. A buxom woman with white skin and blonde hair, an exotic creature in a city of olive hues and wine brown skins, welcomed him inside. Transparent pieces of blue silk covered her breasts and groin, supported by thin chains of brass around her neck and hips.

"Welcome, Panther," she greeted, bowing her head slightly. "I did not imagine you would be visiting today. Come for the pleasures?"

The first chamber of the brothel lay before Manwe. Oil lamps lit the walls in warmth, fluttering red and blue banners draped the ceiling's edge. In one of the room's corners stood a statue of Hertathia herself, her voluptuous body bared to the flickering light as she held the moon up in her hands. Around her hung tapestries depicting every sort of position with every sort of partner, showing man and woman, man and man, woman and woman, and even the beasts of the far-off west in the midst of copulation.

"No, Magera," he said, refocusing on his task. "Is Sophicus here?"

"He's in the back." Magera adjusted the shift over her bosom. "Should I let him know you've come to call?"

"Has he paid you yet?"

"No. In fact, he increased his promissory notes for a later date. I had no choice but to let him in."

"No choice?"

"He brought his guards into this house of peace and serenity," she revealed. "To watch the door of his chamber in case his wife shows up again, of course. It is quite serendipitous you came today, now that I think about it. The goddess works her ways, no?"

Manwe nodded, treading farther into the carnal den. The second room was the public area, where an orgy of men, women, and boys commenced in a fervent tangle of twisted bodies, lost among the heat of the hot stones set in the center of the floor. Past the moans and through a third door was a short split hall that went off to the left and the right. Every few yards lay the door of a private chamber, a cozy bedroom well-off patrons could rent for the evening.

In the left wing, near the end of the passage, stood two tall Gypians dressed in patched tunics. Manwe strode toward them, his hands hidden under the folds of his red cloak.

The man to the right of the door moved to block the way. "Where are you going, kitty cat?"

Manwe looked up at him, placid against the guard's scowl. "I'm here to see Sophicus, Braeus."

"Nobody sees the boss right now," said the second guard, a gap-toothed fellow he knew as Tarsis. "He's busy."

"Not busy enough." Manwe stepped to the side.

Braeus thrust his arm out to bar the way. "Who do you think you—"

Manwe drove his knee into the guard's crotch, putting him on hands and knees. Tarsis lunged at Manwe, who shot his legs out behind him and sprawled, his full weight on the man's head and shoulders. Scooting back up to his feet, he held the Gypian's head in one hand and drove a palm into his large nose. Blood squirted as the second guard fell backward. Braeus, still clutching his groin, rose off his knees to be met with a hard cross to the jaw.

Leaving the two roughs on the floor, Manwe grabbed the handle of the chamber door and pushed it open.

Inside two women writhed on a pallet of linen and cotton, their oiled bodies gleaming in the light of the few lamps set on a tiny shelf. Sandwiched between them lay a man in the throes of ecstasy. Sweat beaded on his forehead as his hands groped and probed the two priestesses, their joined cries of pleasure growing.

Manwe cleared his throat.

"By Adias, can't you see—" Sophicus the Pretty sat up in bed, his mouth opening in protest when he saw who stood in the doorway. The two girls stopped as well, but did little to cover themselves from the gaze of the room's intruder.

"You two should go," Manwe said to them. Both complied without a word.

"I paid my donation for those girls, Panther," Sophicus said.

Manwe shut the door behind him. "No, you extended your credit. Too many times, if the lady of the house is to be believed."

"Braeus," he shouted. "Tarsis?"

"They're taking a break." Manwe stepped over the footboard of the bed and sat down on it, perched like a cat. "I thought the city's top fence and its best thief could chat in private."

"You're middling at best, these days. Revolutionaries don't make money," Sophicus retorted. "What do you want?"

"Where's Toba?"

Sophicus' anger faded, and he pulled a blanket across his lap to cover his genitals. "You should live here and not on those damned plains. You would've heard by now."

"Heard what?"

The Gypian's full lips bent a frown. "You stole too big, Panther. You should have taken the Gem of Acitus and nothing more."

Manwe furrowed his brow. "What are you talking about?"

"The man you stole the gem from. You raped his daughter."

"What?" Manwe shot to his feet. "What treachery is this?"

"That is the word of a Gypian woman, Panther. Her voice holds more weight than some thief's," Sophicus answered, his hand up to stop his advance. "Please. It's just what I heard."

Manwe searched the wall above Sophicus, at a loss for words against such a horrid accusation. "What happened?" he asked after a few moments, aware that something far worse might have already occurred.

Sophicus crossed his legs under his blanket, his elbows on his knees. "Apparently Toba went to take the gem to the buyer and hasn't been seen since. Some think the buyer's guards took him as a way to punish you. One dead Juutan is usually enough to sate us Gypians, in these cases. Count yourself lucky. I doubt anyone's coming after you now."

"Who was the buyer?"

Sophicus waved a finger at him. "A deal is between the fence and his buyer, and only between them. There are rules that not even I would break."

"But you know all the buyers, just as you know all the fences. You put the word out for them when they are looking for men like me." The dim light of the room caught the edge of Manwe's knife when he drew it out. "And it is just you and I in here."

"There are witnesses." Sophicus gulped behind his cocksure grin. "You'd be hunted."

"Did you know that you don't die immediately when your throat is cut? You spend the last few moments gasping for air…" Manwe crawled forward on hands and feet. "And all you hear is the blood bubbling in the wound."

"You've made your point," Sophicus said in a hurried manner, putting up a hand again to stop him. "It was the merchant, Leomachus."

"Where can I find him?"

"Ivory Row."

Manwe slinked off the bed. "Remember to pay your debts to Magera, Sophicus. Next time I won't be so charitable."

THE MANOR OF LEOMACHUS WAS NOT THE GRANDEST MANOR IN THE MERCHANT quarter, not that it mattered next to the fact that it sat in the middle of Ivory Row, where only the wealthiest lived in an area of the city known as Merchant's March. Situated near the northern wall, the square building made up for its lack of elegance and sophisticated design with the many guards patrolling its grounds, a better display of wealth than any gaudy construction or décor could ever convey. More than twenty men walked the perimeter behind the tall iron fence, their spears and shields covered in tar to dampen the reflection of the full moon.

In the southwestern corner of the estate grew a large marula, one of the few trees the Gypians had left when they settled the city. Manwe stood on one of the uppermost branches, tying the long bandages of undyed linen around his wrists. Within them he tucked the tools of his trade, a long iron file worn with use and a few lock picks, delicate lengths of hardened copper bent into all manner of shapes. Hidden behind the wall of thick green leaves and golden fruit, he waited as a pair of guards marched by, lost in conversation.

"Why are we here again?" the first one asked as he adjusted the crest of his helm. "We don't need to be out here, not with all the treasure inside."

"Will you just shut up and march?" said the second man. "We have a few hours and then we can go home."

"But what about all these extra hands? We'll have to split more of the pouch with them."

"Money's money. I'd rather have three coins in my pocket than none."

The pair turned the corner of a thick hedgerow separating the middle of the garden. Manwe dropped from the branch and ran for the wall. His fingers found purchase on a window sill, and after pulling himself up, he drew his knife. He stuck the blade in the gap between two panels of wooden lattice and unlatched the bar.

He slipped into a dark kitchen. The only source of light lay at the other end of the room, where a red clay oven lay open its mouth of embers.

The lone door popped open, forcing Manwe to hide under a preparation table. A dark-skinned servant stepped inside, humming a pleasant tune. He stopped before the oven and raked the coals. After a moment more, he left.

Manwe broke cover and approached the portal. Pushing it open a crack, he spied through the gap an empty hallway. He entered the hall and headed left.

The silence of the night, the oily lines of smoke of the torches, the lack of guards inside Leomachus' halls—none of it was right. There should have been sentries on patrol like the two guards outside had said there would be, but none appeared or stood watch outside the many rooms of the manor. Manwe came to a junction where the hall intersected another, a shorter passage that ended at an open vault.

A stand made of white marble rose in the center of the small chamber, and upon it rested a familiar red satin pillow. Nestled in the middle, the Gem of Acitus shone in the light of the many oil lamps set on the single shelf built into the room's walls, its green facets mocking and cruel.

"This is clearly a trap," Manwe said aloud. Men surged into the hall behind him, their spears at the ready. Standing shoulder to shoulder, they blocked the way, leaving no avenue of escape.

"Not a trap," said a strong, confident voice. A short man stepped into the doorway of the gem's room, draped in a length of light blue cloth. Streaks of silver peppered his beard, and a dark mane framed a wide head and thick cheekbones. "For what wise man tries to capture a wild beast?"

"And yet the beast has not been slain. The hunter has reasons for not releasing his arrow," Manwe said, finishing the old Juutan axiom. "You must be Leomachus."

"And you are a grand thief, sir." The merchant bowed with a flourish. "It pleases me to no end to meet you."

"You knew I was coming?"

"Of course," Leomachus said with a grin, his teeth too large for his mouth.

"With the rumors of your rape of Gonius' daughter and the disappearance of your fence, I knew it was only time before you came to my door."

"I didn't rape that girl," Manwe said.

Leomachus entered the hall. "Oh, I know, but the promise of marriage to my third son is enough to keep the lie on her tongue. After all, such a stain on her reputation…" He came to stand before Manwe, his hands held out at his sides. "Would you like some wine?"

"For a man so close to death, you're a fine host," said Manwe, tensed to attack.

The guards in the hall shuffled, but Leomachus signaled them to stop. "I try." The merchant waved for him to come along, and after a brief pause, Manwe followed.

He and his host let the guards lead them to Leomachus' grand sitting room in the middle of his manor, a common feature in most merchants' homes. Fat pillows made of colored silk lay on the floor around a square table, and set on its polished face was a silver carafe and two goblets.

"Please, sit." Leomachus picked up the carafe. "It is actually quite cool in here tonight."

Manwe watched the wine flow, red and fragrant, as the merchant filled both goblets. "Where's Toba?"

Leomachus slid one of the goblets across the table to him as he sat. "I lost him."

Manwe felt his eye twitch. "You lost him?"

"Please, don't start," said Leomachus, taking his first sip and swallowing. "If you hadn't been caught by the girl, we wouldn't be here now. Your shoddy work made this happen."

"I couldn't predict that she would even be there. I'm a thief, not a bone-reader," he said, gripping his knees. "And you have your gem."

"No, I don't."

"I just saw it in that room."

"A fake." Leomachus swirled the wine in his cup. "A good fake, as long it keeps those thinking I have the real one occupied. That girl who caught you was to be married off to the son of another merchant with the gem as her dowry. I know that merchant, and that old fool would've put it in a vault and leered at it until the day he died. I have better plans."

"And yet you've thrown the bauble out."

Leomachus snorted his disappointment. "Apparently Toba's pockets were deeper than my men could dig through."

Disgusted by the Gypian's flippancy, Manwe focused. "Why all this for a gem?"

"It is more than just a gem, and you know that. The Gem of Acitus sat in the crown of my people's greatest emperor. It is a part of our history, and for years it has passed through the hands of the merchants, treated as nothing more than a trinket to be traded and ogled. It could be used better."

"And you are the one who'd use it," Manwe surmised.

"You are smarter than most of your race, Panther."

"My race has nothing to do with my intelligence. So if not gold or honor, what more can the gem give you?"

"Power." His host refreshed his drink. "Imagine how grateful Gypus' king would be if one of his citizens, a lowly merchant from this backwater city, returned one of history's most prized treasures out of the goodness of his heart."

"He'd make you a lord, and not just in name."

Leomachus snapped his fingers. "Exactly. And this has brought me to felicity. You want your friend and the gold promised to you, and I can remedy those nasty rumors. All you need is to find that gem again."

"Toba has the gem on him. Is he alive?" Manwe repeated, stressing for a real answer.

His host, and now his employer once again, looked over the rim of his goblet. "Whether he is alive is not the question you should worry about. What you should worry over is where he is."

◆

To THE NATIVE TRIBES THAT INHABITED THE SAVANNAH, IT WAS CALLED "THE Mouth of the Mother."

A gaping void in the ground, many believed it led to a place between the living world and the land of the dead, where the gods welcomed the souls of good people before they were sent to their ancestors in a blessed realm. Those

16

who led lives of vice and evil, however, were left tortured in its darkness, torn apart so their essence could be planted back into the soil, where they hopefully grew into something more worthwhile.

Yet to the Gypians this hole was not a sacred place, but just another pit to throw criminals, whether they were dead or not.

They gave it a simpler name: The Maw.

Manwe stood at its edge. Dawn had not come yet, but even in the time between the last twinkle of the stars and the warming of the horizon, the hole seemed blacker than death, a portal to an abode where only the hellish reigned. He had hammered an iron stake into the earth a few feet away and tied to its head a thick rope, long enough to take him to the bottom. He knew the legends spoke of endless tunnels, of the beasts that had fallen in and became more savage without the sunlight, and tales of weird magicks shamans had brought back from the shadows.

He descended down to the stone floor of the mouth and pulled a torch from the band of his loincloth, along with his knife and a piece of flint. After a few minutes, the oiled cloth wrapped around the end of the stick caught fire.

Scattered on the floor were the bones of the dead, touched by warmth for the first time in centuries. Shadows clung to the backs of mountains made of skulls, gathering in the voids of their eyes. It was then Manwe realized how great the space was around him, less the bottom of a hole, and more a cavern. Rock formations melted off the ceiling in glittering stalactites.

"Toba?" Manwe called. He remained staked on the spot, waiting for an echo to return. Even the weight of the knife in his hand did little to calm the frantic beat of his heart. The rope still hung behind him, the last tether to the surface and the sun.

On he went into the bowels of the earth. The way narrowed and widened, diminished and grew, never once a clear path even with his bit of light.

Manwe did not know how far he had gone when he heard a drone beat in the distance. It wasn't like the patting of a hand on stretched goat skin, but a knock, as if someone tapped a stick on a fence post. He went toward the sound. The passage snaked right for a long time before breaking hard to the left.

Around the next corner shuffled feet. Manwe tossed his torch back the way he came and stood perfectly still, shrouded in total darkness.

Four men carried a body by the arms and legs as they trod down the next hall. One of them, the leader, held up a torch to guide their way into the abyss. The white flames revealed his features, a brutish visage more apish than human, with his cheeks swollen and teeth sharpened to wedges.

Manwe could have only guessed at their actual skin tones, which was washed by the torch to the color of gray chalk. He stalked after the four and their captive, staying far enough behind so his own footsteps were lost in the noise of their march.

After a while they entered another cavern. Unlike the first, this one was not a space of pure darkness, but a wide cell lit by a great bonfire. Twenty men danced around the smoky blaze, hands above their heads as they spun and twirled in unison. A pair of percussionists on their own outcropping of rock banged ulnas on rows of skulls set out before them, continuing the rapid beat Manwe had first heard on the way to this hell.

Three corpses swung from the ceiling, their faces bloated purple and red from strangulation. The front of their bodies had been sliced open, allowing their viscera to fall down in great strands to be chewed on by the savages. The four men carrying their unconscious prisoner dumped him near the bonfire. The flames illuminated his face.

Toba, glassy-eyed and mumbling incoherently, convulsed in the throes of a horrified ecstasy. Powder covered his nose and mouth, a fine dust of yellow and green. A smaller man smeared in blood and dirt leapt from a hidden place and marched around him, his leering expression stretched wide as he paraded before the revelers. He held up the shard of a human rib in one hand, its point scraped into an edge. He shouted, and was answered by a chorus of disjointed chants.

Manwe looked from this witchdoctor back to the bodies hanging from the cave's ceiling, knowing what the creature had in mind. He slunk into the chamber and skirted around its perimeter, dodging behind wide stalagmites. The witchdoctor screamed as the drummers fell into frenzy, spinning on his heels with his cruel bone-knife high in the air.

Manwe ducked behind another low rock formation and stepped into a dark patch between two rough columns of granite.

The witchdoctor crouched over Toba. He raised his knife up one last time, shouting at the bodies above him.

The drums stopped and the blade came down.

Manwe bounded from the shadows, the edge of his knife blazing in the flames of the bonfire. Blood sprayed as he sliced open the witchdoctor's throat, knocking the wretch to the side. He gathered Toba in his arms and broke past the masses circled around them. They chased after him into the passage, crowding the narrow channel. Manwe collided with and bounced off the walls and corners until he could no longer hear the screams and growls of the cannibals behind him. When the silence grew steady, he stopped, hunkered down in a tunnel to listen for any sound.

Toba coughed, hacking bloody spit until it dribbled down his chin. "Manwe?"

"Shush, Toba," Manwe whispered, holding the fence's face. He brushed a thumb across his chapped lips. "Keep still. You're bleeding."

Toba shivered, his skin cold to the touch. "You came for me."

Manwe blinked, snatched back to reality. All worry of being caught, the darkness, the question of whether he would ever see the light again—it disappeared, replaced by his own failure. "I couldn't leave you. I would never leave you."

"I'm so sorry." Toba curled himself in Manwe's lap. "I should have been more careful."

Manwe rocked him gently. "It doesn't matter. I'll get you back to the light."

"I know you will."

They held each other until Toba gave away, his final breath a hiss. Manwe searched the corpse's tattered tunic and drew out the gem. He brought Toba close and, for the last time, kissed the lips of the only man he had ever loved.

LEOMACHUS ROLLED THE GIRL ONTO HER BACK, SPREADING HER LEGS. HER bright white body gleamed in the light of the lamps, the ringlets of her hair black and glossy.

For all his anger, Manwe stayed in the bedroom's darkened eave and let them consummate their lust, allowing for one final moment of security. He had stolen into the house hours before—he could wait a bit longer to savor revenge.

Gonius' daughter, the same girl who accused Manwe of rape, rolled atop the ugly merchant, moaning about how much better the father performed than her husband. Leomachus laughed as he held her bucking hips. Their joined climax came in a wild and untamed gasp, and the two collapsed on the mattress.

"Ah, my dear," said Leomachus, a hand on her breast, "You truly are wasted on my boy."

"Waste not, sighed not," she said, grinning lustily. "And you will still give me my part of the money when The Panther returns?"

"If he returns. For all I know the heathen will never rise from The Maw's darkness, lost like his idiot friend. Gem or not, I will be a lord one day, and you shall be basked in splendor."

"A lie is often sweeter than the truth." She scratched her nails across his hairy chest. "Just remember our deal."

The pair talked a bit more until Leomachus, exhausted from his release, fell into a deep sleep. Creeping from the eave on hands and feet, Manwe snuck across the tile floor to the foot of the large bed. Gonius' daughter let out a yawn and fell back into the crook of the merchant's arm, humming a pleasant tune.

Manwe sprung onto the bed, covering her nose and mouth with his wide hand. He cut Leomachus across the throat with his knife, slashing with confidence. The merchant choked on his own life, gurgling as his stained hands tried to cover the bloody smile. Eyes rolled back in death, and a last gush of air escaped in the bubbles popping in his throat.

"Before, this was just thievery. I never harmed anyone for the sake of it." Manwe wiped his blade on the girl's skin, a streak of red across her white stomach. The girl flinched under the stroke. "You've made me do this."

He removed his hand from her mouth. Gasping for air, the girl wrenched away from the corpse beside her.

"Are you going to kill me?" she wheezed, curled into a ball on the bed.

"Kill you?" He shook his head in disgust. "Not today. All I care is that you tell them I did this. Tell them I will no longer come to steal their treasures." Manwe slid off the bed and headed for the window on the far wall. "Tell them I come to steal their lives."

MANYARA BIRDS CHIRPED IN THE TREES, THEIR RED NECKS PUFFED OUT WHILE they sang to welcome the morning. Manwe watched the orb rise from beneath the horizon. The light spread across the plains, an endless field forever dancing in the wild wind. In the birdsong he did not hear sweet melodies, but the beat of the cultists' drums. He had left Toba's body out on the plains, somewhere he hoped the spirit of his dead lover might find the way to his ancestors and a better light than the world where he remained.

Manwe crossed his legs and leaned back against the base of the jackalberry tree, waiting for the rebels to arrive. They appeared not long after sunrise, armed with iron spears and bronze-faced shields. Rangy and with a hungered look in their eyes, the three of them slowly approached.

The lead man, a tall and well-muscled youth stripped to the waist, called out. "Are you The Panther?"

Manwe raised his gloomy eyes at him. "What's your name?"

"I am Kosey." The man lowered his weapon. "I am Toba's brother."

"What is the password?"

"Hippo."

Manwe slowly rose to his feet and dusted his bare backside. "Thank you for meeting me."

Kosey smiled and gave a slight bow. "Toba has told me so much about you, and yet we have never stood face-to-face. I have been sure for a long while that this had to change. But tell me, where is my brother? I hoped to see him here as well."

Manwe looked to the rebel-leader's two companions, one a short but fit woman, and the other a teen barely grown into his body. "I ask that your two friends stay back. My words are for you alone."

Kosey signaled to his friends, and they retreated.

Manwe struggled to find the right words until they came, clear and cold. "Toba's dead."

The man jolted. "Dead?"

"The Gypians killed him for this." He drew the Gem of Acitus from his loincloth. He dared not to look at it, for he knew if he had, he would have thrown the stone to the grasses. "He was to sell it to help support the cause. The man he made the deal with killed him."

"My brother." Kosey dropped his spear and shield, hands over his mouth. Tears flowed, mingled in the thick beard on his narrow face. "All for a stone?"

"A very powerful stone, something with too much history," Manwe said. "Take it. I don't have a fence anymore, but you must know someone who can get you the money for it."

"There are coins that I will never take, even for freedom."

"Then for Toba."

Kosey let his hands fall at his side, and after a deep breath, he took the gem from Manwe's palm. "I will get rid of the damned thing as quickly as I can. But tell me, Panther, what of the people who did this? What of the man who took my brother?"

"I took care of him." Manwe walked into the grass, off in the direction of Tolivius. "Just as I will take care of them all."

THE END

A LIGHT IN THE DARK

The wick in the oil lamp sparked when Manwe touched the burning match to its end, the flame low and dull. The light pushed back at the shadows to reveal the long and narrow passage of the cave. He stooped in the darkness, the ceiling too low in places for even his inconsiderable height. Cool air stuck to his bare back, chilling the sweat from his midnight run.

Farther in, an outline emerged, tall and powerful. The man who owned it turned toward Manwe, his handsome face cramped as he tried for a more comfortable position in the narrow space.

"Greetings, Panther," he said, his voice slow. "Were you followed?"

Manwe lifted his hand off the knife stuck in the band of his loincloth. "Password first, Kosey."

"Right," said the young warrior. "Hippo."

"You risked too much setting up this meeting. I saw your lamp a mile out on my approach." Manwe held a hand over his own lamp, blinking a few times to regain his night-vision. "Your brother would have never made such a mistake."

Kosey stiffened, his scarred shoulders hunched. "I apologize. I only wished for you to see that I was here."

"We could have met at my tree. It is a safe place to do business." Manwe checked over his shoulder, back to the entrance of the cave. The stars gleamed in the dark blue sky through the wide mouth, cold dots of radiance. "Thank the mother Gypians are too civilized to be up at these hours."

"I need your help, Panther," Kosey said, hushed. "There is something that must be stolen. Something powerful."

"Then be quick. My eyes are already beginning to water from the smoke."

Kosey nodded and drew from the ground a piece of rolled parchment. "Can you read?"

"Well enough." Manwe took the offered scroll and opened it, peering hard as he held up his lamp to read the inky script. "What is this? A letter?"

"It is a communication from the Senate Consul of Tolivius to the Lord Governor of Merchants Rows, I was told. There is an object of power being brought through the city on its way to the Glass Jungle. It will arrive tomorrow."

Manwe pressed the parchment against the cave wall, spreading his hand to keep the scroll open. "The Centaurian Torch? Some artifact, then?"

"A great weapon, from what some of our spies in the Lord Governor's house are guessing. It is supposedly an ancient thing from a time when centaurs lived as we did, before they were made wild and violent."

"Time and change are cruel, even to the noblest of beasts." Manwe passed Kosey the parchment and blew out the wick in his lamp. "I'll be in touch."

MANWE LEANED BACK AGAINST ONE OF THE MINARETS, HIS GAZE LEVEL TO take in the city. Tolivius' white walls stood stark in the late morning, freshly cleaned by the previous day's storm. The smell of rain had left with the coming of the sun, replaced by the odor of humanity. Down below in the alley, a scullery maid dumped her master's chamber pot, a puddle of brown liquid that spread through the cracks in the pave stones.

He returned focus on his target, a lavish gate set in the northern wall known as the Gold Door. The full quarter of the city known as Merchant's March stretched out before him, lane upon lane of manors and great homes for the wealthiest of the region. From his place on the high roof of the temple to the Gypians' god Adias, Manwe could see almost every street and alley as the hill sloped upward to the far white wall.

The guards at the gate, forty in total, worked together in a thin line to unbar the iron doors. In rolled a series of wagons. Manwe counted five before the gates shut again, five transports covered in canopies of green canvas. They slowly made their way down the hill and turned to the southeast, onto one of the many avenues. He counted for another forty seconds, expecting the wagons to reappear when they moved behind a particularly tall set of houses.

They had stopped.

"And there is the den," he whispered to himself. Walking to the edge of the temple's roof, he climbed down a tall ladder to the narrow alley below. A woman waited there for him, wrapped in a thick brown cloak.

"Done for today, Panther?" She pulled back her hood, letting free her long blonde curls.

"As always, Magera, you're too kind." He reached into his belted pouch and extracted a small bag. "Please accept my contribution to the Goddess of Love and Life."

The priestess and Madame of one of the city's most luxurious brothels, she smiled as she peeked into the small sack. "These wouldn't be the opals taken from Lady Ophelia's home no more than two nights ago, would they?"

Manwe shrugged on his way to the alley's exit.

He walked onto Monkey Tail Way an hour later, a wide street where the city's few merchants who did not make all of their coin on the black markets resided, relying instead on their collections of contacts and semi-reputable dealings with the larger businesses of the western world. About half a mile down, he found the wagons parked near the low curb. Crews of men unloaded boxes while more guards stood at attention.

Manwe made to go past them, focused on going farther down the street and away from them, when one of the workers caught his attention.

A man clothed in a robe of bright yellow, his tall form leaned against one of the wagons. With his beard trimmed in a tight goatee and his brown hair a shaggy mop, the sun lighting his handsome face sparkled in a pair of bright brown eyes.

Manwe exchanged glances as he passed, offering a smile. "Morning."

"Morning," said the man in yellow. "Off somewhere?"

"Perhaps," said Manwe, slowing his gait. "I carry a message for one of the merchants on The Rows, but I'm a bit lost. Maybe you could help me?"

"Not well, I'm afraid." The man in yellow gave a sincere smile. "My fellows and I are delivering a few items to the merchants, but when it comes to ways and means of Tolivius, I know little."

"Is this your first time here?" Manwe asked. Something about this man intrigued him, something deeper than his handsomeness.

"Aye, but I think I'll be coming around more and more." He straightened to his feet and offered a hand. "Cleon."

"Toba," said Manwe, shaking it. He used the name of his dead lover, a reminder to focus. This man, this Cleon, was a Gypian and an enemy—no matter how handsome. "So what are you delivering? Cloth? Spice?"

"More or less." Cleon's honest grin widened. "So what is there to do in this city? It is much smaller than the capital in Gypus."

"Oh, Tolivius is full of its own excitement," Manwe replied. He stepped away. "Alas, I must go. My message to the masters of coin cannot wait. Farewell."

"Farewell yourself." Cleon nodded. "Hopefully we'll see each other soon."

THE WIND ROARED DOWN THE LANE, SETTING THE TREES ALONG THE SIDEWALKS in a nighttime dance. Manwe shook out his bare arms as the breeze sneaked into the darkened alley where he crouched, his focus on the house across the street. No guards patrolled Monkey Tail Way that night, nor did any stand guard at the door of the many manors. Shadows cut from the moonlit tree spread over the pave stones, paths to where he needed to go.

Patting his wrists to make sure he had bound them in linen correctly, Manwe checked for the lock picks tucked in the folds of cloth. He pawed his waist one last time as well, making sure his knife was secure in the twisted band of his loincloth. The moon's full face sat high in the navy field as he slipped out into the street, so bright it blotted out the stars. He offered a silent prayer to the Goddess, and for a moment, wondered if Cleon was looking up as well.

"Always Toba. Remember Toba," he whispered to himself, angered at the distraction.

The pads of his feet slapped the pavement as he charged between two of the wagons still parked outside the manor's entrance. Slithering between them, he scampered up the stoop and to the manor's door, kneeling before the lock. Manwe pressed an ear to the imported olive-wood door, searching for any sound of life within the home. He extracted a pair of picks and a long bronze file from his wrist wrappings.

After a few moments of diligent work, the door creaked inward.

Sneaking into the hallway, Manwe stopped at the foot of the stairs leading to the next level. Boxes cluttered the halls and chambers instead of expensive furniture, and off in the darkness, the heads of spears on a rack gleamed in the scant light filtered through a nearby window. Glyphs painted the boxes designated oils, spices, iron, cloth of various types, but none stood out as the container for The Centaurian Torch. Truth be told, Manwe did not know what he sought—the artifact could be large or small, an actual torch or something entirely different, only named in a clever manner.

On the second floor of the disguised warehouse, he found an odd room, emptied save for one crate. Darkness clung to the walls and corners around it, blacker and less permeable to the small bits of light encroaching from the outside world. Manwe paused in the threshold, his muscles tight in anticipation. He thumbed the handle of his knife and slowly strode into the room. No trap or surprise sprang to intercept him.

He stuck his blade into the gap of the lid and pried the crate open. Inside he found a glass tube packed in straw. He extracted the object, and inside of the cylinder was a folded slip of paper. Sticking two fingers into one end, he pulled it free and opened it.

A pair of words marked the parchment.

Got you.

The shadows seeped away in a breath, and from the illuminated walls sprang men armed with swords and torches. They descended upon Manwe, knocking him to the ground. Knees pressed on his back and neck as he thrashed to get free. He ceased when the edge of a knife rasped his throat, the edge pressed on an artery.

Someone spoke when the outburst ended. "Get him up."

Dragged to his feet, Manwe stood perfectly still, glaring at the man holding the knife to his throat. The Gypian guardsman grinned like a triumphant bastard, one of his canines missing from the gum.

Manwe's attention was drawn away from his captor when another figure moved into sight. Cleon stepped before him, his hand sparking with power. The last of the shadows wormed their way into his small mouth. He drew close, enough that the smell of sweat and incense found its way into Manwe's nostrils.

"Fancy meeting you here," he said. He palmed Manwe's face, almost lovingly, and grabbed hold of his jaw. "You must be The Panther."

THE WAGONS WHEELS CLATTERED ON THE ROAD, JOLTING THE WAGON UP AND down in a quick motion. Manwe woke from his daze and pulled hard to bring his hands to his waist, instinctively going for his knife. Rope bound both wrists, and he tilted onto the wagon bench with a thud.

"Looking for this?" Cleon sat on the bench across from Manwe's, holding the iron blade up like a prize.

Manwe slowly righted himself. "Where am I?"

"Does it matter?" Cleon reclined on his side of the compartment, un-fazed by the divots in the highway. "You're quite different from what I was expecting, Panther. I thought catching you would require more cunning."

Manwe glanced to the flap of the wagon's canvas canopy. Outside the cover, a road faded into the hills of the savannah, the mounds yellow and dusty. Copses of umber trees, their arms wide and wiry, dotted both sides of the road. Given the shade and the way the sun filtered through the roof, he failed to discern the direction they traveled.

"You're a great topic of conversation in Gypus, you know," Cleon went on, leaning his head against one of the canopy's ribs. "Did you really kill Leomachus in his bed with his son's wife beside him?"

"Does it matter?"

"It might. I never liked the man, given the few times he and I met. Too ambitious. That must have been his undoing."

Manwe stared hard at the sorcerer. Cleon's ease, his tone—the man had a way that reminded him of Toba, never at once serious about the situation at hand, nor dishonest about it, as if things came together simply because they were supposed to.

"You don't have to answer," Cleon said. "I already know what happened. Your fence, that hole out in the savannah, the lord slain for his part. Everything."

They said nothing after that, lost to the silence and the wagon's clatter. The sunlight had dimmed a bit by the time they stopped, and the outline of a figure formed at the back of the wagon, its shape growing as its owner neared the curtain. A tanned hand, roughed from work and dust, parted the flaps to reveal a man decked in a shining cuirass of dark iron. The yellow crest of his war-helm waved in the wind, and from beneath the shallow visor glared a pair of dull eyes.

"Is this him?" the soldier asked Cleon, his gaze fixed on Manwe.

"In the flesh." Cleon rose from his bench and exited the wagon, landing lightly on both feet. "General Talamus, I present the infamous Panther." Cleon flashed Manwe one last smile before he started off. "Careful with him. He has a bite matching the name."

Talamus signaled to someone out of sight, and two more men appeared in the same armor, though their breastplates were less decorated. The pair manhandled Manwe out of the wagon, dumping him onto the dirt. They dragged him to his feet and shoved onward. Stumbling, he slowly turned in a great wheel, acting as if his balance remained unsteady. A quick look at his surroundings confirmed that he was far to the east of Tolivius, more than two days ride on horseback and six on foot. The savannah ended at the edge of the great Glass Jungle, a dark green wall of trees, bushes, and shadows. Green leaves of bright emerald swayed in the steady breath of the wind, enlivened to a slow dance.

"Go on. Get!" said one of the Gypians, shoving him in the side. Manwe moved at their order, set straight for the tree line.

He entered the shade of the massive forest, a place his people believed homed things both natural and supernatural, where beasts lived alongside nightmarish demons of legend. The soft dirt, black and damp, turned to harder rock and pebble. Soon they arrived to a cave in the woods, a tall mound outlined in moss and deep red flowers.

"Where are we?" Manwe asked Cleon, who stood at the edge of the opening.

From the folds of his robe, Cleon extracted a thin rod of copper. "This is just some cave, lost to time and history, a hole in the earth..."

"But?"

"Well, a door is a door, after all."

The two Gypians pushed Manwe after the five entered the gloomy hole. He stopped when he heard Cleon whispering, and a moment later a great light flared, blinding him in a red haze. A point of illumination had blossomed on the end of sorcerer's wand, which he held up to light the passage.

"Come along, children," he said, proud of his working.

Farther and farther on, the path into the bowels of the earth smoothed from a rocky decline into a polished road, wide enough that they could travel clustered instead of single file. The ceiling, once rough cut and stained in streaks of ore, faded to a pale limestone etched in ancient script.

The road ended at a great cavern, a huge vault that went so far back the light of Cleon's wand failed to reach the end. A building cleaved itself from the shadows, its face a series of columns supporting a pyramid roof. On its forward-facing side reared the molded relief of a great centaur, spear in one hand and a torch in the other.

"Let me guess," said Manwe. "A Centaurian Temple."

Cleon nodded with satisfaction. "This is indeed a temple, long ago abandoned in the Golden Age of Juut, when kingdoms of the natural world bowed at the feet of men. If legends are true, this particular site is the home of the Centaurian Torch, a weapon of such great power that the lords of old banded together to wrest it from their former allies, and sometimes protectors, the centaurs."

"Those horse-bred savages made this?" Talamus hooked both thumbs in his sword-belt. The light of Cleon's wand shined on the clean lines of his helm. "It is very...competent."

"Absolutely so, General," replied Cleon. "The centaurs still speak of the old times, when their kingdoms loomed on the world much as man's did. They were masons, artists, warriors... and engineers. Engineers of the age, in fact! This ruin is but a pale ghost of their glory, but one abounding with treasures."

"You never had the torch, did you?" Manwe stared at the temple, his worry beyond its entrance, beyond the cavern, beyond the jungle. He wondered—if Kosey and the rebels could be duped so easily, how did he know that the Gypians did not know everything? To be tricked with such ease carried more than the cost of his hubris.

"Just the idea of it." Cleon brought the tip of his wand to his lips and blew. The illumination flew off the point, down the path to the old steps of the temple. "Unbind him," he instructed Talamus. "The thief and I will go on from here."

The rope around his wrists severed, Manwe rubbed the chaffed skin as he and Cleon continued ahead. When they were out of earshot, the sorcerer cleared his throat.

"You'll have to pardon General Talamus. A brilliant soldier, but a soldier nonetheless. He possesses quite the myopic focus on the mission."

"And what is the mission?" Manwe asked.

"Simple enough, Panther. The Centaurian Torch lies within this temple," he replied, nodding to the old structure. "I do not possess the skill to delve into the darkness, however. One needs a lighter touch and a keen mind for puzzles of the more earthly sort. I am my spells and cunning. You are your skills and wits."

"But my life isn't nearly worth either, is it?"

"A thief is a thief."

They came to the foot of the stair. Cleon reached into his robe and pulled from a hidden pocket a small bundle wrapped in strands of linen. "Your tools, sans the knife. I will hold onto that."

Manwe grunted as he took the offering, feeling the edges and probes of his lock picks. "How do I know you won't kill me if I come out alive?"

Cleon smiled that handsome smile and shrugged silk-clad shoulders. "It will have to be a surprise."

***

MANWE SLIPPED INTO THE SHADOWS OF THE TEMPLE'S FIRST HALL, A WIDE space cluttered in fallen columns and broken tiles that had once been part of a great mosaic floor. Years of running on the hard soil of the savannah had hardened the soles of his feet, leaving the edges of the squares no more annoying than stepping on a hard pebble or sharp twig. Each step crunched, no matter how much he tried to distribute his weight.

He stopped in the center of the floor and let his eyes readjust to the gloom. In his mind he heard a tap, bone on bone, and for a moment he was transported back to the darkness where Toba had died, a hell blacker than even the temple could gather to its corners. This was not that place, he reminded himself—just another house, ready to be robbed.

Past the first chamber was a large rotunda, a room carved into a perfect circle of stone set with more effigies chiseled into the walls. It split off into three separate halls, one forward and two that went right and left. In the center rose the statue of a triumphant centaur, the details and features still crisp after unknown centuries in the dark.

Squatting in the archway, Manwe studied a new pattern set in the tiled floor. This mosaic was made of wider squares colored in pale shades of red and green, bright enough it showed clear in the room's dimness. A small circle dotted the center of each plate, a curious effect he had not seen in any art known to him.

He looked about, his gaze falling to a small scattering of rocks and dust he guessed were once part of a relief column. Picking a few handfuls of the heavier debris, he scattered them in all directions, skipping them in a shower that raced across the way to the two passages now blocked by the statue.

A pop sounded beneath the floor's surface. Spikes shot up on random tiles, tall and sharp.

"A fair roll," he whispered. The pattern formed by the spikes was broken and irregular, too imprecise to stop someone who might traverse the room. He walked carefully to the nearest spike and studied it. At the base was the edge of the center circle, now a ring of yellow.

The ease of crossing the rotunda brought him no peace as he rounded the statue in the center. He stood before the three passages leading further into the temple. The way to the right had collapsed, closed off by rubble, while the center and the left paths remained open. The center was the darker of the two, ominous enough Manwe shirked away from it.

The hall of the left passage, a short jaunt of hewn rock, ended in a larger room with a great pool, wide and long enough that only a narrow ledge allowed a way around. An odd glow issued from beneath the water, and as Manwe hovered at the edge, a strange line caught his eye. A lighter shade of white, it writhed against the bottom, long, thick, and languid.

Slowly Manwe started around the pool's perimeter, never taking an eye off the creature. He reached the other end of the chamber, where he discovered a set of double doors. No lock or bar closed the way, and taking hold of the half-moon handles set near the seam, he pulled gently until they portals cracked open.

Gold gleamed, caught in the light of two arcane torches, marvels of an ancient world where such innovation had allowed them to burn for centuries. Even with the final wisps of fibers charred to black, the points of flame glistened and sparkled on the pile of loot laid at his feet.

Manwe's breath caught, forcing him to stifle an excited gasp. He checked the pool, not knowing if what lay within the water heard him. The surface stayed still, and secure in his safety, he bent down and picked one of the gold off the pile.

Each piece, two small squares connected by an adjoining rod, formed an odd coin of the like of which he had never seen. He threaded one into the wrappings on his wrists, knowing full well he had not found the Centaurian Torch, yet also knowing that a little bit of gold was better than none at all.

He retreated back to the rotunda.

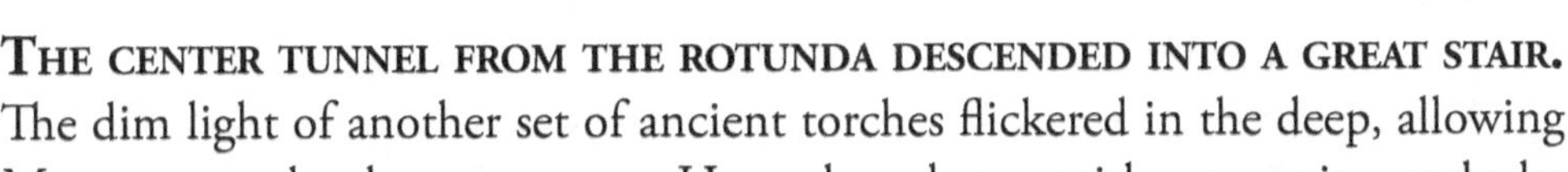

THE CENTER TUNNEL FROM THE ROTUNDA DESCENDED INTO A GREAT STAIR. The dim light of another set of ancient torches flickered in the deep, allowing Manwe to make the stone steps. He took each one with care, using rocks he gathered again from the rotunda room to pressure the faces in search of traps.

At the bottom of the channel stood a massive stone door, its face carved in an intricate lattice. Within the circles swirled jagged geometric patterns of a type Manwe had never seen before. He longed for his knife at that moment, a perfect tool for finding the seams and cracks in such doors. Instead he used fingers, probing and gliding the runs of the stone until he came upon a strange space, a shallow but cleanly cut hole shaped in an "I."

Manwe pawed the gold piece he had secured in the linen wraps around his wrists, much more curious about it now than he had been when he first filched it. Examining both the object and the hole, their matching size and shape offered the solution.

The gold piece slid perfectly into the hole, and a whirring sound preceded the grind of gears and squeaking pulleys from behind the door. The portal slowly rose up, and past it, a small antechamber.

Manwe waited, frozen as he gazed into what he knew to be the final chamber of the temple. In the center rested another statue of a centaur, but unlike the first in the rotunda, this one did not stand proud on a raised platform. Instead his hoofs connected to the stone floors, more real and life-like than any sculpture Manwe had ever seen. In the beast's hand was a sword as long as his arm. Sunshine from a skylight in the domed roof sparkled at the edge of the adamantine blade, cold and sharp.

The sight of daylight itself invigorated Manwe, who strode to the room's center and looked up at the skylight. He could see the glaring skies behind them, the freedom of an escape far out of reach. His gaze back to the ground, he looked about for the item he had come for.

Set on a stone table in a rear alcove, a foot-long tube glittered dully in its holder. Polished smooth with a silver sheen, it went unadorned, a rod of nondescript presentation so simple Manwe wondered if he had actually found the item of Cleon's desires. He came to it with care, blowing the dust off the table to better find any sign of traps. Certain nothing of ill-design, he gingerly lifted the rod from the holder, its weight light but sturdy.

"Never once did I think I'd see this."

Manwe spun around, rod in hand and ready to fight. For a moment he wondered if Cleon succored himself in the few small shadows of the room. He tried to find the origin of the voice, its baritone strong but wizened.

"Who comes?" Manwe called.

"How can one come when they are already here?"

He froze. No real shadows stained the walls or the floor, save one. He stared at the back of the centaur statue, to the delicate runs chiseled into its human back, the powerful curves of his haunches. Manwe forced himself not to blink, making sure he missed not one crucial detail. The dusty hide of the horse-half, striped in streaks of black and white, twitched its muscles, and when he looked long enough, the human shoulders of the centaur rose once and fell in a breath.

And then the centaur turned his head.

Manwe startled, taking a step back in shock.

Muscle and sinew moved at once as the sculpture-made-flesh clopped in a half circle to face him. Old red eyes were framed in the woolly square of his tawny face, the top of his head crowned in a pair of slight black horns. Dust fell from his joints and curves as he took the first few steps, his hooves echoing off the stone.

"Pardon my silence," said the centaur. "I was napping."

"You're..." Manwe mouthed some incomprehensible words, at a loss. "You're impossible."

"Well, nobody's ever called me that," he replied. "And what are you? A spy from the plain folk?"

"The plain folk?" Manwe shook his head, trying to accept the being before him. "No. Not a spy—I'm a thief."

The centaur threw his head back in a deep laugh. Dust fell from his shoulders. "A thief! Oh, it must be an odd age now. Tell me, did you pass my kin on the way in?"

"They're not here. There hasn't been a Centaurian Empire for...well, a very long time." Manwe lowered the rod. "How are you alive?"

"To the chosen goes the curse of their prize. I am Roald, Guardian of The Dome." The centaur brushed off his muscular chest and arms and shook his equine tail. "You must be a good thief to get past the guards and the traps in the hall. Strange that you did not try to steal the door keys, though. It was why we made so many."

Manwe held his arms out to his side, the rod clenched in his right hand. "I'm not here of my own accord. I had no plan to rob you, nor do I truly wish to."

"No?" Roald came closer. "So a slave as well. My indignity continues."

"Prisoner," corrected Manwe. He held up the rod. "Is this the Centaurian Torch?"

Roald froze, all ease banished by the question. "How do you know that name?"

There was no way past the guardian, Manwe knew, no path or dodge quick enough to bypass this personification of power and speed. The warrior skills of the centaurs out in the fields of Juut were legendary, and in cases like this, his only avenue was trickery.

But this centaur, a remnant of an older world, was not deserving of such.

Manwe, so used to illusion and double-speak, chose the truth. "It is sought by my folk for protection or destruction, while the Gypians wish to use it to further their dominance. I was...picked...to serve the latter."

"Fools! You damned fools!" Roald stamped and reared. "You fought us, forced us to surrender, all to ensure such horrid weapons never reached the world again. Have you forgotten the suffering we enacted upon you? Have you forgotten the sins of the past?"

"I know nothing of them."

"Pray to your gods that you never do." Roald snorted through his aquiline nose. He looked over his shoulder to the stair leading back to the main floor of the temple. "How many of these Gypians have come to steal the power of the past? You may be a thief, but at least your words ring true. They, on the other hand…I'll be damned if the Torch is used as a weapon again."

"There are four upstairs. Two soldiers, a general, and a very competent sorcerer."

"Sorcerer?" Roald narrowed his eyes at the word, its tone bitter in his mouth. "Now the plot thickens. And you still need to get past the final trap."

"What trap?" asked Manwe.

The centaur nodded toward the entrance of his dome. "Two stone doors will shut in the antechamber to this dome when you pass the midway point on your return. This is a test, human—a test for all centaurs who wish to guard the Torch until the end of days. In the olden times my kind fought for such honor, but those times…" He sighed. "Well, no matter."

Manwe moved closer, within reach of Roald's mighty arms. "How do we get through?"

"With perfection. The first door will fall down while the second will push upwards. Only an impossible leap will clear it."

"And have you ever made this impossible leap?"

Roald smiled, his square yellow teeth large in his mouth. "Never with a man on my back." He knelt, the knees of his equine forelegs to the stone. "Climb on."

Manwe threw a leg over Roald's powerful midsection. The coarse hair of the centaur's striped flanks bit into the flesh of his inner thighs as he squirmed for a comfortable position.

"Just get on, human," Roald cajoled, rising to his full height. He cantered around the back-half of the dome for a few laps, winding and stretching his shoulders. "Ready?"

Hugged to the centaur's equine back, Manwe clutched the Centaurian Torch. Its smooth shank had warmed in the flesh of his palm, but a cold thought defeated any sense of triumph. "Can this weapon be destroyed?"

Roald chewed on the question. "Better it were lost. If one man can deduce its location, another will as well. If you truly intend to protect it or destroy it, I will throw my sword in with you."

"A fair deal," admitted Manwe. "If this rod is as dangerous as you say, then it can never be used."

The centaur whipped his sword out in a circle, exercising his shoulder one last time. "Ready?"

The answer was torn from Manwe's mouth as Roald charged. Crossing the mid-point of the room, a grinding noise echoed as hidden gears somewhere in the room caught, the ropes snapping after years without movement. The two doors of the antechamber started to close, the nearest rising from its seam and the floor while the rear door descended.

"Stay down," Roald roared, his upper body leaned forward until he was perpendicular to the floor. Manwe shut his eyes as he felt the centaur's hooves leave the ground in a mighty leap. Air rushed in his ears, and for a moment stone grazed his back.

Roald laughed as he landed hard on the staircase. The vault doors to the dome slammed shut.

"Still there?" he asked.

Manwe sat up on his back, dazed for a moment. "That was terrifying."

His laughter booming, Roald waved his sword before him. "To battle, then."

THEY REACHED THE TOP OF THE STONE STAIR, ROALD'S HOOVES CLOPPING on each step. Manwe winced at every echo in the darkness, hoping some small hope that neither Cleon nor his accomplices had heard their clamor.

Manwe signaled for Roald to halt. "Let me check the chamber," he whispered.

The centaur nodded, thumbing the edge of his sword.

Creeping up the last of the flight, Manwe peered over the top step into the rotunda. No one waited in the shadowy space. The spike traps remained sprung. He waved for Roald, who ascended to the landing.

"I..." Roald stopped, his weapon limp in his hand as he took in the temple's state. His mouth worked for the words, but as the frown dominated his blockish face, only sadness seeped out. "I've been down there a long time, haven't I?"

Manwe stood there, looking from Roald to the rotunda and back. He wondered at how different the world would be for this creature once they left the caves, a world where his kind were scattered like his, a once proud folk discarded to the savagery of the savannah and jungles, never deemed to be more than beasts by the kingdoms in the west. Manwe did not miss the comparisons to the plight of his own people.

"The world carries on," he said, hopeful. "And what was old can be refreshed, with time and effort."

The centaur glanced to him with an appreciative grin. "And some things will always be, like the potential of man."

They walked the floor, covering the tiles at a slow pace when a shriek echoed from the first passage, the one that led to the pool and room filled with the golden keys.

Roald raised his sword, stunned by the sound. "No, not that!"

"What?" asked Manwe. "What is it?"

"The Destined Beast," Roald answered, terrified. "Someone woke it."

At that moment, the two Gypian soldiers who served Cleon and General Talamus burst from the passage, unarmed and with their clothes singed to tatters. Thick yellow juice covered the metal of their armor, and the red crests of their helms were burnt to the comb. They skidded to a halt before Roald, who reared at them, his equine forelegs clawing the air. One of the Gypians reached for the short sword strapped to his belt, only to be quickly met with a hoof to the skull. His helmet dented and blood streaming out of his face, he dropped to the floor while the other ran for the temple's exit.

Roald paid him little attention. "To the pool!"

Manwe and the centaur sprinted across the floor, leaping over spikes and tiles, and dashed down the steps. Another scream, high-pitched and warbled, rang the room as they entered. Cleon waved his wand, throwing a streak of light against something at the pool's edge. The serpentine trunk of some hellish thing writhed, its skin slick and slimy as it squeezed the dead body of General Talamus. Cords of light skirted across the soldier's cooked flesh, the skin black and hardened.

The sorcerer looked back, surprised to see Manwe and Roald. "Flee," he shouted. "Flee, Panther!"

He leapt as something darted out of the water, a worm's head complete with a pair of dull blue orbs for eyes. The doors to its wretched soul flickered, lidless, and the thing reared back. Its helmet cracked into four seams that met at the tip. Lips parted, and four mandibles lapped the air, dotted in rows of razor teeth. A sucking hole of darkness groaned open, the weird sound of a lamprey.

Manwe stood in horror of it. A beast of a world long dead, it bellowed in its terrible beauty, and from the maw came a crackle of electricity. It drove for Cleon, sloshing the water of the pool.

"We must flee," Manwe implored Roald.

The centaur bared his teeth. "Never! Such a thing was not meant for the world. Not in my time, nor in yours." Casting his sword away, Roald stuck his open hand out at Manwe. "The torch."

Manwe looked at his treasure for a moment before handing it to its rightful owner. "What do you need me to do?"

"Run for the top of the stair. Wait for me there, if I arise."

Cleon shouted in surprise as the lamprey brushed him. His body shocked ridged, he fell into the water with a splash. Without hesitation, Manwe dove into the pool. Roald charged in beside him, headed straight for the lamprey with the Centaurian Torch bared.

Breaking the surface of the water, Manwe emerged from the warmth of the sloshing reek. The clammy liquid soured his mouth as he searched, and seeing a dim spot of yellow on the white floor of the pool, he squatted in the water. Eyes shut by the stinging salt, he grabbed at whatever he could touch. His fingers closed on the hem of Cleon's robe, and he yanked until the sorcerer was close enough to grab.

Lifting Cleon from the pool's bottom, he rose in the midst of a pitched fight.

Roald batted the lamprey in the mouth, the Torch blazing in a divine light. The rod left black lashes on the pale hide of the monster. They knocked each other around the corners of the pool, striking and whipping until they were spent. The lamprey let out a great wail, a keening cry, and slumped back into the water.

Manwe dragged Cleon out, leaving the sorcerer on the pool's edge so he could check on Roald. The centaur sprawled on the pool's bottom, his equine forelegs broken, but his human half out of the reddened water. Burns and bite marks had left bloody, black holes over his body, and yet through the agony he mustered a smile when Manwe approached. "You can come closer," he said, wheezing.

Manwe touched his burnt arm gently. "Can you stand?"

"No. The Destined Beast is dead, but it has brought me to my end as well." He winced, his arms splayed on the marble edge of the pool. "Tell me, man... was I glorious?"

"You were better," he said, unsure of the question. "What do I do? How do I take care of you?"

"Take care of me?" Roald chuckled weakly. "There is no greater comfort you can provide than what comes for me. I only beg..." He coughed up water and blood, and slowly reached out with the Centaurian Torch, the rod unblemished from the fight. "This cannot reach your world again. It must be left behind or it will set kingdoms ablaze."

"What can I do?"

"When you reach the columns at the temple's entrance, touch them all with the Torch and throw it back into the first hall. My gods will take it from there." He gasped, tensed as he whispered his final words. "Do it for those who live today so they will not... be damned... like we were."

⸻⸻⸻◇⸻

HE TOUCHED THE ROD TO THE FIRST COLUMN ON THE RIGHT. MANWE RAN from one end of the temple's entrance to the other, banging the Centaurian Torch on the stone the way a child ran a stick across a piece of fencing. The tings of the metal rang odd notes, which were lost as the roof groaned. Cracks appeared in the columns, small at first, until the fluted lengths were covered in fissures.

With Cleon set on his shoulder, he tossed the Torch into the waiting maw of the entrance and ran, never looking back to watch the ancient place fall to pieces with a rumble. The ground shook beneath them until Manwe found his way to the cave's mouth. The jungle air outside was cool and fresh, a welcome relief to the stale underground.

Leaving the sorcerer in the grass, he recovered his knife and plopped down beside Cleon, caught in the middle of a starless night. Animals called, the trees roared the wind's song, and past the darkness, the world moved. With no way forward and nothing to do, Manwe sat there and thought on everything that had happened: his choices, the loss of Toba, these mad quests for riches and objects of power.

He wondered if there was a point.

Hours passed by, and the coming day crusted the sky bronze. Cleon sat up on his elbows, his eyes closed to slits as he tried to gain his bearings. "Ah, Panther. Still here?"

Manwe flipped his knife in his long fingers, the blade's iron cold to the touch. "What did you think I'd do?"

"I thought you'd run. Or cut my throat." The sorcerer sat up straight, brushing off the elbows of his dirty yellow robe. "I take it you left the Torch behind?"

"I collapsed the temple as well. Nobody will ever use it. Not my side or yours."

He blew a breath though his pursed lips and chuckled. "And here I thought you'd at least think better."

"Cleon," said Manwe, "how close am I?"

He laughed at the question. "With your little knife?"

"I'm close enough that you won't get the words out in time for a spell, I'd imagine." Manwe looked hard at him. "Aren't I?"

Cleon swallowed, his smile strained. He relaxed his posture. "So I'm to die."

"No."

"No?"

"I don't kill unless I have to." Manwe sunk at the explanation, remembering the lord he had murdered for the death of Toba. Part of him wanted to murder Cleon in the same way, but another part, one shrouded in the subterranean past, felt a tug of temptation. "We lost today. I lost my prize. You failed your mission. There's no need to end this in further ruin."

"So what now?"

Manwe rose to his feet and looked westward, where he knew his savannah waited. "I'm going home. You can follow, but if you try to harm me, I will do what I must."

Cleon moved to his feet, brushing off the skirt of his yellow frock. "And if I do try something?"

Manwe left his enemy behind as he searched for a path in the trees and brush of the jungle. He had almost left the glade when Cleon called to him.

"You surprised me, Panther," said the sorcerer. "A thief is a thief. And you are truly a master."

He stopped at the edge of darkness and turned. "You surprised me as well."

Cleon beamed with his handsome smile. "How so?"

"A sorcerer is just a sorcerer, it seems. I expect better trickery." Manwe returned to his trek. "Next time."

THE END

BY THE TEARS

Manwe ducked into the narrow lane between the manor's perimeter wall and the next home beside it, checking behind him to see if he had been followed. He palmed the linen wrappings tied around his hands and wrists in the dark, counting his lock picks until he was satisfied they were all there.

A pair of the manor's guards walked past the alley's northern mouth, talking to themselves while paying little attention to the world around them. Manwe stood frozen in the shadows, clutching at the knife tucked in the back of his loincloth's waistband. When they were gone, he eased, beginning his search of the two walls sandwiching him. As his eyes adjusted to the dimness, he spotted cracks in the plaster, exposed bricks that offered worthy edges for his roughened feet.

Manwe charged to the right. He brought his right foot up and pushed off of one of the exposed bricks, propelling himself hard to the left. He kicked hard to reach the top of the barrier.

Pulling himself up, he found himself blocked by the great girth of an old mopane tree, its butterfly leaves alive in the breeze. On hands and feet, Manwe crawled through the foliage, slinking and slipping past the branches.

Through the boughs he spied a great party on the lawn as far as he could see. Patrons in bright linen robes and tunics traipsed about the green wearing garish masks, their wine cups loose in their hands while naked black servants refreshed them with the finest libations the Senate Consul of Tolivius could afford in a frontier territory.

More importantly, Manwe noticed that no guards patrolled the gathering.

These lords and ladies of the city, lost in their revelry, barely noticed when he dropped from the tree. One woman near the wall laughed and pointed as he calmly walked by, whispering something to the man she hung on about how overdressed he was in his loincloth. He ignored the pair and filtered into the crowd, grabbing a tray of half-eaten food that someone had left on one of the feasting tables. Holding up the square of bronze, he grunted under its weight as more people loaded it with empty cups and pieces of partially-chewed food.

"Really, Taeus," said one of the ladies he passed by, her face covered in the glaring mask of a centaur. "Have you seen her? The Senate Consul's wife acts positively the part of a whore."

"Well, it is an orgy, dear," said her partner, a slight of a man who held his annoyance behind a fine lion mask, complete with a pair of teeth and a full mane. They tottered off, mumbling more insults about their hosts.

The crowds thickened the closer he came to the main home, and strange cries rose over the musicians set beneath a nearby veranda. Parting the sea of bodies, Manwe pierced the multitudes until he reached a patio set before a series of double stairs leading up to the household. He stopped dead in his tracks when he saw the red marble terrace.

A throng of people, naked and greased with oil, twisted and meshed together in an intense orgy before the eyes of the other guests. Women moaned in pleasure as they gyrated atop, beneath, and before their partners, nude men who ignored those watching them to focus on their singular pleasures.

Manwe watched in shocked awe as these people, some of them prostitutes he knew through contacts in Tolivius' underworld, slammed themselves into each other. He almost wondered why the Senate Consul would put on such a display until he scanned the party-goers mashed around him. Rich lords and ladies stared luridly, their hands lifting the hems of tunics to free their penises or probe areas no decent aristocrat would dare to in public. Some even engaged, throwing their partner onto the grass or a table to mount them.

The satin gleam on the muscular chest of one man drew his eyes. Another's legs and butt caught his attention, and a stirring rose from the depths of his being. This stirring was shattered when he noticed one person in the center of the orgy was having a better time than others, a woman he recognized almost immediately.

Sweat beaded Lady Nelo's body as she bounced atop a man who was not her husband, the Senate Consul of Tolivius. Her narrow face and high cheekbones shone in the light of the bonfires set around the patio, her pouty lips twisted in delicate ecstasy. Losing herself in a mixture of laughter and orgasm as her consort spent himself in her, she rose and moved to the next man, an amazed noble no older than seventeen. It was not her wantonness or beauty that beguiled Manwe, but the chain of sparkling lights that waved and bounced upon her full breasts. Around her neck draped a wondrous necklace, the only piece of garb on her bared form. Each bead was pure diamond, one of dozens, a rare treasure known as "The Savannah's Tears." An artifact of the old world where Manwe's people had ruled the plains, such a treasure would secure more than a fat payday for a thief—he could fund a rebellion.

"There she is," Manwe said, more to himself than anyone around him.

"Oh, quite," said one of the ladies beside him in the crowd. She had lifted the skirt of her floor-length white dress up her hips, exposing her groin so she could rub herself. "But I'll show her."

He ignored the noblewoman, refocused on the task at hand. He had begun to plan his theft when he caught a flash of movement at the edge of his vision. A shadow passed from the manor wall far to his right, darting into the bushes. Manwe's attention to his prize went away against a troubling new truth:

Someone else had decided to work the party tonight.

MANWE ENTERED THE HOUSEHOLD, MIXING WITH THE OTHER BLACK SERVANTS who paid him no mind as if he were one of their own. He ambled behind a pair of servers on the way to the kitchen. Spotting an alcove farther down the side hall, he jogged past them when they turned into the busy storm of cooks screaming at each other to rush out more food. Waiting for a few minutes, he ducked out from his hiding place to hunt down the second thief.

Passing by the chambers of the inner halls, doors lay open to more orgies, more drinking, and a few stunk of yellow lotus, a potent drug used by many wealthy westerners. The stench of burnt resin muddied the air.

A door cracked open. A woman stepped out, no older than twenty. She wore a tight canvas shirt to flatten her breasts to her chest, as well as a loincloth much like Manwe's. Lengths of linen wrapped her hands and forearms all the way up to the elbow, a common practice among the city's smarter thieves.

She looked at Manwe with curiosity, which bloomed into recognition before settling into smug satisfaction. "My, my, my... the Panther prowls."

"And the Songbird settles in the wrong tree. Again." Manwe stood at his full height, a head taller than her. He held his hands out to the sides in a gesture of non-aggression. "Folami."

"It is quite interesting to see you here, Panther." Folami put her hands out as well, a common sign among thieves for parlay. "I never thought these kinds of jobs attracted you."

"Why are you here?" he asked. "I sent out my notice to Sophicus and his fences. I claimed this party for the entire night."

"Did you?" she asked in mock innocence, putting a hand to her chest. "I must not have heard the call."

"Then rectify your mistake. Get out of here."

"No."

He balked at her. "Excuse me?"

"I said no," she reaffirmed, meeting his edged tone. "Just because you're the favorite of the fences doesn't mean you get to pick and choose your targets. I saw this house first."

"There are rules and traditions. They keep us from each other's throats."

"Says the man who cuts the necks of his buyers."

He quieted at the retort, his shoulders slack. "Why are you even here?"

"The rich throw a party, they break out their jewels and gold and silver..." Folami threw her hands up and twirled on her toes in a sensuous circle. "How could one resist?"

"I'm here for The Savannah's Tears. All the brooches, bangles, earrings, jewels... whatever you want, take it, but that strand of diamonds is mine."

"If you can get it first."

"I dare you to try it. If one thief steals another's claim...well, I would be within my rights. This time, at least."

"Oh, would you?" Folami asked, the levity of her posture replaced with a rigid stance. "And what happens then, Panther? In the last three months you've lost your fence because of your recklessness, you slew a buyer, and rumor abound that you were captured by the Gypians. I doubt the fences of the city will remain as idle when they see more blood on your hands, especially the blood of a thief. There is only so much a reputation can cover."

"Leave it alone, Folami. I need those diamonds."

"For your petty revolution?" she asked, scoffing.

"Yes."

She dimmed at the answer, the tension leaving her smooth cheeks and pouting her mouth. A quick smile reclaimed her a moment later. "Let's play a game. Something simple, in the tradition of the best thieves. Fences still think you're the best, if not the best in the entire Gypian Empire. I think they're mistaken."

"Get to the point."

Folami nodded slightly, her grin wider. "I will let you have the Tears. If they are the only thing you are here for, why stop you? But I say I can get to them first. If I do, you will never ever step on my jobs again, no matter if you claimed them before or not. You arrive to knock over a house and I'm there, you turn and walk away."

"And if I win?" asked Manwe.

"If you win, you get the necklace, credit for the job, and more importantly, I will put in a fair word for you next time I meet my fence. You know how a good word bolsters and spreads."

"Not as quickly as a poor one." The idea of a better reputation aside, something old and vigorous reignited within, a call back to a time when the future was not weighted on burning cities and hard-won freedom. Manwe let go of his knife. "I want any loot that is taken during the contest, yours and mine. I will hand it over if I lose."

She put out her hand. "Done."

As they shook, a great commotion rang out, one so loud that the participants of the various room parties emerged to follow it. Swept up in the sudden traffic, Manwe and Folami marched in the surge. The lines shambled back out to the lawn at the rear of the manor, where the main orgy had paused to take in a spectacle of sight and sound.

Fireworks sparked the night sky as writhing serpents slithered between explosions of multicolored light, leaving behind paths of flame and lightning. Fresh stars appeared, blazing as they rained glimmering sparks that faded before they touched naked flesh. Some remained as they fell, slowing their descent until they floated like dancing fireflies.

Beneath this wonder of lights and explosions stood a tall man in a yellow robe, his wide sleeves pulled back to expose his sinewy and tattooed arms. Silky brown hair hung down to his shoulders to frame a narrow and handsome face fitted with a beaming smile. The sorcerer spun with his hands out, dancing as he loosed another volley of magic.

People cheered and clapped, but for Manwe there was no happiness to be found in what he saw. "Oh, no," he said. "Not now."

"Friend of yours?" asked Folami, crushed into the spot next to him.

"That's Cleon, a thief-chaser and sorcerer." Manwe let out a great sigh. "And this night just became harder for the both of us."

LADY NELO, STILL WEARING THE SAVANNAH'S TEARS, CLAPPED AS CLEON'S display ended, her coated body shining in the light of his lingering magic. "Fantastic, Lord Cleon," she proclaimed loudly, wet hands slapping together. "If only my husband could have torn himself from whatever he's doing to witness such wonder."

Manwe watched from afar as the sorcerer bowed deeply before her. "Lady Nelo, I am simply happy to have pleased you with my skill. I'm so very thankful to have been invited to celebrate such auspicious guests," he replied, equally loud and equally contrived.

"Why are they shouting?" Folami asked Manwe.

Manwe waited for the conversation to continue between Cleon and Nelo, but the two drew closer to each other and kept their words between them. "There's always time to reaffirm relationships between the law and the wealthy. We just caught the first act."

"Gypians are so odd."

He hummed in agreement. Lady Nelo and the sorcerer conversed, and suddenly she placed a hand on Cleon's face. The latter froze, his smile forced as he quickly spoke a string of unreadable words. Her hand came down and she turned, not as pleased as she had been.

Strangely satisfied by Cleon's rejection, Manwe chuckled as she sauntered back to the patio where the orgy had recommenced. "Working around Cleon will be a task, and more the better if neither of us runs into him. What do you think, Folami?" He looked to his side and discovered she had disappeared. "Folami?" Turning about in place, he spotted her in the crowds, her hand already on the belt of some lord. It came away with a small bag of coins.

He nodded, appreciating her ploy. "Time to work."

A caress of a hand, an "accidental" bump into a guest, and more than a few longing glances with some interested gentlemen, Manwe soon walked back toward the manor, slipping crumpled strands of stones and silver into the front of his loincloth. Ascending the stair, he re-entered the house, thinking the more precious valuable items would be kept there.

Returned to the inner halls of the manor, he treaded the tiled passages and found a bedroom door ajar. Within the dimly lit chamber a smaller party commenced, a gathering of four drug-addled ladies and some young men they had roped into their carnal pleasures. Drunk on wine and euphoric from the ample pots of lotus spread around the chamber, they half-heartedly went about their frolics, too inebriated to fully perform lustful deeds.

Manwe almost passed them on when the gleam of gold flashed in the dark. He stepped into the room, wincing as the door's hinges creaked.

One of the ladies looked up from atop her boy, heavy-lidded and smiling like a fool. A line of large pearls draped from her neck. "Oh, perfect! More wine, slave."

Half-grinning, half-gritting his teeth, Manwe took on a tall posture and bent at the waist. "Unfortunately my lady, I'm not a provider for this fine soiree. I am, however, looking for a party who demanded the party magician."

"You're the magician, you say?" One of the boys extracted himself from the tangle of women. "Wait, of course you are. I heard about your display out in the manor yard a few minutes ago! You have found your party, sirrah."

Manwe tilted his head playfully. "Are you sure, my lord? I wouldn't want to dismay another group of fine individuals such as this one."

"Oh, shush," said the first lady with the pearls. She stood and came to Manwe, her sagging breasts and fleshy hips jiggling with each skip. She took his hand and led him close to the bed. "A trick. Now."

Manwe clapped his hands together, looking into the eyes of his seven targets. He smiled broadly as they stared back, absent of any sense. "Well, for my first act I will need a small to medium-sized bag...perhaps one of the pillow cases on your fine bed?"

"How utterly mysterious," drawled a second lady with glittering earrings crusted with emeralds. She grabbed a nearby pillow and stripped it of its cover, handing it to Manwe.

"So," Manwe said, holding the bag in one hand. He pointed to the boy who pointed him out as a 'magician'. "I can't do the same trick with my fire and lights, but..." He pinched his chin. "Ah! An illusion, if you all will permit me."

"Of course," said a third lady, her fingers roped in rings set with gemstones. "I needed a break, anyway."

"My illusion is quite simple." Manwe balled up the pillow case in his hands and snapped it back out, returning it to its original shape. "I will make things disappear."

"How wonderful," said a fourth lady, her arms dripping with gold and silver bangles. Bleary-eyed, she shoveled more dried lotus into her mouth with two fingers stained yellow and blue before passing the bowl onto the next nude participant. She licked her lips to clean off the dust. "We must find something to put in the bag."

"How about we make it interesting?" Manwe proposed, opening the mouth of the pillow case. Bewildered as he watched each member of his audience consume more of the potent drug, he maintained his happy façade. "Ladies, if you would, deposit your jewels. I will make them vanish and reappear."

"Fantastic! An illusion of risk," said the first one with the pearls. The women removed their jewelry and dropped it into the bag. While the ladies cajoled their younger studs to ingest more lotus, Manwe twisted the pillow case lengthwise until it was tightly bound, so much so the gems of the third lady's rings could be seen poking through the fabric.

"And now you'll make them disappear?" one of the boys asked, more interested in the trick than the hand pawing his genitals.

"Oh, but to make them disappear would be such a waste of time," said Manwe clicking his tongue. "Riches like these...well, such baubles are not meant for this world." He gathered the rope of stolen jewels in his hands and crumpled them into a ball like a piece of trash.

The third lady, now bereft of her rings, stood from the bed. "Sirrah! Those were priceless Juutan heirlooms that once belonged to the daughter of a noble savage chieftain. They were liberated by my father who was once the commander of the third Gypian army under Gypisius! I demand you return them at once!"

"And with such wonderful history behind them…" Manwe grinned at her and unbound the ball with a second snap. The pillow case unfurled. "By all means, they're yours," he said, presenting it to her.

Red-eyed and drowsy, the third lady's anger vanished as she turned over the pillow case. Nothing fell out of the sleeve. Confused, she searched the bag until she broke out in laughter. "By Hya's glossy tits, he did it," she exclaimed, showing everyone on the bed.

"And, for the next part of the trick…" Manwe dipped low in his bow, a display he had once witnessed an actor perform in a play. "The treasure has been secured in a hidden place upstairs. We must go and search for it."

"Ah-hah, an illusion and a game!" the first lady jumped up in excitement. "Come on," she waved with spastic vigor, addled to a point beyond control. The occupants of the room emptied out, not forgetting their lotus pot, and scampered off into the hallways in search of their lost treasure.

Manwe looked into his full hands, clutching tightly to the pearls, earrings, rings, and bangles left behind by his audience.

⁂

HIS LOOT COLLECTED IN THE PILLOW CASE HE HAD USED FOR HIS "MAGIC" trick, Manwe strutted down the hall in search of his audience members, hoping the drugged fools would lead him to even greater treasure. On his way to the grand stair in the main foyer of the manor, he was stopped by the trilling of a woman's voice. It grew louder the farther he drew to the foyer, and stepping from the shadowy hallway, he arrived in time to see Folami in the middle of her own impromptu show.

"The Songbird" danced around the many people milling about in the anteroom. It was an old poem set to a common melody used by their tribes out on the savannah. She was joined by a few of the servants who knew the words.

Guessing she had paid them off, Manwe sidestepped into the shadow of an archway, curious to see how her ruse would work.

"*Don't seek too much fame,*" she intoned. She scooted by a drunk couple, stopping to lean toward the husband, her lithe body bent backward. Providing him and his interested wife a long look at her ample bosom, she took both their wrists and spun them on the spot. Delighted by the attention, the rich lord and his lady played their parts, laughing as they turned.

Manwe chuckled from his place in the dark, impressed as Folami slipped off one of the gold bangles hanging loose on the lady's wrist. Before he could blink, it was gone, somewhere out of sight.

Folami backed away from them, gesturing luridly with her arms as she moved onto the next target. She landed her curvaceous body into the lap of a drunken man who had sat down beside the stair, his flagon of wine in one hand and a bag of coins hanging from his belt. "*But don't fear obscurity...*" Writhing on him, all eyes drew to her liberated movements as the servants added a chorus.

"*Don't fear,*" they cooed in harmony.

Folami turned on the drunken man's lap, and facing him, wiggled for the amusement of the crowd. "Be Proud." Her thumb stuck out on her left hand, and staring hard, Manwe noticed the edge of a razor glisten in the haze of the lamp-lit hall. With a quick slice she severed the draw strings tying the pouch to his belt, and spinning off of him, she pushed it into a potted plant beside them, leaving it to be picked up later. Her victim, dazed and delighted, fell back on the steps, where he was patted on the chest and shoulders for his participation by some onlookers.

"*But...do...not...remind the world of your deeds,*" Folami sang, a sad smile on her delicate lips. A man near her reached out and groped the swell of her right buttock, whispering lewd things to his wife while others clapped and cheered.

Manwe noticed a change come over Folami and the servants who sang along, a hint of anger. That same anger welled in the pit of his own stomach, a tell-tale reminder of a plain fact—no matter how rich the culture he, Folami, and the subjugated shared, it would always be considered a trifle to those in power, something to be taken for granted.

The servants in the foyer chorused. "*Your deeds,*" they echoed, the words edged with a dire promise.

His face scrunched at the edge of rage and tears, affected by the hidden message. One day Gypian deeds would be remembered. One day his voice, and the voice of his people, would not be taken for granted.

Folami danced past another couple, her movements smooth and practiced. She grinned at them like a lioness smiling at two old wildebeests. "*Excel when you must.*" She closed in on the pair, throwing her arms around the lady's shoulder and linking her hands behind the woman's slender neck. Clearly the lady had spent near a fortune on her blonde coif that evening, a peculiar fashion popular among the Gypians that formed long hair into a cone held by dozens of jeweled pins.

"*But don't excel the world,*" Folami sighed loudly, supported by her backing singers. She came away, her hands held out at her sides. Manwe found his smile again, noticing that the noble woman's cone was missing more than a few of those expensive needles.

Storing her unseen prizes away in the skirt of her canvas shift, Folami took the center of the room, landing lightly atop a long table weighed with food and jugs of wine. Dancing among the oil lamps set in a line down the length of the wooden top, she spun and floated like a swan, snatching up coins and other baubles carelessly left behind. Through the sheer grace of her voice and the song, she remained clean of her obvious crimes, having transfixed the audience with her performance.

"*Many heroes have not yet been born,*" she shouted melodically.

"*Many have already died,*" thundered the servants, clapping and stamping to a beat and meter only they knew in their hearts, a hearkening call back to former glories and forgotten times.

Swept up by the urge to join them, by the urge to be swept up in his people's faded pride, Manwe stepped into the light of the room.

"*But to be alive to hear this song...*" Folami stretched that final word, dragging it from the depths of her being. She squatted in the middle of the table and lifted up one of the burning lamps. The wick, its end a long line of bright and smoky flame, hung before her face.

"*...is victory,*" mouthed Manwe.

Folami blew out the light.

Manwe let out a deep breath of satisfaction right as Cleon stepped in front of him.

<hr>

"FANCY MEETING YOU HERE."

Manwe gaped in surprise, struck silent.

Cleon stood there, inches away from his face. Clad in his simple yellow robe, a belt made of polished glass squares cinched it around his thin waist, pulling the cloth tight to his well-firmed torso and strong shoulders.

"Don't stare too long, Panther," the sorcerer teased. "People might talk."

Closing his mouth, Manwe realized his hand had slipped behind his back and grabbed his knife. He hid his bag of loot behind the mass of his bare leg as well, his body turned away from his opponent. "We don't have to do this in here. Not with all these people."

"What does a revolutionary care about casualties when he is in the den of his enemy?" Cleon straightened, letting out of a light laugh. "I take it we're indulging in old pastimes tonight, from the display we just witnessed. So who is this girl to you?" He motioned at Folami as she hopped off the table and weaved through the room to collect more loot. "A student, perhaps? A lover?"

"Just a rival."

Cleon puckered his lips and whistled. "Fascinating, you thieves. Your lot is so industrious for so very little." Shaking his head and clicking his tongue, his eyes roamed the room in search of something. "You're too good to be here, Panther. Stealing little things like hair pins and what I imagine to be gaudy jewelry in that bag you're holding is beneath a man of your talents. Something drew you here."

It was then Nelo appeared, draped in a length of translucent silk and The Savannah's Tears. People gasped as she entered the foyer on the way to the stair, entranced by her majesty. The diamonds strewn along her oiled collarbone dazzled.

"Ah," said Cleon. His lips split in a grin. "A fair treasure, Panther. So are you and the little girl racing for it?"

Manwe looked to the sorcerer, his expression muted to hide his surprise at the deduction. "You can only catch one of us."

"You think so?" He took a step back, acting as if he had been struck. "I'm here alone tonight."

"So?"

"So trying to catch both of you would be a waste of time and talent. Added to the fact that I really don't care if you rob some insufferable nobles, I hate being here. Parties are not my scene, but you've proposed an interesting distraction."

"What are you talking about?" asked Manwe.

"Oh, don't be thick," chided Cleon. "I'll go get something to drink and when I am done sipping, I am going to catch one of you. I have fine feelings for you, Panther, but this little songbird..."

Manwe leaned away from the sorcerer. "Why?"

Cleon rolled his eyes, his posture slouched and lifeless. "I'm rich. I just want to make the days go by."

"Then come after me," Manwe said quickly. "Leave her be. You want to take me in anyway."

"Not to the authorities, at least," Cleon said, flirty. "What is this worth to you?"

"If you can catch either of us by morning, we will give up our pursuit of the Tears. If not, you leave us be to go on however we wish, with whatever loot we wish."

"And if I catch you, can I keep you?"

For all of his distrust of the sorcerer, for their sordid history with each other, Manwe found himself laughing at the absurdity of the man. "Not in shackles."

"Oh, of course not. I would tie you up with something far softer."

Immediately discomforted by the ease of their words, Manwe grew serious. "Do we have a deal?" he asked, offering a hand.

Cleon looked down at it, perplexed. "You have an hour."

MANWE SPOTTED FOLAMI AS SHE DEPARTED INTO A NEARBY HALLWAY. Dodging and darting past the mass of drunken wealth and obliterated excess, he closed the distance before she disappeared.

He reached for her arm. "Folami!"

Folami flinched when his hand touched her skin, turning about on her rear foot while stepping back with the front. Small blades tied to the insides of her thumbs and forefingers flared from behind their respective digits, bared to damage. She ceased her clawing when she saw who had stopped her.

"What is wrong with you?" she said, whining. "We are in the middle of the game."

"Not for much longer," said Manwe. "Cleon caught me in the crowd. He is giving us an hour before he comes looking for us."

"What does he want with me? I've caused him no problems."

"Cleon doesn't care about problems. This is a game for him to catch me, but if he gets you, he will not be so kind."

"Typical men."

Manwe made a sour face at her. "Either way, the game is over. We need to find Nelo, or at the very least a place to hide. You can have all the loot. Just leave me the necklace."

Drawing up her toned body in a strained sigh, Folami nodded as she pushed the air through her nostrils.

They remained in the foyer, where Nelo still basked in the strange adoration of her guests. Men reached out to touch her naked breasts or kiss her body while the women scratched at her exposed flesh, some of them reaching between her legs. Headed for the stairs, she picked members out of the crowd, forming a chain behind her as she ascended.

"Hurry," said Folami, dashing forward.

Back into the field of party-goers, Manwe kept after her until they were at the end of the procession following Nelo as she rose to the second floor. Unlike the base level, this floor was a circular hall of rooms, each one shut off by a stout door made of olive. No torches or lamps lit the passages, leaving the group to tread in a concealing darkness.

They were ready to follow Nelo into whatever chamber she would enter when a hand grasped Manwe's bare shoulder. He started, turning to find Cleon standing behind them. The sorcerer grabbed him and Folami by the arms, his pale fingers dug into the flesh of their dark skin.

"And look at that. A kitty and a birdie," he said, smirking.

"You promised an hour," said Manwe, panicked.

Folami shucked out of Cleon's hold, her hands spread to reveal her razors. "I care little for your feud with The Panther, sorcerer," she said, nodding at Manwe. "Leave me be or I'll cut your throat."

Cleon hummed in disappointment. "You're definitely not as fun," he told her. "I'd watch your tongue, girl. Little black ladies tend to disappear when a suggestion is made by an upstanding member of this city's authority." He stepped between them and set his arms around his captives' shoulders. "But I'm a fair sport. Let's let these little fools go to their orgies and binges first," he proposed, signaling ahead to the crowds disappearing into the bedrooms. "We'll just wait right here."

"Why are you doing this?" Folami asked. "You have us. There's no need to play games."

"I completely disagree." Cleon pulled her in close enough to whisper. "You see, my little songbird, as I've previously explained to Manwe, I don't really care if you rob the wealthy. Most of them robbed someone else for their riches anyway. What I do care about is seeing the best in this city. As the designated thief-chaser, it's good for me to know the capabilities of my opposition. So..." He looked ahead, a leering smile on his thin face. "You and the Panther have five minutes to pick a room. Maybe it's the one Nelo is in. Maybe it's not. Either way, once that five minutes is over, I will catch who ever walks back out into the shadows."

"This isn't a game," Folami retorted. "This is sick."

"You give them one chance and all they do is whine about that chance. Youths," Cleon grumbled to Manwe.

The final doors shut in the dark.

"You first," Cleon told Folami, freeing her from the crook of his arm. "Go on. Go on, little bird. I'll catch up."

Folami backed away, her eyes on the sorcerer. After a few steps, she turned and ran into the halls.

"Your turn," he whispered to Manwe. "Don't be long."

Manwe ran, not looking back. His bare feet padded the wooden floor as he sank into shadows, darting to the left wing of the upper level. He made a full circuit of the floor, passing Cleon once, who gave a friendly wave at him as he went by. He ignored him as he counted the doors. There were six—two in the left and right wings of floor, one in the hall at the back, and a single door that led to a chamber situated in the center.

He ignored that single door to the center, thinking on the fact that Nelo had spent the entire night at her debauchery, and at some point all bodies weakened under such strain. His thought was confirmed when he heard groans from behind the portal, too fresh and too enthused. That left him the door in the rear hallway and the four in the wings.

At some point he knew full well no amount of calculation could exceed his luck in this case. Stopping in the left wing of the upper floor, he picked the second door on the right. He grabbed the handle and pushed, diving for a roll into the bedroom. Carpet prickled his back, and when he landed on his feet, he froze.

Lying on the gigantic bed in the center of the room was Nelo.

The wife of the Senate Consul of Tolivius rested upon her plush cotton mattress, smiling dreamily as calm rays of moonlight entered through the balcony outside. Her eyes shut, she moaned as she turned over, her sensuous body twisting luridly in silk.

Manwe almost grinned at his own dumb luck until a secret door opened and in stepped a man. Drunk and blinking, he looked at Nelo on her bed, taking a few furtive steps in her direction.

"Nelo," this stranger whispered. "Is that you?"

Manwe dropped, belly down.

Nelo stirred. "Taeus? Is that you finally?"

"It's I, my love. Where is your husband?"

"In the basement with some ten year-olds," she answered. "The pig almost dared to think he would touch me tonight."

"Ugh," said Taeus. The lord climbed onto the bed. "I lost my shrew somewhere on the lawn. She's such a sanctimonious little bitch. She doesn't understand anything like you do."

"We are animals, you and I," Nelo replied. Lips met, wet and smacking. Nelo murmured something and groaned. "...we are chosen by the true gods."

The couple rolled and thrashed on the bed for a moment, gasping and calling each other's names, and then silence.

They started to snore.

Manwe rose, incredulous. Taeus and Nelo had sprawled in two different areas of the bed, far from each other's reach. Taeus drooled on the cotton, his hand still reaching for Nelo's leg.

It only took a blink of an eye for Manwe to walk around the bed and remove her necklace. A quick pull of the silk in the back freed it from her body, and he waited for Nelo to turn over in her sleep, leaving behind the treasure.

With the diamond beads hidden with the rest of his loot in the front of his loin cloth, Manwe went to the balcony in search of an easy escape. Out on the suspended platform of wood and stone, he looked out, seeing the roof of the manor's first level only a few feet below him. He hopped the thigh-high fencing and ran for the next edge. He leapt to a bare patch of grass on an empty piece of lawn, clearing a row of bushes as he landed hard on his knees.

Looking up and wincing, he tilted his head in surprise when he saw a figure run across the grass.

Folami sprinted as two men in yellow robes chased after her. To Manwe's surprise, they were exact matches of Cleon.

"Ah, there you are."

Manwe rolled to his back to find the sorcerer standing over him. "Impossible."

"Is it?" Cleon asked. "Well, go on, Panther. Run."

"Don't you want to know whether or not I have The Savannah's Tears?" he asked.

"I really don't care."

"Then why chase her?"

The sorcerer shrugged his shoulders. "Fun."

Manwe turned to check on Folami. To his sincere happiness she had cleared the yard, scaling up one of the many trees before the manor wall. The two clones of Cleon had stopped at the base of one of the trunks, arguing with each other about who was to blame. "So what now?"

Cleon offered his hand.

Helped to his feet, Manwe stood before the cunning Gypian. Their eyes met, and he stared into Cleon's luminous brown pools, transfixed by the life within them. They reminded him of Toba's eyes—full of joy. "Why do you do this, Cleon? You're supposed to hunt me, and I'm supposed to run."

"What can I say? I don't like rules."

"You're such a peculiar man."

"And you're a riddle."

"How so?" asked Manwe.

Cleon took a step toward him, close enough that only a few inches separated their faces. He hesitated, a breath held back, until he leaned forward. The warmth of their lips together almost made Manwe weak in his legs, if only for a second, before the sorcerer backed away.

"You're my riddle," said Cleon. "What do I find so alluring about a rebel?"

It was a question Manwe knew well, and one he couldn't answer himself.

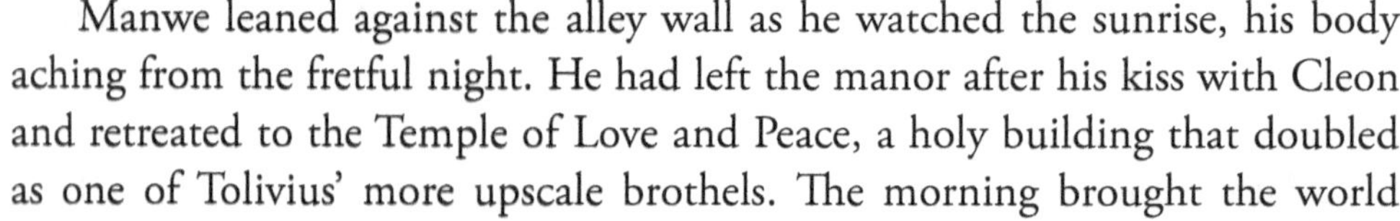

Manwe leaned against the alley wall as he watched the sunrise, his body aching from the fretful night. He had left the manor after his kiss with Cleon and retreated to the Temple of Love and Peace, a holy building that doubled as one of Tolivius' more upscale brothels. The morning brought the world warmth, pushing away the dreariness of the night. The sun settled on his wall, blasting him in its light.

"I thought you were dead."

He looked to his right, into the alley's shadows. There stood Folami, her hands behind her back as she leaned against the opposing wall. "Morning."

"How did you get away?" she asked. "I saw Cleon standing over you."

"He let me go."

They fell to silence, neither speaking nor making eye contact for long minutes. Dawn seeped into their narrow lane.

"Did you get it?" Folami asked.

Manwe reached into his loin cloth and pulled out the Savannah's Tears, each diamond bead a spark of fire. "Oh, and I have these." He bent down at his side and picked up two knotted pillow cases. Tossing them to her, they struck the cobblestones by her feet.

"Now you'll tell me you just walked back into the manor and recovered all of it," Folami said, sarcastic.

"If you must know..."

"Save it." She gathered what was accorded to her, a small sack she threw over his shoulder. "This day's been long enough as it is."

"I heard you tonight. When you sang." Manwe rolled the line of diamonds in his hands. "You know the cause is just."

"What if it is, Panther?" she replied, tired. "We're thieves. Criminals. Justice doesn't apply to us, nor do we wish it to."

"Just because we're criminals doesn't mean we deserve indignity. The Gypian occupation must end."

"Then I'll leave you to end it." She turned to slink deeper into the twisting paths of the city, but stopped at the blind corner of the next building. "Manwe?"

"Yes, Folami?"

She tossed back one of the loot bags. "I'll put a good word in."

Left alone, Manwe returned his attention to the necklace in his possession. Pleased by the diamonds' sparkle, he gathered the line into a ball and squeezed them in his hand, ready for what came next.

THE END

THIEF OF SECRETS

WHEN SHADOWS WALKED ON LEGENDS

KAARLE RAN UNTIL HIS KNEES BURNED. MILE AFTER MILE PASSED UNDERFOOT, until the skin on the bottom of his feet peeled and bled, each step a plea for him to stop, give up—anything to ease the agony shooting up his legs. Tears ran from his eyes, hot and salted.

The darkness of the Glass Jungles, filled with their green-leafed shadows and silence, echoed his labored gasps as he came to the edge of the great forests, where the sunlit hills of the yellow savannah burned under the early autumn sun, a white wheel brighter than any jewel.

At the edge of consciousness, Kaarle tripped on a small rock hidden in the hard soil. His big toe ripped open by its gray edge, he tumbled headfirst to the earth, rolling onto his neck and shoulder, the latter popping out of its joint with a sear of frozen fire that numbed his body. Flopping onto his naked back, he stared up into the bright blue vault of the sky, its cloudless expanse lifeless and parched.

"Please, Anga," he whispered through dry, broken lips. "Please. Please save me."

The Goddess of Life said nothing.

The light of the sky shimmered at the edge of sight, and as he blinked, Kaarle knew he would soon see no more. The wind filled his ears as the light faded.

For an eternity he mired in the dark, corporality a far-off thought among the starry drifts of an endless night. Somewhere between eternity and death, warmth found its way to him. A notion of sense returned—his face, at first, then the rest of his body, until one moment he woke from his slumber to a chilling voice he knew all too well.

"Best to leave him out on the plains, where the gods will claim his flesh and free his soul," said Voduni Calla, his tone bleak.

"The Panther would skin me alive for it," said another voice, this one firm and deep. "If he wakes, he wakes, and if he dies then we will pay him the greatest of respect. The boy has given much for his people. Just like his friends did."

Voduni Calla hissed at the response. "One boy does not win a war."

"But many brave ones do," said Kaarle, his throat sore as he finished the rest of the old Juutan saying. He opened his eyes, squinting against the small light of the oil lamp set beside his bed. The glimmer of the wick revealed the faint walls of a cavern, and as his eyes adjusted, he made out the forms of the two men at the foot of his pallet.

He recognized Kosey first, elated when the rebel lord smiled upon him with his curve of silver moonlight. A strapping man who was younger than he looked, he sat sturdy on a tall wooden stool, his short spear resting across his lap and a cowhide shield by his feet. The scratches and dents in his iron breastplate gleamed like the honey rings of his eyes, the irises made bright by the contrast of the thick beard on his black face and his unkempt shock of woolen hair.

"Ah, there he is," Kosey said, spreading his arms open in celebration.

One of Kosey's ebon limbs almost touched Voduni Calla, who took a slight jerk away with a sneer. The skinny man's umber arms and shoulders, exposed from the cut outs of his black robes, revealed flesh layered in thick lines left by a slave master's whip. Around the old man's neck hung a necklace made of small bones, bits of quail, and monkey toes, all of which hung taut by a single skull that served as a pendant—the bleached head of a vulture. His sneer transformed into a frown as he looked to Kaarle, his eyes two points of hatred.

"Where am I?" Kaarle asked, looking around the cavern.

"You're at the new camp," said Kosey. "You've been asleep for two days."

"Two days?" Kaarle tried to sit up, but a sharp pain from his shoulder spread across his chest. His breath sucked from his body, he fell back onto the hay. Wheezing, he dipped his chin to look at the bandages binding his shoulder. "Where is he? Where's Manwe?"

"There will be plenty of time for that later, Kaarle," said Kosey, unmoved by the young man's pain. Elbows rested on the shaft of his spear, his posture relaxed. "For now you need to tell me what happened."

"What do you mean?"

"Aemon's Fort, boy," cawed Voduni Calla. "You were sent there to help the thief free our captured lieutenants of the Glass Jungles campaign before they were executed. Word of the events are skewed."

"I'm sorry, Voduni, but I don't know what you mean." Kaarle eyed the old witchdoctor with fear—it never paid to upset one of their like. "I remember the Glass Jungle. I remember..."

Kosey rose from his stool and went over to a small bucket near a chest. Drawing a mouthful of water with a carved ladle, he brought it over to Kaarle and held it by his mouth. "Calm, little brother. Take a sip and tell us what you can."

The cool water slaked the dryness in his throat, and swallowing for the first time without pain, Kaarle breathed. Through the cobwebs of the mind he saw the white walls of Tolivius. "As Voduni Calla said, we were to meet The Panther for a raid on the fort."

LEADING NOBOU AND SIMO INTO THE DARKENED ALLEY BETWEEN THE Gypian temple of the Goddess of Love and a second dedicated to yet one more of the invaders' deities, Kaarle looked wide-eyed into the passage, expecting their contact to already be there. His hand on the iron knife he held beneath his blue cloak, he stopped a few feet past the threshold, his eyes darting from the ground to the two roofs above him.

"He's not here," said Simo, the youngest of the trio. "We should leave."

"Our orders were clear," Kaarle replied, standing still on the paved stones. He spied a set of stairs at the end of the alley, a decline leading down to an olive door of the Goddess of Love's temple. "Are we in the wrong alley?"

"It doesn't matter if this is the right one or the wrong one," Simo argued. "Voduni Calla said we can't trust a murderer of shamans and lords."

"And yet Voduni Calla is quick to send boys to their deaths," called a strong voice behind them.

Turning in an instant, Kaarle reached forward and stopped Simo before he charged, recognizing immediately the figure in the alley's mouth.

His face shadowed by the sun's angle, the man's short stature was made up for by a set of powerful shoulders and the flair of his defined hips. His upper body was draped in a dusty red cloak. A curved iron dagger hung in the band of his loincloth. Dressed only in this simple garb, it was his eyes that drew Kaarle's attention. Within those black eyes gleamed the cold light of a killer, though the gleam held no great or natural malice. A rough beard covered a pointed chin, and the hair on his head grew out in a large, woolen mass.

Manwe the Panther stared at the three rebels. "Password."

Kaarle broke ahead of Simo and placed his hand on Nobou's forearm, forcing his weapon down. "The cranes fly at dusk."

"For the panther hunts where shadows walk," said Manwe, completing the phrase. He studied the three of them. "Are you all Kosey sent?"

"We are more than enough, thief," said Simo, his eyes narrowed with insult. He held his knife down, keeping it at the ready.

Manwe shifted toward the boy, his posture slouched. "Are you enough to spot the soldiers marching behind you?"

Once again the three turned on their heels. Out in the daylight of Tolivius' corrupt metropolis marched an endless column three men wide. Even Simo hid his knife as the three retreated deeper into the building's shade. The four watched in dread quiet as the center of the line passed by. Riding in a gilded chariot driven by a slender man in a fine tunic cut from cloth of gold, the rider standing behind him that chilled Kaarle's blood.

Upright and lean, the tallest Gypian he had ever seen surveyed the street before him with a dispassionate gaze. Too far to see the finer features of his face, what became clear to Kaarle was that this man, this mountain of bronze muscle and honey-brown hair, was far more than any soldier or lord the western invaders often sent to rape his people's land. This one was like a god, and if the people of Juut's conquered savannah knew anything, the gods of the Gypians were the heralds of ruin.

"Who is he?" asked Nobou, sounding more like a boy than ever.

"Someone to be considered." Manwe headed for the steps leading down to the Goddess of Love's temple, every movement smooth and assured. "Come along."

Seeing his fellows glance at him for direction, Kaarle nodded for them to follow the thief down the short flight of stairs. Manwe knocked three times on the door and waited until the viewing slot slid open. A pair of bright blue eyes looked out from the space.

"What is the goddess' secret?" a woman's voice asked.

"The goddess has no secrets," the thief replied. "I'm bringing three in with me, Magera."

Her eyes slid to Kaarle and his two friends. "Are they armed?" she asked, not unbarring the door.

"I have it on good authority that they will behave themselves." He raised the hem of his cloak, revealing the iron knife tucked in his band. "I'll make sure of it."

A bar slid free, and the door opened to reveal a beguiling woman. Blonde hair framed a tanned face, tresses that fell down her sleek shoulders to frame a pair of firm breasts covered in translucent blue silk. The same material girded her loins, held up by a band of polished bronze rings that pressed into the flesh of her hips. A few bronze keys dangled from a hook forged into one of these rings.

Barefoot, she stepped to the side, allowing them space to enter.

Simo protested as Manwe broke forward. "I'm not going into a Gypian whorehouse, Kaarle," he said, his voice pitched high. "She is the enemy!"

"Whether you enter or not, this door will always be open to those seeking solace," Magera replied, offering a wounded smile. "But if you do not wish to enter then you do not have to."

"Pardon me a moment," said Manwe, raising his hand to stop her. "Would you kindly close the door?"

Her wounded smile dimmed as the silk-clad priestess looked at the thief for a moment and nodded, closing the door gently. Manwe faced Simo and stepped close. Nose to nose with the young man, the whites of his eyes seemed to glow as he spoke. "Whose orders do you follow?"

Chest out and his arms tight, Simo sneered at him. "Kosey, thief. A man who doesn't murder lords in their bed, but faces them, brave on battlefields."

"That's enough, Simo." Kaarle placed himself between the two of them. "If that is true then we are to follow Kosey's order, and his order was to follow The Panther's. If succeeding in this mission requires us to go into a Gypian temple, so be it."

"But Kaarle, she is a whore," said Simo. "Voduni Calla says that Gypian whores are—"

"Watch your tongue," rumbled Manwe. His face a mask of quiet promise, the thief's words muted the rebel and his defiant pose. Simo looked down at his feet with a half-frown, half-snarl, hands away from his knife.

Kaarle sighed, his scarred shoulders rising and falling as he nodded to Manwe. The thief knocked on the door for a second time; Magera answered, slowly opening the portal. Her expression of concern faded when she saw all four men still standing, and with a quiet wave, she welcomed them into the bordello.

The first room, a simple chamber littered in the things one expected to find in Gypian temples—prayer flags, mosaic floors, offering fires—but joined with a population of different reliefs and statues, each one an effigy to acts of romance and carnal pleasure. Manwe and the priestess walked past rows of tapestries nailed to the walls, scenes of men and women caught in the throes of pleasure, sometimes in pairs, sometimes with animals and gods. Kaarle averted his eyes and smiled as he followed, a heat still finding its way into his cheeks.

The next room, however, stopped him in his tracks.

Basking in the light of a hundred oil lamps, a knot of bodies writhed upon the hard floor, lost among an uncountable number of brightly colored and beaded pillows. A mass of both Gypians and native Juutans, men's tongues met with other men's tongues while women's fingers probed places left uncovered for all to see.

Some couples engaged in the deepest acts of love groaned and thrust at each other, flesh slapping flesh in uncontrolled beats of ecstasy. Oil dripped down curves and crannies of toned, lithe forms. Some of those who partook in the orgy wore masks carved in the manner of the invader's gentler gods, or the beasts and birds that were to be found out on the savannah. Incense hazed the air, heady scents of vanilla and rose, mingling with the fragrant potpourri of the dried flowers hanging from the ceiling's supports.

Manwe glanced back at Kaarle, paying the scene little attention. "Are you three coming, or do you need more time to gawk?"

Kaarle blinked a few times before he realized he had been staring at one Gypian, who looked back with a tawdry grin as she pushed her fingers into the opening of her vagina. Breaking eye contact, he checked on his two compatriots.

Much to his amusement, Nobou had indeed stood there the entire time, gawking as the young man reached in his loin cloth to fondle himself. Kaarle slapped at the offending arm, shoving Nobou along with a chuckle and light insult.

Simo, standing to Kaarle's left, could not have been more the opposite—his white teeth clenched tight as he held firm to the handle of the knife in his belt, muttering quiet curses.

"Come on," Kaarle whispered, tugging on his arm. "We're not here for bloodshed. Not yet, anyway."

"Look at this evil," his friend seethed. "Gypians and our brothers...our sisters! How could our people defile their own flesh with such..."

"Just come on." Kaarle pulled Simo toward the next doorway.

THEY ENTERED A LONG HALL, ITS WALLS CARVED FROM THE DARK ROCK THE temple proper rested upon. Manwe had followed Magera to the left, down past a series of stout wooden doors set on both sides of the hall. They came to the last door on the right.

Magera extracted a key from one of the rings holding up the silk around her hips and handed it to Manwe. "Let me know when your meeting is finished. I'll have rooms made up for you and your friends." The priestess glided past Kaarle, grinning at the young man as his eyes followed the sway of her hips.

Manwe slid the bronze fork into the gilded slot, lifting the latch bar to free the lock. "Say nothing," he told them, glaring at Simo with warning.

The four entered the lone chamber, a medium-sized bedroom furnished with a pair of chairs, a bed, and a small table. Sitting beside a lit oil lamp, a thin man waited on the down mattress, wearing nothing but a red chiton and a pair of road-worn sandals that laced up to his knees. He glanced up from the pile of papers on his lap, quiet as he caught sight of Manwe.

"Good evening, Sophicus," said the thief as he approached the foot of the bed. "Does the night find you well?"

"Well enough for a traitor's work." Sophicus reached down and lifted a bottle of putrid wine. He slaked his thirst with a long draw and wiped his bearded face with a forearm. "Let's not dally, Panther. These boys part of that damned rebellion out in the hills?"

"They are my guests. That is all you should concern yourself with." Manwe placed his hands out to the side, a common gesture of peace among both Gypians and Juutans. "Do you have what I need?"

"Depends," said the man sitting on the bed, taking another draw of wine. "Do you have it?"

"Allow me a moment." Manwe pulled forward the band of his loin cloth, using his free hand to fish out a long, glittering strand. Kaarle's breath caught when he recognized the diamonds, a legendary length of glory held together with interwoven leather thongs.

"The Savannah's Tears, as promised," said Manwe, laying the necklace on the end of the mattress.

Sophicus, his face cut into two by the lamp's light, frowned. "Oh shit, Manwe."

"Is there a problem?" the thief inquired.

The Gypian sighed deep as he reached forward to collect his payment. "I thought you were joking when you said you'd steal it. I never thought you'd actually..."

"You're the best fence in Tolivius, Sophicus," Manwe said, taking up the tense silence. "You'll find a way."

Sophicus rose to his feet and headed toward the door, shaking his head with every step. "If I don't end up dead first."

The fence exited the room quickly without farewell or warning and, left on their own, Manwe bade the three over to the bed. "Sit down, all of you. We only have so many hours to plan out tomorrow morning."

"You gave away the Savannah's Tears," Simo said as he neared. "That was our people's treasure."

"Baubles or freedom, boy," said Manwe, spreading the sheets of parchment out on the bedding. "Which do you want more?"

Simo plodded his way to one of the chairs in the room. Kaarle sat down at the foot of the bed while Nobou leaned against the chamber's door.

"These are maps of Aemon's Fort, which is located on the eastern side of the city's center, near the Senate Consul's sanctum and his philosopher courts."

Manwe moved the lamp off the side table and rested it on the bed, taking great care to ensure it did not tip over and spill its contents. On the hide was sketched a series of careful designs in a firm hand, the black ink sharp and defined. The thief rotated each sheet and layered them. The corners connected into a large view of the city's layout, which revealed the entirety of the fort and the surrounding governmental buildings.

Manwe looked to Kaarle. "How many of Kosey's lieutenants were captured?"

"Twelve, but we know at least six of them were tortured to death," Kaarle said. "Many of them are the sons of loyal chieftains who have given much to The Cause. To lose these men would be too much of a blow. Kosey worries that they might withdraw support."

"That happens when you don't win battles," replied Manwe, rubbing his eyes with his dark fingers. "Aemon's Fort is penetrable, more of a showpiece than an actual garrison. This execution is just a show for visiting dignitaries who will be in attendance. The Senate Consul must be worried enough about the rebellion to put on such a display."

Nobou spoke, his youthful baritone filled with hurt. "You make us sound like flies to the invaders as they supper."

"Everyone is an insect to the rich." Manwe tapped the spot where the maps' corners met. "Most of the city's guard will be at the walls tomorrow morning, or in the streets. There are too many spears and shields to keep at the fort and that can make a lord sweat with worry. With The Latian Lion in attendance, they will pay deference to their hero before they embarrass him with the notion he cannot keep them safe."

"Who?" asked Kaarle, his rough hands rested on his lap.

"The man in the chariot," said Simo, his belligerence opening to realization. "That was who passed by us outside, wasn't it?"

"Indeed," said Manwe. "He's a great champion of a kingdom to the south of Gypus, a legend in his own time who pulls the heads off of his enemies with his bare hands and may be the son of Adias, the lightning king of their gods."

"Why is he here for an execution?" Simo asked. "What does a Latian have to do with Gypus?"

"Nothing. Everything." Manwe glanced up from the constructed map, searching the liminal space of darkness and light for something, an idea Kaarle imagined no other man would think of besides the thief, a figure that was spoken of in many of the same tones as this "Latian Lion" supposedly was. "For what I know of Latia, I'm glad we only have to throw back Gypians. Most likely this visit from one of their dignitaries is a show that all things are in order as well as a reminder to the Latians that Gypus enforces its sovereignty, even on the frontier."

"So what are we to do?" asked Kaarle.

Manwe returned to his study of the map. A dangerous grin formed. "We show both sides otherwise."

"THAT BLASPHEMOUS, TRAITOROUS, SAVAGE WHELP OF A WHORE," SCREAMED Voduni Calla, his arms up and waving. Shadows played on the cave wall, one an outline that matched the enraged mystic's, the other a tall, stoic silhouette that remained firm in its bearing.

Kosey stared hard at his co-conspirator. "The Panther has his reasons for giving up The Savannah's Tears, and like Kaarle relates, what is a mere bauble for the freedom of our people?"

"Don't you dare defend him! I tire of your defending this lout," shouted Voduni Calla with a long, skeletal finger pointed at Kosey. "To sell the Gem of Acitus to the Gypians was a sweet irony I could abide, but to sell drops of starlight stained with the blood of our ancient queens..." The shaman's frail body shook within the confines of his black wrap, a writhing shadow disturbed by every movement. He noticed Kaarle's stare. "And then to take our young men, the pride of Juut, into a Gypian whorehouse, where race traitors are rutting with western filth? What indignities will you allow this cur to stain us with before you finally see him for what he is?"

"Who Manwe works with is who Manwe works with," Kosey said, bordering on anger. "We must take our allies where we can get them, Voduni. No man is an island, and no island can turn the tides of a sea."

"Cease with pretty poems, Kosey," Voduni Calla snarled, his hairless face screwed in a mask of discontent. "I tolerated your brother, both his larcenous habits and his baser ones."

Kosey's jaw clenched. More than six feet tall and carved from hard, black ebony, his intense eyes fixed on the mystic, and for a moment Kaarle feared that the leader of Juut's just rebellion would attack this holy man for ill words spoken of a heroic brother—even if the man had fenced for Tolivius' greatest thief. The silver taken from The Panther's exploits had gone back into the fight for freedom, and to hear someone speak so poorly of one who had gone to join their ancestors was a grave insult.

Yet much to Kaarle's surprise, Kosey merely turned away and retook his seat on the stool. Voduni Calla stared daggers at the warrior but remained on his spot, neither leaving nor coming as close as he had been to the bed.

Kosey's exhaustion, trapped in the crevices of his face, shoulders, and legs, revealed itself as he spoke to Kaarle. "Go on, little brother. What happened at Aemon's Fort?"

Stuck between the shock of his leader cowed and the seething voduni, Kaarle remained quiet for a moment. He recalled the hot day, the stale scent of the fort's limestone, and the first question.

"CAN THEY RUN FAST?" MANWE ASKED, HIS ATTENTION TIED TO THE LONG strips of black linen he bound to his hands and wrists. He walked down the narrow lane at a brisk pace, paying no attention to the rats or beggars who scurried out of his way. A cat, feasting on the carcass of one of the diseased vermin, hissed at him as he passed.

Kaarle followed, buckling on the sword belt the thief had handed him the moment they had left Tolivius' busy streets. "Nobou, definitely." He jammed the metal bit into one of the belt's ragged holes, hoping the length of leather would hold tight enough that the sword's naked blade could not bite with its uneven edge. "Simo might run the wrong way, toward the enemy."

"A fool is a fool, alive or dead."

Behind them the long lines of rabble choked the road, a morass of olive and black bodies stinking of oil and sweat. Seagulls flying above the cluttered roofs cried out in the sweltering morning, the rare day where the humidity of the city's wells, baths, and latrines coated all things in a layer of almost-invisible grime. The farther into the alley they went, the more the metropolitan sounds faded, replaced with the patting of bare feet on stone and dirt, the skitter of the rodents, and a foreboding quiet. Up ahead loomed a towering wall of limestone, pitted and scarred, which made up the western side of Aemon's Fort.

Kaarle felt his eyes widen the higher he craned to look for the edge, a bare line that he knew separated him and the thief from the den of their great enemy. The fort had once been the site of a temple dedicated to Ogan-Badah; the Iron Prince of his gods, long before the Gypians demolished what had been there and erected a place of death and punishment.

Never shy from battle, Kaarle muttered a small prayer, hoping the Lord of Bravery and Change still resided somewhere in the behemoth—at least enough so to see him out alive.

"When we get up there, you need to follow me and not get lost," said Manwe, showing no trepidation. Loose and relaxed, he shed his red cloak when he finished tying the wrappings around his hands and wrists. "Stay close."

"There's no way," Kaarle exclaimed, his eyes to the wall. "We aren't monkeys."

"No one is anything beyond what they do." The thief grabbed one of the pits in the wall, finding a handhold that Kaarle had not detected. Like some black spider, he started to climb, hands and feet finding every crack, hole, or seam in the wall that allowed him to ascend. Amazed at this feat of strength and dexterity, he followed beneath Manwe, his fingers hurting every time he touched the stone.

Foot after foot, nose to the wall, a shock set in after a few short minutes when Kaarle's hand grasped a soft yet defined edge, the grit in his palms powdery. Manwe offered a hand to help pull him over, and standing at the top of the wall, the young rebel looked back down into the alley, shocked at the feat he had achieved.

"How?"

"Simply do." Manwe started along the parapets, crouched low to avoid being seen by any of the guards who patrolled the tops of the walls. Much to Kaarle's surprise, the heights of Aemon's Fort were remarkably empty, a series of flights and landings that crisscrossed the entire inside of the fort in a sloping lattice.

Down below and set before the wall stood a long, wooden platform in the sun, home to a series of simple gibbets and a few posts for the lashings of the Gypians often held before the public as reminders to the enslaved. Stark in its bleached wood and dingy appearance, it remained apart from the fort's great keep, a pyramid bricked in the same limestone as the walls.

"They really did take everything, didn't they?" Kaarle asked aloud, more to himself than his companion.

Manwe descended the steps like a liquid shadow. "Only what we allowed."

The pair came to the last few levels above the gory stage, and looking around, Manwe pointed to a series of wagons set in the courtyard holding pallets of upright clay amphorae. "See those pots? If the notes given to me by Sophicus are accurate, those are containers of serpent's blood. I want you to sneak over there during the execution, when the crowds have arrived, and use them to cause a distraction. If Simo and Nobou are able to kill a few senators in the offices of the government district, the guards left behind will be forced to converge there out of necessity, leaving me time to free the hostages."

"By yourself, Panther? Even with your great skills, one man cannot face off against the might of the Gypian guards by himself."

The thief's eyes flashed in challenge of the statement. "Why not?"

"All the things they say about you cannot be true," Kaarle said. "Some of it is just impossible."

Manwe looked ahead with a different sort of focus, a curiosity that did not seem worried, Kaarle thought, but a mindfulness of what was said and of how it was said. He crouched down on hands and feet, knelt much in the way of his namesake, a ferocious beast of cunning and surprising resourcefulness.

"What do they say?" the thief questioned.

Sitting down beside the squatting shadow, Kaarle studied the layout of the dusty courtyard, trying to imagine what his companion saw. "Lots of things. Did you truly slay a Gypian lord in his bed while his lover slept beside him?"

Manwe's chest rose with a sigh. "She was quite awake. Probably still is."

"But you did do it?" Kaarle's voice heightened with hope. "Just like you stole the Gem of Acitus from the depths of the underworld?"

"So they told you I went to the underworld, did they?"

"Of course. You entered two mouths in the mother, the places from where we rose. They say that true vodunis spend years in that darkness, finding out the secrets of the oldest ancients."

When Manwe spoke, his tone was bleak in both brevity and emotion. "If that is where souls go after they die, I'd rather be a ghost."

Kaarle gasped at the idea. "A ghost? Unsown and unfinished?"

"Why not?" Manwe tilted his head. "Maybe I'll be a new spirit of The Highest One, and one day you'll all pray to me."

People entered the fort through the main gates to the south, gigantic doors of hardwood studded in nails with heads the size of shields. Many had brought bottles of wine, a flaky loaf, even their wives and children to see native Juutans die, a gross celebration of one people's domination.

"Why are you fighting for freedom?" Kaarle asked. "Many of us hope the murder of the lord is real, though we don't say so out loud in front of the holy folk."

"It was real." Manwe stared down at the gibbets, his gaze faraway. "I was angry."

Kaarle turned his head in The Panther's direction, keen to know the inside of this freedom fighter's mind. "And then there is a whisper of a party. They say that you and another of the city's cut-purses fended off a Gypian sorcerer and stole the Savannah's Tears. I know you did that."

"And what do you think of it?" Manwe asked, hinting at annoyance.

"I think you're the hero Kosey needs beside him. It's not him supporting the forces. It is the wealth you bring us. We have weapons and armor because of you. We are nowhere near the strength of the Gypians, but you're doing more than the rest of us. The few battles we have won came from your thieving."

Squatted on his heels, Manwe crouched at the edge of the landing like some dark demon from the old tales Kaarle's grandmother used to tell, or like one of the whispered horrors vodunis conjured on the battlefield when things were at their most desperate. Kaarle shook his head and shut his eyes, trying not to remember how many times he has witnessed such hell.

"I don't do well with the other group," said Manwe. "There are those like Voduni Calla who would rather have their power than freedom. Call me an atheist, but I've been in the dark depths where the unclean souls go, and I found things worse than legends. I found something real. Something we have forgotten about this world is dangerous, and I think we might wake up things we don't like around us, let alone within ourselves. And vodunis are willing to do that for the sake of their might. "

The point, quick and mindful, quieted Kaarle as he and the thief waited for the show to begin. Herds of people finished filing into the massive courtyard of Aemon's Fort, some of them there to celebrate a community brought together by death, while some were there to feed their quiet lusts, knowing one race, one society, was better than the other.

The sun towered high when Kaarle parted through the crowds, down to where the wagons full of a volatile distraction waited. Much to his surprise, there were indeed fewer guards, and the ones he came across paid a slave master's attention to seeing yet another slave. He drew his knife and a small piece of flint he had traded a kiss for with the Gypian priestess back at the temple.

A great voice boomed on the air.

"We punish those who do not know their place. Our kingdoms are jewels in the light of knowledge, ability, and innovation. All men will be made equal, in time, but only by adherence to our law. Consider this as we bring justice to those who chose otherwise."

Working at a desperate speed to tear a piece of his clothing, Kaarle gave up the futile notion and searched his surroundings. He heard the trumpets, silver and bold, signal the executioner's march.

The great doors of the keep opened. Chained and shackled in bright iron, the Sons of Juut plodded out into the daylight, a condemned line of five men guarded by at least fifteen armored warriors, the heads of their spears and shields glinting in the sun. Kaarle recognized these prisoners, the princes of Juut's savannah tribes, men who had gone out to fight for freedom—and lost. Black flesh and muscle clung to emaciated, bruised bodies, clear signs of torture.

A needling thought came to him in that moment: what if the Gypians had broken these men? What if they knew where Kosey was, or about whom Voduni Calla reported himself to be, or The Panther? What if they knew that the rebels were here, right now, trying something so foolhardy that benefited no one but some poor nobles left out of the Gypians plans?

Pushing those doubts down, Kaarle spotted a torch sputtering its last wisps of flame in an alcove near one of the doors to the fort's many storage areas. He retrieved it without a big fuss, holding it low at his side as he walked back to the wagons. The princes of the savannah rose to the weathered platform and posted beneath the nooses that would soon stretch their necks.

Kaarle removed the lid from one of the green painted pots, the stink of pine sap and sulfur assailing his nose. He looked up again, waiting for The Panther to move.

An executioner ascended the steps, crowned in white lilies and black thorns. He slipped the first noose onto one of the princes, who hung his heads in a passive fashion, unbecoming of the proud man he should have been.

Kaarle upended the torch in his hand and held it over the pot's mouth.

The executioner grabbed the lever at the side of the stage just as a gasp slit open the quiet. A shadow ran across, slicing a dagger through the Sons of Juut's wrist restraints. Before any could stop this flash of movement, the executioner fell backward, pounced upon by this same shape.

Manwe the Panther slashed the man in the throat and winced at the spray of blood.

"The rebels are upon us," someone in the crowd cried.

Dropping the torch into the serpent's blood, Kaarle leapt hard from the wagon, landing among some the Gypians who had massed around it.

The world went out in a blast of fury.

The smell of fire and seared flesh woke him, followed by a sharp ache that throbbed in his eyes. Wiggling his fingers and toes first, Kaarle pushed up on his hands and knees. A fallen body slipped off his back, the bronze flesh of the man's face black and oozing. He turned onto his bottom and scooted away with a cry, his bloody knees brushed harshly by the hot wind. The wagons burned before him, the impact point of an explosion that had flattened the crowd. Among them, the princes of Juut slew their captors as they escaped, swinging stolen weapons and stopping every so often to stab Gypians in their backs.

Unable to balance his steps, Kaarle staggered away from the blaze, taking hold of the sword that still hung from his belt. He drew the old blade, standing in exhausted agony as he waited for the first enemy to appear.

What he saw instead was impossible.

Kaarle stared, gloomy as he focused on the memory. He still smelled the roasted flesh in his nose, heard the sounds of the dying. The lamplight in the cavern chamber shifted the shadows of Kosey and Voduni Calla. Jubilant that he had quieted them, he lay back into the bedding atop his pallet, clear-minded for the first time in days.

"What did you see?" asked Kosey, his dark eyes gleaming onyx as he looked back. His posture had lifted since the story began, his shoulders squared, knees set apart. Kaarle saw his friend and mentor in a way he had never seen him before, and it brought a slight smile to his haggard face.

His eyes did not shift over to the hunched shape of Voduni Calla, who stood at the back of the room like some conspirator worried of something in the shadows. Hardened by slavery and vengeance, the mystic's eyes glowed like nightmare coals, their fire from another world.

"I saw a shadow walk across a legend," Kaarle said, settled to finish his account.

A sharper, cooler wind blew in from the east, pushing at the cinder walls that obscured the fort's courtyard. The roasted bodies of lords and poor alike, splattered in the resinous, burning serpent's blood, writhed on cobblestones and patches of barren dirt, their blood baked into their melted skins and snarled clothes.

Kaarle lowered the sword in his hand, glad that no enemy charged to attack him, but froze when he saw two figures emerge in the hazy, weird light made by the sun and smoke.

Yards away, enough that he could not directly hear them above the roaring wall of wagons he had set ablaze, Kaarle watched The Panther square off with The Latian Lion.

The lord of another western empire had appeared, dressed in his full armor, a shining iron cuirass strapped to his great frame. A helm crested in black horse hair fluttered on the smoldered breeze, and on one arm was strapped a small shield, a round disk made of gold inlaid wood. In his other hand, the sharp, wide head of his spear glared silver in catches of sunlight.

The thief across from him could not have been more different. Shorter by a full head, Manwe presented a more complex image, a wiry frame packed with spring-tight muscle and lithe fluidity, even when he remained in a placid stance. A wicked knife, curved and hard-pointed, shone bloody in a more lurid light, the weapon of a true killer. When one looked at the thief, his namesake was appropriate.

The soldier of the west charged Juut's natural born assassin. Manwe tilted right as he thrust his knife, letting the head of the spear go by as he penetrated past the Lion's reach. The Latian turned quickly to bring his shield around, but not before Manwe poked his knife into the man's unarmored thigh. The thief danced away, leaving the warrior who lumbered after him.

Jogging in a wide circle, Manwe called to Kaarle. "Find us a way out, boy!"

Brought back to his senses, Kaarle turned toward the gates, through which hundreds of bodies clawed and shoved for an escape from the carnage. Untended in the mindless rush were a few chariots, bereft of their riders and harnessed with their frightened chargers. He hopped onto the frame of one of these riggings, grabbing the reins. Shouting at the horse, Kaarle drove the beast forward, back in the direction of Manwe and the enemy.

The two were locked in another skirmish as Kaarle approached. He directed the horse close as Manwe dodged a series of spear thrusts from The Latian Lion, who had pushed forward with both hands on his spear, having lost his gold-shod shield. Blood trickled from under his helmet.

Manwe turned and caught hold of the rail as the chariot rolled by. Perched on the edge of the frame, he sat back with a relaxed breath, poking at the sliced flesh on his shoulder. Blood sluiced down his sinewy arm, which he paid little attention to as he worked to staunch the wound.

"Do I need to stop?" Kaarle shouted. He turned them toward the gate, and to his relief found the gates empty of most of the bodies. Hundreds of people scattered into the streets of Tolivius, leaving the way open.

Manwe sat cross-legged and used some of the black canvas binding his wrists to bandage the wound. His knife rested between his legs, stained red. "Drive us out of the city. Take the east gate."

"That means we will force our way back across the south," Kaarle said, his heart pounding with their horse's hooves. "That's madness!"

"I don't want to go south," Manwe said. "Keep us east, toward the Glass Jungles. Our friend may be following us."

"The Lion?"

"Just drive. I need rest."

The banded wheels of the chariot clattered on the gray paths. Buildings passed by, lonesome towers of shanties built atop other shanties. The sun, pinned to the piece of heaven directly above them, bleached the alleys bright and open. Rats, stray animals, the sick, and the poor were made to be seen in those moments, as was the ugliness of what the Gypians considered artistic and modern, where fresh paint captured the grime in the air. They arrived at the eastern gates and the paved road turned to red clay. A highway that faded on the horizon where the yellow hills of the savannah gave way to black tree forests waited beyond.

Their beast bore the two men past groves of umber trees and thorny thickets home to lions, zebras, and gazelles, who supped from gentle ponds of emerald waters. At some point Manwe woke from his nap and relieved Kaarle of the reins. They carried forward to the border of the Glass Jungles, where they were met by the princes of the savannah in the shadowed glades. These freed men, all stalwart warriors of failed campaigns, welcomed The Panther with open arms and led him to their fire where a forest boar roasted on a spit.

Birds broke the trees somewhere near sunset, and a line of white dust trailed in the last foothills of the hot plains. Manwe and Kaarle guarded the edge of the Glass Jungles, situated on a thick tree branch fanned with broad green leaves.

"You were right. He followed us."

"Of course he did," said the thief, his feet dangling. Reinvigorated by his meal, he rested on the branch in a lazy fashion, unhampered by the spear wound now covered with a dry salve of berries, herbs, and wet oats. Manwe looked as much as he had during his first bout with The Latian Lion, completely at ease with what was to come. "I told him to come here."

"You did?"

In his hands, the thief examined his knife, an iron edge with a tied leather handle. He thumbed the blade, watching the line of far-off dust draw closer and closer. "I challenged him to finish our fight, for me to show him why Latia should leave Gypus to its own demise. I have to kill him to convince his people that the Gypians have too much on their hands with the rebellion, and if I know westerners, they like taking advantage of each other."

"They might go against each other." Kaarle flattened his mouth, thinking on the things he had seen in the last day. "You live up to your name, Panther."

"There's a point to it," the thief admitted. "At some juncture in this war, we are going to have to pick sides and make friends with those who will make friends with us. We might have to ally with those we do not expect, consider our friends our enemies, and truly decide the fate of Tolivius. This either ends in peace or it ends in ruin. Either way, I am ready."

"You're worried about people like Simo."

"I'm more worried about the people that Simo listens to. I don't hear much of Kosey's words in anything anymore."

"I want our people to be free, but only in the truest sense."

"Then question who you choose for your friends," Manwe said. "Question wisely."

THE LATIAN LION PULLED HIS CHARIOT INTO THE FIRST CLEARING PAST THE forest's perimeter; his horse dragged to a heavy stop. The hulking warrior removed his helmet to let his honey brown hair free, and he stepped off the back of the frame with only a sword in his hand, its short blade heavy and curved. As he walked toward the mossy meadow's natural center, he favored his left leg with a steady but tender step.

Kaarle spied from between the massive trees, hidden from sight. A long spear rested across his lap, its length a promise he had made to The Panther before dawn…

If the thief fell, it would be his turn next.

The Latian Lion spoke aloud, his voice the boom of a god made flesh. "Come out, thief." He loosened his sword arm, swinging his blade in wide arcs. "Let's see if your miserable race has a better honor than the Gypians."

"There will be no worries there."

84

Perched on the tree branch directly above the Latian, Manwe stood in an easy pose. His curved knife glittered in a sunrise ray that pierced the heavy green canopy as the wind seeped through the leaves.

The Latian, one eye squinted from a scab on his eyebrow, smiled wide and showed his clean teeth. He took a few steps back and presented the battlefield, a mock invitation.

Manwe leapt from the high place, landing on the soft black soil with nary a sound. He scampered back on all fours, hands and feet patting the ground in rapid beats. The Latian stalked after him, a grim smile on his shaved face. He cut off angles by stepping to the left and right, cornering the thief into one of the trees.

Pivoting on one foot, Manwe pressed the other against the trunk of the iroko, throwing himself forward like a dart. His entire body zipped past the Latian's ill-timed slash, and with a quick cut, he sliced at the larger man's elbow, opening a shallow wound.

Manwe came up on his feet and leaned away from the Latian's next heavy cut. The two traded attacks, their iron deflecting away the points of their weapons, the armored warrior at a better advantage. He shoved the thief, forcing him backward.

"I like chasing you," the Latian Lion bellowed.

Manwe turned onto his heels, cartwheeling away from the Latian's slashes. The pair fought their way back to the grove's shaded center. The Latian's eyes reflected his utter contempt for his opponent, a wasp with a sting harder than iron.

For his part, the thief did not retreat without his own scores. He poked and prodded, nipped and stabbed, opening several small cuts and punctures on the westerner's face, neck, and arms. The Panther, brown-eyed and taciturn, moved with the grace of a dancer. Without effort he dodged, always giving ground.

Reaching forward with a quick grab, the Latian snatched Manwe by the throat and jerked him close to butt heads. The thief teetered backward on his feet, trying to keep the horizontal guard he had formed with his knife. A hard slash roared out of the Latian as he smacked the knife from Manwe's hand, twisting the thief to a knee. The Latian reared back for his next attack.

Kaarle, without a single thought, charged from the shadows. Letting his spear lead, he plunged the point into the Latian's bare thigh, piercing meat and muscle.

The sword fell from the Latian's hand as he looked down at the wound for a moment with grim acceptance. He grabbed the spear's shaft with both hands and snapped it with a strike of his callous palm.

Kaarle stumbled into a heavy chop from the warrior. A fire seized his body as he felt his knees quiver and he landed hard with a groan. The Latian Lion held his limp body up by the wrist and began to kick at his body and face, smashing him at a steady, measured pace.

From light to dark, the world played out in flashes of consciousness. He saw the Latian sneer, bringing back his bloody fist as his own life seeped from between his teeth.

Begging through broken lips, Kaarle whispered a prayer when the Latian let go.

Manwe appeared before him, his nose broken and swollen. "Run, you damned fool," he shouted, yanking Kaarle from the ground and toward the light. The young rebel stumbled toward the edge of the jungle, back to the wild hills where lions roared, hyenas cackled, and the thunder of the herds carried on the wind.

***

VODUNI CALLA STORMED OUT OF THE CHAMBER, MUTTERING UNDER HIS breath about the damnations the thief would endure, the shame he brought to their cause, and whatever else the mystic hated about Manwe the Panther. Kosey simply remained on his stool, his expression contemplative.

"I don't remember anything else," said Kaarle. He had thrown off his blankets, too hot for their warmth. His joints and sides ached as he slowly rose to his feet, holding his shoulder in discomfort. "I just ran as fast as I could. I don't know what happened after that."

Glancing to the floor at his left, the rebel leader spotted his fallen spear and hide shield and slowly moved to retrieve them. Leaning on his shield when he set it right, Kosey broke into a slight chuckle. "It's almost too amazing to hear the other side of what happened."

"What do you mean?"

"Come, little brother," Kosey said, reverential. "Only Simo made it home to us. Nobou was cut down by the guards, and while those princes were recovered, what man wants to follow the defeated onto the next battlefield? To listen to your story..." He sighed, stood, and left.

Kaarle remained in the little chamber of the cave, his shadow left lonesome by the lamplight. The flame eating at the cotton wick soaked in oil put off a sour smell, one that gathered itself in a slight cloud that hazed the room. When the stench became too much, he turned and marched out the door, only the find Manwe waiting for him beside the entrance.

"Manwe," Kaarle cried, almost reaching to embrace the thief. He stopped when he saw the smile on Manwe's face infused with an appreciative hint of warning. "What happened? What did you do with The Latian Lion?"

His grin diminished, he spoke in a serious tone. "The Latians have been sent their warning."

"Meaning?"

Manwe padded into the cave's dim tunnels, off in the darkness and, one guessed, whatever lay in the light beyond. "When they find their lord's head on Tolivius' gates, I'll tell you."

THE END

LOSS

A BRIGHT, BLUE FLOWER MOON HUNG IN THE NIGHT SKY, LOST AMONG SHEETS of stars where the great gods made love. The wind of the savannah, wet and warm, licked the grasses and trees into a frenzied dance, its music a roar through the boughs. Somewhere in the hills an elephant sang, calling to the herds as they had found one of the black ponds pocking the dried heath.

Manwe the Panther rested against the trunk of his jackalberry tree, the place where he lived and slept and thought, away from the stifled streets and choking air of Tolivius, the Gypian outpost city western invaders had long ago settled and won. He preferred clean, fresh air, the feel of the soft red soil beneath his heels.

He held his knife in his hands. The iron shone silver-black like the sky itself, glowing in the lunar light.

It had been sixth months since Toba died.

The corners of his eyes dewed tears, and he sniffed as he thumbed the edge of the blade. He imagined the look on the face of the lord he had slain, the shock on his young lover's features as Manwe gained vengeance for what had been taken from him. Had they known this had all been over a fence, some life they had thrown into a pit with the very emerald the lord had sought?

Those tears dripped into Manwe's rough black beard as he stared at the moon.

"Silver thoughts on silver nights, I take it."

Cleon the Yellow, sorcerer and spy of Gypus' secret intelligence networks, emerged from the shadows of the tall glades, his saffron robe glittering like some faraway star. The dimness of that amber light bronzed his face brown face to a honey blond that made his eyes sparkle and expression seem kind.

Manwe ceased fiddling with his knife, his eyes drawn to the intruder. He kept his surprise held in check, presenting an immovable facade of focus. "Very few know this location. Fewer so remain alive."

"Oh, come now, Panther," said Cleon. "It's not like you and I don't have fun."

"Not tonight." He let his head slump to the side. "Have you ever loved, Sorcerer? Or does your kind only vex upon your powers?"

"Oh, this is one of those stories, is it?" Cleon questioned, his tone raised in annoyance. "There have been other men. Sometimes they were mentors who taught me of the world and the way it works, and they doted on me. There were, of course, soldiers and statesmen, for what good is a spy that does not pry open secrets from mouths on high? I've even tempted a senator or general a time or two."

Manwe had never considered someone else after Toba. For a thief of his ability, finding such an experienced fence had been a rare feat of luck. It had been wonderful to share the thrills that came with the perfect heist, the finesse one had to have to thrive in Tolivius' poor but bustling streets, where outcasts of the west mingled with the conquered, be they enslaved or otherwise.

And when the fence who sold all of his nefarious prizes tugged at the heart of a tribesman's patriotism, he had fallen in love during their midnight alley meetings and bathhouse visits. Such a love, spoken freely in an older time but now regarded as base degeneracy, often meant it remained silent.

"And you?" Cleon asked. "How many honey lips have sweetened that sharp mouth of yours?"

"I've only known one," Manwe said. Slowly he rose from his place under the tree, stretched his arms and shoulders, and waited for Cleon. The sorcerer's yellow robes dimmed as the Gypian neared. He kept his knife at his side, unsure of whether he should strike out or not.

Cleon scratched the point of his bare chin and grinned. "That is remarkably less than I imagined, though if I received that dour look every time we met, I would reconsider you as well."

"Why are you here, Cleon? Did you come to finally hunt me down? Are you here to break me apart with your magics until I reveal what my heart truly holds?"

"The first question's answer is obvious, the second moot, and the third is the greatest of mysteries."

The sorcerer in yellow closed in, his hands out in a reaching, begging fashion. He took hold of Manwe's shoulder and face, his lips pressing into the hard line that was the Panther's mouth. At first Manwe thought to resist, but the boldness of this Gypian's unexpected, unpredictable actions—they demolished the final wall between what he knew was best and what he felt was completely right.

He pulled Cleon into him, his hands on the man's hips as fingers dug into tight, defined muscle. Their mouths hungered for each other, and without another word of doubt, Manwe allowed himself to fall into the darkness of one he had failed to deny.

A RED SUN LIFTED OVER THE EARTH AND CASTED A WARM WAVE OF LIGHT, pushing back the darkness foot by foot until it bathed the front of Manwe's body. The night's cool needles, touched by this heat, disappeared as he blinked sleepily at the dawn. Flat on his back and his head propped on one of his tree's roots for a pillow, he paid no attention to the naked sorcerer beside him. Cleon snored softly, his body wrapped in the yellow robes they had used as a blanket for their lovemaking.

When the hot disk freed itself from the clutches of the horizon, he rose, dusting his bare bottom and the backs of his legs as he marched the open groves of the savannah, shady places filled with tall trees and sleepy ponds where herds, hunters, and prey slaked their morning thirsts. He brought along his loin cloth and knife; the first he dressed in so he could carry the second in its band. Quiet yet troubled, Manwe brooded as he came across one of the small glens where a small, hip deep hole of water waited, free of any animal who would soon wander in.

Squatted at the edge, Manwe looked upon his appearance caught in the silver surface. His black hair, a wild shock, carried the leaves and dirt he had slept in. He looked up at the brightening skies and wondered what he would do.

There was a shadow on the water, born from some strange angle. It shaped into a slighter frame, tall and corded. "I can see why you live out here," said Cleon, his hands clasped behind his back. He stood to Manwe's right, his gaze roaming the pond. "It's quite beautiful."

"So the humor goes first?" Manwe asked, cracking a smile. "You were more talkative last night."

Crossing his arms over his chest, Cleon shivered in morning chill, wearing nothing under the thin wrap of his yellow robes. The pair waited at the edge of the water for a long time before either said anything. Lilac birds shattered the silence with a sudden flight as the wind eddied through the branches.

"Are you going to keep hunting me down?" Manwe asked.

"I don't know," said Cleon. "I thought I knew what I was doing last night. Now I don't."

"Is this the first time you don't have all the steps worked out?" Manwe's own chuckle sounded hollow in his chest, his grin quaking. He had slept with a Gypian without real concern at what happened afterward. Standing up, he glanced to the sorcerer.

Cleon turned his head and looked square at Manwe. "You don't know what it is like always having to be at the ready. Maybe you do, but in Gypus, a man can never allow himself to be swayed by such things as passion in the pursuit of his own perfection. 'Beauty before death', my people say, but it is never simple. If the Senate Consul were to find out that I have lain with our shared foe..." He chewed the inside of his cheeks and exhaled. "Sometimes I understand why you want to bring it all down."

"I don't want to bring it all down," said Manwe. "My people were making themselves their own civilization before the Gypians invaded all those centuries ago. They never were allowed to find their own way, to make up their own minds, or have their own futures."

"And you think your rebels will make a future where people like you and I will be free?" Cleon shook his head, morose as he stepped into the pond. The water reached his ankles and rippled out in wavering rings. "Do you actually think they'll have room for people like us?"

Manwe stared at the water, playing games in his head with the shadows that stretched and danced on the water's surface. He'd opened his mouth to answer when a horn sounded in the east, long and low. A second soon joined it, a clarion note from a silver trumpet. Hundreds of nearby voices shouted in unison from all directions as Gypians rushed the grove, clattering in their bronze armor and crested helms.

Grabbing Manwe in a tight hug, Cleon pitched them forward into the pond's depths.

MANWE ROSE IN THE MIDDLE OF A BATTLE.

Off through wide-set trees, dozens of men fought around the area leading back to his camp. Drawing his knife, he blinked hard as he searched the depths beneath him for Cleon. No hint of yellow, no writhing form waited in the pond.

He escaped for the nearest grove, away from the fight. Hidden behind an uneven ridge of bushes, Manwe crept along one of the streams that fed the pond, a muddy clay ditch that sucked at his feet. At the next bend, he halted, crouched beneath an embankment.

Bronze-armored Gypians clashed with Juutan rebels who fought bare-chested with white paint and hide harnesses as their only garb. Armed with iron spears, axes, and clubs, these homespun warriors held their hide shields against the sharp swords and cunning formations of the invaders.

Blood misted the air and mingled with the dust thrown up by sandaled feet, a choking cloud that rumbled and clanged with the storm. Smart enough to know there was no place for him in that fight, Manwe sneaked by the edges of the thundering battlefields.

He made it to where his tree stood only to find a camp had been set up around its base. Dozens of Juutan women and older men busied around the site, erecting tents and cots while groups of warriors rested beneath his jackalberry's budding fronds. One of the central figures, a tall man with powerful shoulders traced in white reliefs of a maned lion, doled out orders with his voice and point of his spear.

Manwe emerged from his cover when he saw Kosey, the leader of the savannah's revolution against the Gypians, and all thought of subterfuge banished. A great celebration sparked in the camp when one of the perimeter guards spotted him, and all the warriors stood in time to meet the savannah's greatest thief.

Kosey led their welcoming party. "Manwe," the rebel leader cried. A sincere smile creased his face. "You escaped the Gypian ambush!"

"Ambush?" Confused by the expressions of relief spread on the faces of the fighters massed behind Kosey, Manwe set both hands on his hips. "What are you talking about?"

"We were given word by one of our contacts in Tolivius that the Senate Consul had sent Cleon the Yellow to murder you while you slept," Kosey said, gesturing to the flatlands around them. "I collected who I could and marched them from our base near the Glass Jungles. On the way, we ran into a Gypian unit that was sent to support the sorcerer in his hunt."

"The sorcerer never appeared," Manwe said with the practiced measure, his lie hard and assured. "How many did you bring?"

Kosey tilted his head to the side, his bright brown eyes filled with suspicion. "Two hundred."

"You need to get them out of here," said Manwe, much to the derision of those who had come to rescue him. "We need to retreat from this area completely."

"Leave?" one of the warriors questioned, an unarmored youth with a gangly frame. "But the first wounded are coming. We just started fighting!"

A chorus of agreement sounded from the hot-blooded fighters, and Kosey raised his eyebrows in a considerate expression. For his part, Manwe knew better than to try to convince them otherwise, his lips pursed in an annoyed line. He studied the grove he had long called home, the place where he had rested his head—and shared his first moments of happiness with Toba.

And Cleon.

Wise to the cruel ways of the world, Manwe knew the time of him and his tree was over.

The young rebels went back to their rest as they waited for the next group of skirmishers to come and take their places. The racket of battle in the distance, the eerie calm of this camp, the desecration of his home after a night where he had allowed himself to be happy for a moment, laid a thick tension upon Manwe's shoulders.

Kosey noticed his disappointment. "I'm sorry, Panther," said the rebel leader. He squeezed the handle of his weapon in frustration. "We only meant to make sure that you were all right. Things are harder now after Aemon's Fort. The Gypians hunt us with a keener focus, which is a sign that we have done damage. We owe so much of it to you. We would not leave you."

Manwe raised a dirty hand to stay the words of Toba's brother, caught between the shallow grief of homelessness and the knowledge that in revolution things were destined to be lost. He offered Kosey a small false smile. "This is where your brother and I used to meet after he started fencing for me. Over time, it became my home. His too."

Kosey, his mouth shut, rose up in a deep breath. "I know, Manwe. I know what this place meant to you and him."

He flashed a nervous glance. "Freedom comes from suffering. At least that is what your Voduni tells the rest of you, isn't it?"

"The kingdoms of the old savannah are dead and gone," said Kosey. "We will restore what was remained and built from there."

"We lost those old ideas with the Gypians," Manwe said, embittered. "We replaced them with purity and religion and heritage, never remembering that it was those very things that made our old kings and queens fight on the savannah. Those royals are bought or dead now. Our young are enslaved or dying at the point of a sword. Will the new kingdom be one of diversity and faith and community, or will we still be worrying about purity and religion and..."

Kosey swiped the air with his spear. "Say your piece, Panther."

At that moment, another contingent of rebels charged the camp led by a wild presence, a wiry man of ichor skin who whooped and wailed fragments of old songs and spells. A necklace of bones weighted by a vulture's skull ringed the man's bird-like throat. His scraps of armor tied with small amulets rattled as he approached, followed by a horde of rough men covered in blood, much of it their own. Thrusting his gnarled staff in the air, he paraded before Kosey on a victorious warpath as his men collapsed behind him.

Manwe motioned at this man. "What else do I need to say?" he asked Kosey.

"The soil of freedom is nourished in righteous sacrifice," Voduni Calla cawed at Kosey. He glared at Manwe, his scarred shoulders hunched in incredulity. "And look, we have found the precious snake, one worthy of life after the flood."

"Looks like it will be a dry, barren one," said Manwe as the older folk came along to treat the wounded, picking up the exhausted where they fell. "Or is the water too impure for our people's soil as well?"

A wicked smile worked its way across Voduni Calla's skeletal face, his cheeks bunched into two sharp mounds of tight, taut flesh. "Famine will produce a better yield in the spring of victory."

"Enough," called Kosey, shouldering into the small space between Manwe and the mystic. A wall of black muscle and sinew, he paid Voduni Calla a glare, a slight the mystic did not fail to notice. For a moment the bone-thin man stood against Kosey, who towered over him by a full head. Voduni Calla eased back, his staff hanging at his side.

"Let the men rest another ten minutes before we call the retreat," said Kosey when peace resumed. "We'll withdraw westward, toward the ravines down near the low forests. Calla, your group and mine will provide—"

"Retreat?" Voduni Calla shouted. "We cannot retreat! Our young men and women have found battle and glory! We must stay and finish these Gypian dogs."

"We completed our mission when we found Manwe," Kosey replied. "To stay here for your ego would only get more people killed."

"Better dead and free than alive and enslaved," countered Voduni Calla. "The heart of every true revolutionary welcomes bold death." He turned his baleful eyes on Manwe. "It is far better to fight and fall for the next world than to sneak away into the shadows."

A second band of rebels charged into the camp, running headlong as fast as their dusty feet could carry them. Manwe recognized the young lad who led those men, nodding to Kaarle as the two caught sight of each other.

"Reporting in, sir," Kaarle told Kosey as he approached.

"You weren't due for another half-hour," said Kosey, confused. "Why have you returned?"

Kaarle turned back to his brothers-in-arms and waved them in with his spear. "Where's Abo?"

"Right here," called a young boy, his face a flaky mask of blood. Shivering from the toll of battle, the one known as Abo fidgeted as he broke from Kaarle's main pack, trying to steady his hands that held his spear and shield. He coughed when he noticed his commander's glance. "Pardon, sir. Reporting."

"It is fine, little brother," Kosey said with a forgiving smile. "What do you have to report?"

Abo shrank at the question. He raised his shield upright like he would soon defend himself. "We were sneaking atop a ridge when I heard some Gypians below us. I spotted them in an empty old grove."

"I stopped when I noticed how Abo had tarried," Kaarle informed.

Abo set his spear down and tried to brush the dry blood off his eyelids with equally bloody hands. "They were saying…"

Manwe stepped forward and put a hand on Abo's shoulder. "Do you need a moment?"

"No," said Abo, fighting tears. He set his shoulders square, his mouth into a resolute line. "I heard the Gypians reveal the real reason why they came out here. It wasn't to catch you," he said to Manwe. "They're out here searching for Cleon the Yellow."

Manwe froze as he heard Voduni Calla's gasp. The witch-doctor grabbed Abo's other shoulder with a skeletal hand, his eyes lit in a hungered light. "Gypus' sorcerer is in these hills?"

Abo nodded in a broken manner.

His perpetual sneer transformed, Voduni Calla looked to Kosey with a calculated grin. "We must slay this man! To do so would cause the Gypians a blow that will shake them like Aemon's Fort did. It will show the strength of our cause!"

"Cleon is a mighty sorcerer," Manwe said quickly. He studied the young solider in front of him, still focused on Abo as the young fighter tried desperately to remain placid in the mortality painted upon him. "Hunting him will be no simple task. Maybe even a waste of life."

"Then perhaps a single hunter should prove his patriotism, to the cause and to our people," Voduni Calla suggested.

"This is an opportunity we might never have again," admitted Kosey. His tired brow furrowed in thought, the warrior craned his head toward the clear morning sky. Bringing his gaze back to earth, he spoke to Manwe. "You've dealt with him before, Panther. What would you suggest?"

With no escape and no excuses available, Manwe felt his stomach sour as he watched Voduni Calla's grin widen. The loss of his home, already compounded by the guilt over a blissful night, drove nails into his heart as he continued to behold the ruins of revolution. He saw the bloodied and broken anguishing in stained cots, the terror on Abo's face reflected in perfect suffering. Now the evil of change—of freedom—demanded further sacrifice.

Bound to freedom, Manwe gritted his teeth. "I'll find him," he said, sinking into the cold killer he knew himself to be. "I'll hunt him down."

RUNNING UPON THE SHADOWS LATTICED ON THE GROUND, MANWE WOVE through the cool glades, his dagger freed in one hand. He returned to the edge of the pond where he and Cleon had hidden, a spot that had remained untouched by the ferocious skirmishes and howling charges that had thrown the savannah into chaos. Their individual trails, printed onto soft banks, separated in two distinct tracks, with his sandaled gait headed north while another, toes and a heel, wandered east in the direction of Tolivius.

Creeping on the sorcerer's trail, he slipped into the shadows of a burgeoning afternoon. The din of combat still raged in clashing echoes, but fevered hearts had weakened, bodies tired, and more fighters searched for positions of strength instead of outright engagements.

Manwe used this lull to his advantage, combing the groves of umber and boga trees. Cleon's trail carried for miles before it stopped at the edge of a narrow goat path, a long road broken by thousands of different feet, most of them sandaled. Two parallel ruts in the red clay, set wide apart, indicated a transport wagon had lumbered through that day.

Manwe followed the wheel marks. Those ruts led to a longer ridge that served as a boundary of the rustic farmlands that grew around Tolivius, its border a series of low hills where palatial plantations and fenced ranches stretched across its swath.

The Gypian forces had set camp at the southernmost stead where a huge manor stood in sharp relief with its white-peaked roofs and marbled columns. Hundreds of servants, soldiers, messengers, whores, dealers, craftsmen, lords, ladies, and slaves buzzed in and out, set to chaos by the battle taking place at edge of their posh domains.

Manwe crossed the flowering wheat fields in the direction of the clotheslines, where the garb of slaves and lords alike fluttered in the mid-morning sun. Freeing a tattered green tunic, he slipped it over his sinewy body and put his eyes to the ground, taking on the broken man's slouch he had seen far too often in Tolivius' alleys.

Setting out from the drying fields, Manwe wandered toward the manor, folding into the constant traffic until he found himself inside the long, palatial halls. Filing in with the weary slaves who manned the kitchens, he spied lines of soldiers posted at the stairs leading to the top floor. Volunteering to take a tray of bandages and slaves to a master's quarters, he carried the load as his ticket to explore the manor.

At the top of the stairs, he was directed left by one of the helmed Gypians, who ushered him to a bedroom. The door opened from the inside, allowing him to slip in.

An older man, his stomach swollen with years of vice, sipped from a polished silver goblet. Wiping his fat face of red wine dribbles with the corner of his embroidered robe, he refreshed his cup from a stone pitcher. "Dreadful business hunting by yourself, Cleon. This Juutan should have been treated with more concern."

Lying in bed, Cleon rested beneath a few light blankets as a healer applied a salve to a scattering of wounds on his face and neck. With both hands bandaged, he lazed about the plush mattress, his attention far away. "Beg my pardon, Senate Consul, but by the time I handled the proper documentation, he would have been gone. I've demonstrated my skill time and time again against such brigands, whether they were Thom Flightfeet or The Knives of the Jade Emperor."

"But this brigand has eluded you three times so far. Perhaps we frontiersmen deal with hardier stuff than you do in Gypus," said the Senate Consul with an air of superiority. "And you brought a full-scale battle with you, no less."

"Restless remains the vaunted security of Tolivius," Cleon said in a mock boast. "Was it my government that allowed a cherished dignitary like The Latian Lion to disappear into the jungle, forever missing in its timeless dark? How goes the repairs of Aemon's Fort, by the by?"

The lord's satisfaction diminished as he slugged wine. "Well, we both have swords upon our backs."

Manwe looked down at the contents of his tray: bandages, herbal pastes, and salve pots. He attended to the healer in the bed beside Cleon, an older gentleman with eyes faded from cataracts. This healer nodded to him when he approached, muttering some blessing about helpful slaves as he started to unwrap the bandages around the sorcerer's hand. The strips of linen peeled wetly off.

Cleon winced as the cuts and punctures were exposed to the air. "Careful, old man," he said with a quick, pained grin. "I'll need those for later." The sorcerer laughed and checked on Manwe, silenced when he caught eyes with him.

Manwe stared dire warning back at the sorcerer.

"So what do we do, Sorcerer?" asked the Senate Consul. "You failed to capture this Panther, and now we have rebels at our city's borders. Seeing that we are fighting for the very land we have rightfully claimed, I say we need a plan if we are both to be free of this mess when it is all said and done. The Empire can hardly afford another loss to these rebels."

Manwe glanced to the official, which drew a brief cough from Cleon.

The Senate Consul picked up his pitcher and offered it in the sorcerer's direction.

"Ugh, no," said Cleon dismissively. Smiling at Manwe, he bit his lip seductively, a hint of mischief in the nibble. "Do you dare imagine us losing to these rapscallions?"

"Before Aemon's Fort?" asked the Senate Consul. "That thief went beyond stealing my wife's jewels, Cleon. His prizes and victories bond legends to his shadow, and this dirty little rebellion has co-opted it, never knowing the cost of what they do."

"Because we all fear Gypus," said Cleon, his expression thoughtful as he nodded at Manwe.

His back to the both of them, the Senate Consul rested his large bottom on a couch in the middle of the room, facing the small stove used to heat the space on the savannah's chillier nights. A goblet on one knee, he sighed. "I'd rather face those savages in the hills than the Empire's armies. They would fall hard on everyone's back if summoned, Gypian or not."

"Perhaps we should leave savage lands to savages," said Cleon.

"Perhaps we should have in the first place," the Senate Consul replied.

Manwe heard this conversation in perfect stillness, holding his tray as the healer took what bandages and pastes were needed to redress Cleon's wounded hands. The fear he heard in these Gypians' voices when they spoke of their own homeland—what if they had come to Tolivius to flee, choosing waste against the suffocating tyranny they left behind? He and Cleon locked eyes again, sharing a concern beyond the personal attachment they had created behind the lies they had told.

Manwe knew the answer Kosey would give to such knowledge, something brave but foolish.

How Voduni Calla would respond could be disastrous.

"Everyone could die," said Cleon.

Even the healer paused at what seemed to be a random comment applied to the battle outside the manor, but Manwe understood its true depth. He swallowed hard, refocused on what went on in the room. The healer bound the last bandage on Cleon's hands.

"I'll come back," Manwe said, his lips moving soundlessly.

The sorcerer nodded and sank back into his plush pillow.

LONG AFTER THE SUN HAD SET AND THE ROARING IN THE HILLS QUIETED, Manwe returned to Cleon's bedroom where the open windows looked out over smoking fields and the firefly clusters of torches, spots where rebels and Gypians dueled in the deep night. Starlight wreathed a full moon, though it all shone ruddy behind the smoky clouds. Some form of peace came to the farmlands and manor houses, a tense calm amid the scared whispers and worried rumors. He slipped inside the calm, cool darkness of the chamber, his knife held tight in one hand.

A single lamp, its light low and troubled, wavered a glow on the walls and cut shadows on Cleon's handsome, tired face.

"Do you come for my life?" the sorcerer asked aloud.

As lonesome as they were, Manwe checked the hidden places a spy could occupy, expecting someone to rise for his capture. When nothing moved, he calmed. "I'm supposed to."

"Will you?"

He approached the foot of Cleon's bed, a four-posted frame carved of ebony and with pearls inset on the headboard. The softness of the mattress met Manwe's knees as he climbed atop of it, his curved blade moving like the liquid tail of his namesake. He perched beside the sorcerer, who did not move to defend himself.

Cleon scooted himself taller in the bed. "Well, Panther? Am I pardoned or prey?"

Manwe shut his eyes at the question, a hard distinction he wondered himself. "We cannot continue this war this way. Not if you're telling the truth."

"Gypus' reach is far for distance and cruelty. There is a reason why they send dissenters out here, hoping we grab more land as the east slowly picks at our dead."

"Dissenters who are still part of the empire they flee from," reminded Manwe. He knelt on the mattress beside Cleon. "But I know jackals that see power in destruction, who would invite hell upon all of us for the sake of pride."

"So what will you do, Panther?" asked Cleon. "You spare me and you become a traitor; you fail to kill me and you will lose face to one of those jackals you clearly worry about. Your choices are few and less than kind."

At a loss for an immediate answer, he looked to the sorcerer's bandaged hands. "What happened to you after you drove us into that pond?"

"Oh, this," Cleon said with a sigh. He set both hands on his robed lap. "Probably what happened to you—wandered in one direction trying to stay out of the fray. Unfortunately, I wandered into one of those pernicious thorn bushes."

Unable to contain a snort of laughter, Manwe covered his mouth with his hands and chuckled furiously. Cleon put on a wounded expression before the pair of them sat there on the bed, snickering like some old couple. The moment, clear and defined, brought Manwe back to balmy days out in the grasslands with Toba, lazing beneath the sun while elephants drank from muddy ponds and zebras foraged out in the hills. The gentleness of the oil lamp on the bedside table, the silk of the sheets, and the quiet of the night—these scenes fought with each other, a cold guilt set against fierier passions.

When their shared mirth died, the sorcerer glanced toward that single point of flame. "What do we do about us, Panther?"

Manwe let his gaze drift to the bed's canopy. He stared at the hanging fabric, a light, airy material used to keep the insects that climbed through the windows away from the occupant when they slept. He looked at Cleon with curiosity.

"Where's your robe?" he asked.

Cleon nodded to the lone desk in the chamber, and on the chair set before it rested his yellow robe, its velvet fabric torn to shreds. Small smears of blood streaked the lapels.

Manwe climbed across the bed and onto the floor, going to retrieve the garment. He held it in his hands like some sacred shawl. "You'll never be able to be Cleon the Yellow again."

"True," said the sorcerer with a defeated look. "Ah, well," he said with a casual wave of dismissal. "We don't get to keep everything, do we?"

"Not everything." Manwe stared blankly at the sorcerer before turning away, headed for the door out to the manor's halls. "I'll see you soon."

"Where?" Cleon called.

"Wherever there is solace in the dark."

FREE OF THE MANOR, THE PLANTATIONS, AND THE SCRATCHY TUNIC HE HAD stolen from the clothing lines, Manwe strode the dark woods of his homeland, at ease in that nighttime realm. The stars glimmered through the thick branches of the high trees and past the sounds of the nocturnal world, lion's roars and hyena's yelps. He melded into the shadows on his way back to the rebel camp.

Broken packs of Gypian hoplites and Juutan freedom fighters stalked the groves, on the hunt for each other in the narrowing hours between midnight and dawn. Slinking through the trees, Manwe neared the ridge between him and the glen where the rebel camp rested.

Five odd shapes rose from the grasses.

Dark-skinned men coated in hot wood gum that scalded their flesh into pockets of yellow puss lurched forward, each movement a display of gross will through unnatural agony. They wore the brown loincloths and tattered armor of the rebels, but as they stalked toward him, Manwe knew these men were not men—at least not anymore.

He drew his knife as he met them. Rolling into a dive, Manwe slashed the first ghoul open at the ribs when he came up before drawing a cut across the next opponent's throat.

The final three attacked in an organized trio as the first two fell, thrusting from behind their shields with iron spears, poking and prodding to catch Manwe's flowing limbs and shifting movement. He cut at the nearest ghoul as he wheeled to the left, opened one of the dead thing's forearms. Black sludge leaked from the wound.

Manwe bounded up the muddy incline toward the ridge's apex, clawing clay and small rocks. He grabbed at the dry crust near the top and forced a handhold. Pulling himself over, he rolled down the other side of the hill, covered in muck until he splashed into a watering hole.

Manwe wiped his eyes clean of silt as the three ghouls tumbled down the slope after their prey. Their pitch-covered bodies hissed with steam when they hit the shallow waters. Backed against the nearest bank, Manwe stabbed the closest ghoul in the throat when the dead men clamored towards him. The other two surged forward as the first sank to his knees, still crawling to reach his mortal prey.

Forced toward the grove where Kosey's camp waited, Manwe fled past shrubs that scored his skin with their hard thorns as the ghouls' haunting wails followed after him. He halted at the edge of the clearing, horrified beyond measure as he saw what lay before him.

Their limbs dusted white, dozens of men and women skipped and twirled in a wide circle over a field of bodies half-buried in the dirt. They avoided those prone forms, which sizzled as a strange substance oozed and spread like the fingers of some dread beast. The charred smell of human flesh choked the air with its awful steam.

Beyond this first ring lay a smaller ring made of Voduni Calla's devotees, who chanted a droning song, their weird words crackling with the flames. Off to the side stood Kosey and his most loyal followers, who watched the proceedings clutching the shafts of their short spears, their shields up and at the ready.

Yet beyond these weird shadows and shifting forms, it was what happened at the epicenter of this ritual that drew Manwe's full attention.

A cauldron forged of black iron rested in the center of a pit dug into the ground, a bubbling container of tar that roiled in the flames. The heinous liquid splashed over the sides in gross curtains that seared the dirt where it landed.

Standing barefoot in the pool his pot created, yet miraculously unharmed, Voduni Calla waved his staff over the cauldron's mouth. His eyes rolled to white as he shouted spells at the night sky. With each pass of his blood-splattered stick, the tar's surface escaped the rim. The pond of black goo in the depression crawled from its hole like snakes from a nest. These tendrils snared the corpses buried the dirt beyond his devotees, enveloping them in viscious hell.

The bodies started to rise.

The devilish mystic smiled at the grotesqueness he had made.

Manwe's mind took him from the scene without choice, back to the dim shadows of the recent past when he plied the underworld beneath his beloved savannah in search of his dead Toba. The hollow chorus of drumbeats droned on as he watched these ghouls begin their new existences—damned, dead, and doomed to burn forever.

At the edge of madness, Manwe focused when a great crash sounded from behind, the sign that the first ghouls he met had found him. Two burnt forms limped into view, their dead limbs torn to shreds by the thorn bushes.

Manwe's fear dissipated when he surmised who had made them. Returning his attention to Voduni Calla, he drew his iron knife, remembering how he had ended the life of the shaman who had slain Toba. He sprinted forward, arms pumping as his bare feet pounded the dirt. He outdistanced the ghouls, hurtling forward at a breakneck pace. He crashed into the first line of dancers as Kosey's men intervened.

"They were your men," Manwe screamed at Kosey, reaching for the rebel lord through the limbs of the warriors fighting to bar him. These soldiers, many of them boys and teens, struggled to hold him. "They were your men!"

"Back away from him," shouted Kosey, dropping his spear and shield to pull them apart. The knot of chaos subsided in a series of shoves, kicks, and curses as the two sides split in the middle over Manwe. Avoiding the violence of Voduni Calla's adherents, he was pulled to the rebel's side, held by the arms and neck.

Kicking at Kosey as he approached, Manwe seethed. "How could you?"

"What are you going on about?" Kosey demanded.

Manwe drove himself forward in an attempt to free himself from the hold, choking on the stout arm looping his neck. "You damned them," he wheezed. "Look at them." He pointed accusingly at the ghouls that had risen before Calla's fire, their black skin shimmering with a sick gleam before the light of the blaze. More than a dozen had risen to stand silent guard, their boiled eyes searching for whatever horrors the dead craved.

Kosey glanced back at Voduni Calla, who had remained vigilant beside his fire and flanked by his followers. "Do away with them, Calla. Do it now."

Voduni Calla approached the ghouls, mumbling incoherent verses as his eyes rolled back once more. The ghouls took notice of their maker before he finished his incantation. When the string of words from the mystic's mouth ceased they issued a great cry. Onlookers gasped as the victims woke from their ensorcelled state, alive again for one last moment. In terrified agony they fell, unable to mouth pleas as death's mercy took them.

Manwe wriggled free of Kosey's men and walked away from the camp, the rebels, Voduni Calla, and the revolution.

Kosey chased after him alone. "Manwe, please speak to me."

"Walk away from me." He made for the shadows, hands bound to fists. "Do not utter a word."

Kosey grabbed his wrist. "You need to listen."

Turning, Manwe leveled a straight kick at Kosey's chest, thudding his solar plexus. Knocked to his bottom by the blow, Kosey wheezed as his men came to defend their leader. He flopped over quickly and held up a hand, a pained order to halt.

"You miserable bastards," Manwe shouted at them all. "Is this the freedom we wanted? Is this what we settle for?" He motioned to the dead ghouls lying in the dirt. "Is the dirt we battle for truly worth this?"

"So the traitor reveals himself," cawed Voduni Calla. "Poison from the mouth of a snake!"

Manwe spotted a stone near his foot. Plucking it from the earth, he launched it at his true enemy and sent the treacherous voduni down in a heap. Calla cried out in horrified shock as a trickle of blood dripped down the side of his hawk-like nose.

Kosey found his voice, though he wheezed. "Nothing is simple, Panther." He coughed to clear his throat as he rose to his feet. "The Gypians are legion to we few, and there will be more. There will always be more."

"So your solution is to let that bastard, that evil bastard, create abominations?" Manwe shook his head in disgust. "What of the savannah's children? What of their mothers? What would you tell them?"

"That they will be free." Voduni Calla rejoined them, lifted to his feet by his men. Unable to walk, he let those scared youths carry him in their arms like some vaunted king, his full weight on their shoulders and necks. "We will all be freed by the gods, above and below us! Free of that slave city! Free of the lords who hold the whips!" He glowered at Manwe, his bloodstained teeth bared in the scant firelight. "Free of corrupt thugs like you."

Seeing the people standing around his desecrated tree, Manwe knew the fear the Senate Consul had expressed to Cleon upon his sickbed was destiny. "Thugs like me," Manwe said in a half-hearted whisper, looking to Kosey. "A thug you and your priest have exploited."

"He said that, not I," said Kosey. His hands held over the spot Manwe had struck him, he stood battered and bruised. "Please, Manwe. Do not leave me like this. Let us talk."

"Would you have Toba covered in pitch and raised?"

Kosey's black face slackened. "What?"

"Answer me," demanded Manwe, no longer caring who saw his defiance. "Would you have let Voduni Calla raise your brother?"

Kosey heaved at the question.

Manwe pressed. "Would you let Toba be raised?"

Kosey found his breath. "For my country and my countrymen, I'd let Voduni Calla raise *me*."

Heartbroken, Manwe left without another word.

IN THE TEMPLE DISTRICT OF TOLIVIUS' DINGY METROPOLIS STOOD A PLACE dedicated to the Goddess of Love, one of the few Gypians gods more becoming than the tyrannical Adias Cloud-lord or the violent Myrm, a dread god whose bloody words had justified the enslavement and death of Manwe's people. Carved of pink marble and held up by smooth yellow columns that shone bright in the morning rays of sunshine, he paid it little attention other than a tired sigh as he entered the alley cut between it and the next temple.

The cobblestone lane descended in a set of stone steps that led to an olive wood door. Knocking twice on its surface, Manwe waited for the viewing hole to slide open. When it did a few moments later, a woman's bright azure eyes blinked a few times at him, filled with a troubled curiosity.

"Manwe?" Magera asked. "Is that you?"

"May I come in?" he asked, averting his gaze.

"What is the goddess' sec—oh, bloody hell, does it matter?" The priestess unbarred her door and let him in. His shoulders slack and exhaustion weighing his eyes, Manwe stood there in the doorway, unable to take a step forward.

Magera laid a bare hand on his shoulder. A beautiful woman no younger than thirty, she carried a motherly air that transcended her silken garments, a blue shift that covered her large breasts and a loin cloth she belted to her hips with a chain of linked golden rings. Her blonde hair seemed to glow in the light of the oil lamps strewn around the altars and small shelves in the room. "Manwe, what's wrong?"

He looked at her, quiet to the question as the guilt of the past years caught in his chest, a knot of shame when he realized he had been fighting for such a long time. Tiredness reared again and he covered his eyes with his hand.

"I..." Manwe began, but paused. "I'm so sorry for coming here. I didn't know where to go."

"You came to where you'd be welcome." Magera pulled him in by the hand and shut the door behind him. "We were expecting you anyway."

Manwe furrowed his brow. "We?"

"Yes." She motioned him to follow deeper into the temple undercroft. "He was quite insistent that you'd come here sooner or later."

Manwe followed Magera into the next room, the space where a fervent orgy would have been taking place if not for the early hour of the day. Instead, six bodies slumbered on the mats in the dim chamber, men and women entangled together after long hours of love-making and worship to a deity who asked nothing more from her followers than that. Beyond this place was another door that led to a darker hall cut from the bedrock the temple's foundation rested upon, which went off to the right and left. Doors set on both sides of the passage opened to a series of empty bed chambers, small hideaways for wealthier patrons who could afford the privacy. These doors remained ajar, readied for newcomers.

Save one.

Manwe knew who lay behind it. "I don't have any money to pay you," he told Magera. "I don't know when I'll be able to."

"Manwe..." She took his sinewy arm in her hands and stroked the black flesh. "If the goddess of love cared only about coin then I'd be a pimp. This is a house of love and you are loved. You are welcome here as long as you can walk through my door."

THE FIRST THING MANWE SAW WHEN HE OPENED THE DOOR TO THE BEDROOM was a small oil lamp resting on the bedside table, its wick burning bright as it hung over the side of the clay bowl. The ruddy light illuminated the white cotton linens of the bed centered in the middle of the floor in a soft color, a simple set complete with two plush pillows and a faded blue blanket.

Cleon sat in the center of that simple mattress, propped up on his bandaged hands with his legs out in front of him. His smile widened when Manwe opened the door the rest of the way. "Well, hello there."

Slouching where he stood, Manwe did not offer a match to the sorcerer's pleasantness. "When did you get away from the manor?"

"Oh, I left not long after you did." His thin face halved in a shadow cast by the lamp, Cleon's playfulness ebbed. "What troubles you, Panther? What happened?"

Manwe softly closed the door and leaned against it, rubbing the heel of his hand against his right eye, trying to steady his voice as an answer formed. "I went back to my home after I left you. There in the night I came across..." Giving in to the torrent of emotions he had forbidden himself to feel since fleeing the savannah, tears formed at the edges of his vision, blurring the scant light in the room.

Cleon rose from the bed and limped to the door. He led Manwe by the hand, sitting him down on the edge of the bed before kneeling down on one knee. "What happened?"

Slowly, the sorcerer coaxed the story from Manwe between snatches of sobs. When the story finished, Cleon glanced into the shadowed corners of the room, his expression blank save for the horror in his eyes. He sat next to Manwe on the edge of the bed, still holding his hand as the silence emptied between them.

Thumbing tears from his eyes, Manwe glanced in Cleon's direction. "What do you think?"

Cleon puckered his lips and blew out a steady breath. He stewed on the question. "I've known sorcerers all of my life. Most were just academics, some soldiers, but I have known necromancers, though they are few and far between. The ones I've come across study the bounds of life and death to understand it, to shape it in ways that benefit their patients." The sorcerer shuddered. "But they'd never do what this Voduni Calla has done. They would never raise abominations."

"Kosey let him do it," Manwe added. "Those ghouls were just boys."

"That's the problem with revolutionaries. There is often no line they won't cross."

Manwe widened his eyes at the point and considered all the things he had done to help his people's rebellion—the thefts, the attacks, the souls he had taken with his own blade. Shame welled in the pit of his stomach, a shame he wondered if he could exorcise from his soul. He thought of Toba, too—he questioned if the fence ever considered how far Kosey's devotion went, if he would have agreed with the horrid idea of raising the dead.

Manwe spoke. "We cannot let this happen. The destruction that would happen if the Gypian army marched on Kosey and his rebels... Voduni Calla would not halt to raise our—his—enemies against themselves."

"The land would be filled with the undead. No one would be freed." Cleon leaned forward, his elbows rested on his knees. "I'll have to inform the Senate Consul."

"We'll have to inform everyone. The people of this city, the clans out in the savannah."

Cleon's mouth curved upward. "We, Panther?"

"Yes, you fool." Manwe scooted back onto the mattress and sank along its length, releasing the last two days of tension, pain, and frustration. Again the tears came, flowing free as he realized that everything had been lost. Lying there, he closed his eyes and wished that it was all just some terrible nightmare, one he would wake from when he opened his eyes back to the world.

He nearly seized when Cleon rolled to his side and wrapped both arms around him. "What are you—?"

"Quiet, Manwe," said the sorcerer. "You've lost enough today as it is."

Caught in an embrace he dared not fight, Manwe let himself turn into Cleon and weep.

THE END

THE FREE AND THE DAMNED

MANWE STOOD THERE IN THE UNLIT BEDROOM, LOST IN DARKNESS AS HE TIED the last knot of his loincloth. He pawed the table next to the bed, patting the wooden surface until his fingers brushed the sharp edge of his knife. On natural instinct, he grabbed its handle. His eyes set forward toward the glowing outline of the door. Weak light seeped past the cracks as he stretched the tension from his shoulders.

"I rarely have the other person run out on me first." The man in bed rolled over and pointed at the unlit oil lamp resting on the bed stand, whispering as he did so. The wick, burned to a blackened nub, caught a long flame. The small light illuminated a sea of creamy blankets where a pair of rich brown eyes sparkled.

"You cad," Cleon whispered with a smile, sitting up on the mattress.

"I'm going out for a bit," said Manwe.

"Where?"

Manwe flashed a glare at his lover.

Cleon chuckled deeply as he turned over, revealing his muscled contours to the scant lamplight. "You and I will have to get used to each other, Panther. You are now no better than a thief, and I, a compromised sorcerer who sees the cards falling down."

"And where do you think you will fall?" Manwe asked.

The sorcerer's perpetual smirk dimmed at the questions. "I'd like to think you and I would be the dashing hands."

Manwe smiled at the idea. "I'm going to go meet a friend in the city. He's a good source to see where everyone is. I imagine everyone will be buzzing about last week's battle outside the walls."

Cleon rubbed his eyes. "I guess I'll go buy a new robe. What's your favorite color?"

Grabbing the handle of the bedroom door, Manwe lifted the bar and pushed it open. "I've never had time to have one. Surprise me."

Near the western walls of the city, right where the gates opened to the outlying farms and the savannah, a great market sprawled in a splotch of more well-to-do natives and a fair number of Gypians who made up the lower echelons of the merchant and service classes. Intermarried and dependent on each other, these multi-generational families lived at the outskirts of finer society, one foot in poverty and the other always at the edge of opportunity.

And then there were the poor. Those left out of this liminal class had stepped fully into the impoverished realm wasted in alleys and back streets of Tolivius' market squares, smeared in mud and shit as they wandered lost. The saner ones were able to dress themselves in rags and soiled clothes, while some went fully naked, impaired by some physical deformity or malady of the wit. Those with the malady cried out from the gutter, begging in babbles and fragments of clear thought.

Manwe knew better of them.

Many of those who had "the malady" were talented actors too worn or ugly for Gypian playhouses, or the wrong race, leaving many of them to cobble together a decent living through graft and simple thieveries by pickpocket. They knew every bit of news commoners thoughtlessly spoke when they passed. Snatches of knowledge could quickly turn to full statements.

In one particular alley Manwe found the particular beggar who owned it, an old snot named Legbas, who some spoke of as a fallen mystic who had been beneath the earth like the vodunis out on the beloved savannah, but Manwe knew better. The hunched form he found doling orders to his local toughs rested too upright for the cane he leaned upon, a practiced pose so effortless it could be missed.

"Now this is how you get into the dairy down the street," he proclaimed, adding an authoritative nod for effect. "The old Gypian who runs that dairy always leaves at noon to go meet his dark momma. While they are out noodling with each other he usually forgets to lock the back door. Mostly because he needs that herb the emperor of Gypus takes because otherwise his noodle stays wiggly. Go in there and steal five rounds of his finest cheese, bring half of a wheel back to me, and I'll cut you a three sacks silver apiece. That cheese will sell very well at the local kitchens, and people hate that old lecher so no worries about getting handed later on. You got me?"

The local toughs, a mix of western and Juutan blood, blinked hard before they nodded and marched away, with one of the uglier ones repeating the plan first.

Manwe covered his mouth with a hand to muffle a laugh. "Memories."

"That ugly one might actually have a future in our traditions, Panther," said Legbas, turning in the shadows. He tottered forward, leaning in as he closed the distance. "What you here for?"

Comfortable in the cool alley, Manwe placed his hands behind his back—away from his knife. "I need information. I went under for the last few weeks."

"After you stole that necklace." Legbas smiled wildly. "Don't try get one on me, boy. I told you to never do that."

"Yes, god," said Manwe. "I have information to trade. I don't need a job or something to pick up. I just need to talk."

Legbas made an odd expression, aware and focused, though a hint of burden furrowed his brow. The old beggar stood straight up, holding his cane in one hand like a club. "Who'd you want to talk to?"

Manwe bounced on the balls of his feet, his heels lightly slapping the dry stone beneath them. He searched the bluing slice of sky above them, a crack in the limestone roofs that allowed for a piece of heaven to be seen—a fair blessing to those who lived in squalor. He noticed how the silver flecks in Legbas' hair caught in the light.

"The Five Fences, of course," said Manwe. "The Songbird. Any of the vodunis who don't like Calla. I have a feeling we would meet well after midnight."

"The Five Fences don't like you." Legbas' smile broadened. "They won't come around unless you prove yourself of grand taste."

He sighed at the insistence in the beggar-lord's voice. "What would you all like?"

Legbas laughed at the question. "You had any of that new sugar drink the Gypians are fermenting with coconuts brought from their port-towns?"

"We get coconuts up here?" Manwe said, surprised at how cultured Tolivius had become in his absence.

"Rich folk like having things to have them. Someone needs to use them, though," Legbas pointed out, drawing an agreeable nod from Manwe. "Four cases."

"Four cases." Manwe held his hands up. "I can carry one."

"You wanted to call the Five Fences, boy," said Legbas. "I'm going to have to put a lot of work in just to get those black merchants in the same room as crazy vodunis. The Songbird is just not going to show up because Manwe the Panther has a sit-down. I haven't even started to mention the story we'll need to make this work."

"You're planning a party!"

"Damn right." Legbas thrust his staff toward the mouth of the alley. "There's a war going on in those hills, and you rebels aren't going to stop until you kill us all. Some of us are losing our homes soon, Manwe, and the least you can do is give us a party for what you're stealing from us."

"I'm not stealing anything," Manwe said. "Not this time."

Legbas half-winked at him. "What's coming?"

"The dead," Manwe said. "I'll bring two cases, one to split among the Five Fences, one for the vodunis and yourself, and I'll grab two more bottles—one for me and one for the Songbird. The vodunis will like a more exploratory sacrament. Can you find cannabis?"

"I know a field hand. I'll get me some, too—for my ankles, you know. See you at Bacchs for the meeting?"

"They'd gut me anywhere else." Manwe stalked out of the alley, headed for the morning.

⎯⎯⎯◇⎯⎯⎯

WALKING A SUNNY LANE, **M**ANWE SKIRTED A ROW OF SHOPS, A SERIES OF interconnected guildhalls and stalls. At the midway point, Cleon stumbled out of a tailor's shop, clutching two robes in one hand while jogging in his brown tunic to catch up.

"Are you crazy?" Manwe halted in the middle of the dirt road. Relieved at the lack of traffic around them, he quickly met the sorcerer under an awning, out of view of the local guard who turned the corner down the street. Sheltered in the shade, they hit the sweltering heat of the day.

"Which one?" Cleon asked, holding up the robes as sweat ran down his angular face. "I like the mint green, but the idea of 'Cleon the Green' sounds stupid, and 'Cleon the Mint' is a bit too on the nose no matter how handsome I am." He presented the other garment, an unfinished outer robe sewn from purple. "I like what this one does with my hair and eyes, but what do you think?"

"Did you follow me?" Manwe scanned the shops, spying out for anyone who looked at him a tad too long or those who simply paid more attention than they should have. He thanked his luck that the vendors stayed in their shops. "Were you followed?"

"Followed?" Cleon's handsome face wrinkled in confusion. "Manwe, you walked by. If we are going to continue our partnership, whatever that may be, you must cease with this excitability every time we meet. Now, do you like the green or the purple?"

Standing perfectly still, Manwe ground his teeth. "The mint looks awful, and with the other you might as well be called 'Cleon the Eggplant.' Neither."

Cleon dropped both robes in the dirt and hugged Manwe. "Thank you!" Releasing the embrace, he turned on the heels of his fine hobnailed sandals and started off. "Come on. We have business to attend to."

Fretting on these fine robes being left tattered or stained, Manwe threw his hands up as he squatted down, flinging the robes onto an open window sill and a cart-table He caught up to the sorcerer at the next urban intersection, falling in line with his easy pace. "What business are you talking about?" he asked, side by side with his lover.

"Ah, it is of little worry to you right now. If I can even get his time we will need something important to say." Cleon looked about with a pleasant eye, examining the busy stalls as they passed by, nodding and grinning at spice merchants, the vegetable hawkers, the meat cutters, the clothiers. He directed Manwe toward a second little shop on the lane, this one complete with an actual model who stood outside the door, draped in silks and different robes, vests, and tawdrier things.

"This one," said Cleon, stopping before the girl. He fingered the brocade of sequins crusting the bodice she wore, which to Manwe's surprise elicited a curious smile out of her. "Do you think they have these in blue?"

"Cleon." Manwe pulled away the sorcerer's hand before he bothered the model further.

"Oh fine, Panther," he said, yawning. He instructed the girl to go and find her six finest silks, two best linens, and what wool she had, pushing her into her shop with a firm shove to the rear. Turning back on Manwe, he leaned forward, close enough to kiss. "How was your friend?"

"Talkative," said Manwe, frozen on the spot. The smell of the sorcerer, the hints of tea and vanilla and broom, put him at ease. For a moment he wondered if Cleon had cast a spell. "I need your help tonight. I have to rob a lord of two cases of sugar drink, plus two extra bottles."

"And you need my extra muscle?"

Manwe rolled his eyes at the question. "What can I do?"

Cleon glanced past Manwe, quiet for a moment. His brown eyes widened a bit when he spoke. "You wouldn't happen to still have that necklace you stole from Lady Nelo at that party, would you?"

"Of course not. I fenced it to Sophicus and he took it to Merchants' Row to pawn it back out to—" A sudden realization tightened Manwe's face. He locked eyes with Cleon and nodded. "It's been sold by now, but if I can find the broker..."

"...then you can find the buyer and steal it back." Cleon's grin grew wide again. "I'll work on the sugar drink and my lead; you work on that necklace. Come back to the temple when you're done."

⁂

It did not take Manwe long to discover which families in Tolivius could afford a strand of pure diamonds like The Savannah's Tears, and when he found out who had purchased them, he regretted returning to the place fate had sent him to. Near the back of Merchants' Row, a series of white hills ascended to a green plateau, the next level of the savannah headed northward. Atop of these rises were erected large manors, some regal and well-appointed, others gaudy and reflective of more lurid tastes, depending on the carvings of the columns holding up the triangular roofs.

This common fashion made Manwe's destination distinct. A low, flat building made up of a single floor, it lay secluded behind its high white walls, the inside perimeter lined with a series of old marula trees, their boughs heavy with golden fruit. This manor, austere in presentation, belonged to a man Manwe had murdered—Lord Leomachus, merchant and kidnapper.

Or at least it had.

Few guards patrolled its grounds, replaced by a staff of common folk and a few slaves, who toiled in the gardens as they grew barley, cabbage, and millet, simple crops that were pollinated by a small aviary that swelled bees and comb. But the most startling replacement for the dense security was the children.

Boys and girls, most of them barely five, ran around the bustling lawns where people worked, playing and helping their parents with their chores. It was easy for Manwe to conclude which child belonged to which adult, but his eyes drew to one of the most lonesome figures, a young woman who tarried by herself in a small and recently-built barn, handling the goats the best she could around a pregnant belly. Something about the darkness of her hair and the shape of her face drew him to her.

Sneaking his way atop the white walls, he climbed through branches, his steps ginger as he avoided the stray people who would come near the walls. The sun had reached the apex in the sky when he slipped down into the gardens and silently approached the bar, penetrating its shade while the day's heat soared.

The pregnant woman stood at one of the milking stations near the back of the little rectangle of space, humming a song while she gently pulled on the udders of a nanny goat.

Sheltered in a deep shadow created by the door and the way the sun seeped into the barn, Manwe cleared his throat in the dark.

The woman turned toward him, her eyes searching. Strung along her neck, gleaming in a thousand points of starlight, The Savannah's Tears called its lust-song to him, the perfect prize for the perfect thief. Manwe looked at the necklace and the woman wearing it—she was the same lord's daughter who had falsely accused him of raping her, a claim that had led to the death of his lover.

The woman's soiled hands went to her stomach, a mother's first concern. "Have you come to finally kill me?"

Manwe stared, betraying no emotion in his stare or in bearing.

She shuddered. "I'm so sorry. I didn't know that would happen. I didn't know so many people would die."

Manwe leaned back against the wall. His attention went to her belly. "How far along?"

"My midwife says I'm seven months along, maybe less."

"So I guess it's his. That is Leomachus' child."

"If it is, it is," the woman said, eyes averted. "I hope not."

"You hope not?" Manwe asked, surprised.

"I know what I did to you, thief, and to Leomachus. And to his son..." She trembled, unable to hold back tears. Holding her belly in one hand and covering her face with the other, she sobbed aloud, unable to catch her breath.

"Oh, I gather it now," said Manwe. "Does your husband know?"

"Will you spare me if he does?"

Manwe released a shallow sigh. "I'm not here to kill you."

"Why not?" she shouted, hands balled to fists, startling the nanny goat. Taken aback by the outburst, Manwe felt his knees wobble. He clutched the wall, hoping that she had not drawn the attention of someone outside the barn. She seethed despair and anger.

He held out a hand to her, begging calm. "Because I'm not."

"How do I know?" she exclaimed. "How do I know you're not one of those terrorists out in the hills coming to kill my family because of something that happened hundreds of years ago? How do I know you're not here to finish what you started?"

He stood there on his toes, poised to spring if anyone entered the barn. When no one came, Manwe relaxed, but his attention did not return to the necklace; instead, it settled on her. "What's your name?"

"If—"

"What's your name?"

She sucked in a breath. "Crisa."

Manwe relaxed his stance, his hands held out at the sides. He checked the doorway again to see if any shadows broke the edge of the light, and assuming they were safe, he let his hands finally fall. "Let's talk. Can we talk, Crisa?"

Crisa thumbed the tears from her cheeks. "About?"

"Why are you scared about what is happening in the hills?"

The question stilled Crisa. Her hands returned to her belly as the question worked its way across her fine features. "This is my home. Who does not fear for their home?"

"Why do you fear?" asked Manwe.

"No one in Tolivius is not a slave to something. At least that is what my father thinks," she replied, her brow knitted with a hint of conceiving what she said. "'Beauty before death,' they say in the emperor's courts. More beauty means more grandeur, and more grandeur means more danger, and more danger always ends in ruin. The games the people play there are cruel and cold." The glow off the hay warmed her face. "Leomachus was caught in this old foolishness. You may have been the one to cut his throat, but I know he had earned it. I thought I had, too…"

"You're the children of invaders," Manwe reminded her.

"How can you invade the place you were born?"

It was Manwe's turn to be halted.

"Did you come all this way to ask me questions?" Crisa inquired. No longer fearful of Manwe's wrath, she lowered her hands, standing taller.

Manwe gathered himself. "I was hoping to steal that necklace off your neck."

Crisa's brown-eyed stare hardened before she laughed, bursting in tinkling, hysteric pants that ended in a happy sob. She reached behind her neck and undid the clasp, letting the strand of diamonds fall into her other hand.

"Here." She offered the necklace to him freely. "Take it. I told my husband that I didn't need it, but he thinks I need to be coddled all the time. I'll tell him I provided it to the temples to keep in trust. He'll like to think I did that."

Stunned by the display of charity, Manwe was entranced by the prize before him, more so than he had been when he first stole it. Taking a step away from the wall, he approached Crisa and reached with a gentle touch, carefully accepting The Savannah's Tears.

"Why?" he asked.

"Because I shouldn't have lied about the rape," she said.

He marveled at the pool of wonder in his hand. The ancient queens of the Juutan savannah had worn this necklace for a thousand years before the Gypians had come and raped them of their treasures, passing around gems like toys until they became more than something to play with—something to kill for. Worried he would get lost in the sparkling lust he possessed, he closed his hand over the necklace before slipping it into his loincloth.

Manwe and Crisa shared a brief stare before he departed.

MANWE KNOCKED THREE TIMES ON THE DOOR.

The viewing slot slid open, and Magera looked out with her blue eyes. "What is the goddess's secret?"

"The goddess has no secrets," replied Manwe.

The priestess opened the door to her underground bordello, a series of excavated chambers and halls where the cries and pants of pleasure mingled with the whispers of those devoted to the embrace of souls. Dressed in a provocative outfit, flimsy blue silk covered a healthy bust and girded his host's loins, that material sheer enough that one could plainly see what waited beneath.

"Back already?" Magera asked.

Manwe nodded as he entered, feeling the edges of the diamond beads on his testicles. The walk back from Merchants' Row had been long and ponderous, a time of hard thoughts and harder epiphanies. He stood in the center of the first chamber. The warm light from a thousand lamps bathed his dark body. The sweat of the day dried almost in an instant, and he looked at all the little statues, satyrs, and monkey charms beneath clay effigies of the Goddess of Love.

"What thoughts, my friend?" Magera stepped beside him as Manwe studied one of the tapestries, a woven scene of a bull mounting a voluptuous human woman who clung to the beast in rapturous joy.

Manwe focused on nothing in particular. "Were you born here, Magera?"

"No, I was assigned. From Gypus."

"Did you like it?" he asked. "Did you like the imperial city?"

"It was a splendid metropolis."

"That was not my question."

Magera sighed at the observation. "There are only so many ways to be alive, Manwe. For a very few, Gypus holds nothing but treasure and opportunity, a place to live and live well. For the rest of us it is a place of struggle, fear, and insecurity. An interesting arena for an interesting game."

"Being a priestess is not suited for the game, I take it?"

She held her hands behind her back. "One might say that."

"What would you say about the revolution?" he asked bluntly.

A second sigh, deeper than the first, moved her. "I can only ask questions as a devotee to the ideals of love and companionship, not politics and nation-craft. Those are below my vows and my post."

Manwe arched his brow. "And so what would you ask?"

"What made you deter from the path?" She turned her head to study him. "You were out in the hills when the battle happened. What did you see?"

"Nightmares from my childhood, from the darkest corners of magic," Manwe revealed, simple and to the point. He trained his eyes on one of the lamps at the foot of the goddess, its simple flame a match for a more recent, more horrid memory of a cackling shaman and fell ghouls. "I saw good men sell their souls."

"So you aren't aligned at the moment."

Manwe squinted against the flame. "I'd say not."

Magera grabbed his hand, held it firm. "Then what would you see as fair, if you had your way?"

"I would keep you all well," Manwe answered. "No man a slave, no woman a whore. Love and let live and be left alone. End the plight of the poor. That's what I would want for myself."

"Then perhaps you are not as un-aligned as you thought," Magera suggested.

"Did you just give me spiritual advice?"

"Did I?" She smirked as a knock came at the temple bordello's door.

Magera went and opened up the viewing slot. She glanced back at Manwe and rolled her eyes, opening the door to let Cleon barge inside the foyer. The hem of his new robe fluttered in the warm air, its trim made of a luxurious gold cloth that shimmered in the wavering light of the many lamps. Made of cotton died varying hues of red, the stitching formed feathered patterns that seemed to almost dance upon the fabric.

His face freshly shaven, Cleon smiled adoringly at Manwe and posed for review. "Well?" he asked, whimsical. "What do you think?"

Magera excused herself to the next room where the orgies took place. "If I didn't know you I'd think you a whore."

"So is everyone to call you 'Cleon the Apple'?" asked Manwe, somewhat bewildered.

"Oh, hush. You know you like it." Cleon waggled his finger for Manwe to come closer. "I found the proper supply of this sugar drink you larcenous kind all rave about."

"Have you?" said Manwe.

"Indeed." Cleon opened his hand. "But first, did you retrieve the bauble?"

"I'd rather you paid it reverence." Manwe withdrew The Savannah's Tears from his loincloth and handed it to the sorcerer who let it hang between his fingers, sparkling like a string of stars caught by one of his mysterious spells. "I have a hard enough time giving it back."

"It will go to a place where it will be well taken care of." Cleon hid the necklace in a pocket of his new red robe. "Now, away! We haven't got much time."

⊱━━━━━━━━━━━━━━━◆───

"I DID NOT EXPECT YOU TO BE TELLING THE TRUTH," SAID MANWE, A BIT perturbed. "At least not about coming here."

Cleon huffed, re-tying the golden sash to hold his red robe more tightly to his body. He looked around the front of the Senate Consul's manor nervously, scanning the grassy lawn ahead for guards. "Well, you wanted help and I wanted you to meet someone important to the house of cards." He shrugged his shoulders on the way. "Like your people say—one net, many fish."

"Not unless we're the fish," said Manwe, keeping pace as they stopped at the manor gates.

"Watch this," said Cleon, who rang the guard bell.

Manwe panicked, grabbing the hilt of his knife in an instant. "What are you doing?"

A sentry appeared, a Juutan whose light skin and pale eyes spoke of mixed parentage. Armed with a small buckler and patinated sword the length of his forearm, he blinked a few times, as if waking from a snooze. "What do you want?"

Cleon drew close, his eyes flashing with an unnatural light. "Do you remember me this morning, boy?"

The youth perked at the sorcerer's question, sudden in his awareness. "Lord Cleon! Forgive my mistake!" He dropped his sword reaching for the keys on his belt. The gates creaked open.

Cleon nodded to Manwe to follow. "What are my orders, boy?" he called to the guard.

The guard stood at attention, his arms presented in salute. "If anyone comes and says, 'Cleon said so,' I should let them out of the gate and leave the manor."

"Man your post," the sorcerer said.

Striding toward the manor with a cautious gait that mismatched his lover's march, Manwe watched in complete wonder as every person Cleon met along the way repeated this exact sequence, with the appropriate changes made for gender and station, their gazes transfixed by the sorcerer's enchanted stare. When they were within the confines of the manor's foyer Manwe could no longer hold his tongue.

"How did you charm this many people?" he asked, lacking a better word for what he saw.

Cleon's enigmatic grin broadened as he climbed the main stair of the Senate Consul's house, his sandaled feet smacking the wood while Manwe's feet made quiet pats.

They reached the top of the stair and went down a short hall that opened to an opulent chamber of hand-hewn stonework shaped in the visages of Gypus' gods and emperors. Seated on a couch set on a pair of lion hides, a rotund man in a tunic and cheetah-skin wrap stared into the fire of his hearth, his bloodshot eyes dull. In his late forties and balding, the salt fuzz on his face was stark against his olive skin.

Cleon called on him. "Senate Consul."

"Are you back, sorcerer?" the governor of Tolivius and Gypus' imperial representative asked, his tone withdrawn.

"As promised, my lord," Cleon said upon entering the chamber with Manwe. "May we approach?"

"You've ensorcelled my staff, enslaved my wife to your works, and now I'm committing treason by meeting with a rebel. Do you really give a damn?"

Cleon led Manwe to the back of the couch the lord sat on and posted him there. "I could have killed you and assumed control of the city. I was within my rights."

"Until you brought him here." The Senate Consul turned and looked at Manwe with an inebriated smile. "So, you must be The Panther. I've heard a good bit about you for years now."

"And I've seen a good bit of you and your kind's abuse," Manwe replied, placid against the acid slathering the man's voice. He spotted a chair to the immediate left of the couch and went to it. "You have thirty minutes, Cleon. No more."

"More than I need." The red mage sauntered past the furniture to take a place before the fireplace, putting himself in both Manwe and the lord's immediate view. "You two will be doing most of the work, putting together a transition and all."

"A transition?" asked the Senate Consul. "I was told this criminal had information on the rebels he would betray for special favor. I did not get drunk and put on my best to play statecraft with one who has no right to it."

Manwe failed to resist his own answer. "Typical Gypian response," he said, chewing every word with derision. "You think you can own something that is unconquerable."

"My people's swords and spears said otherwise," the politician was quick to remind. "And they still do."

"Gentlemen." Cleon stepped forward and picked up the clay jug of wine the Senate Consul had been nursing, looking about the room for some chalices. "We are not here to discuss the past, only the present and the future. Now," he said as he recovered a pair of clay cups from a nearby serving cart, "let's seek common ground. The rebels clearly want their revolution and are willing to go further than they should in obtaining their desires, even to the point of raising abominations. Gypus, on the other hand, has become more and more concerned about Tolivius' stability as a launching point into the rest of Juut's eastern jungles and the independent kingdoms of the Eastern Glories, probably because the emperor believes in providence."

"Get to your fucking point, Cleon," said the Senate Consul.

Cleon smiled as he sipped from the cup he filled. "Fine vintage, my lord. Where was it made?"

"In my vineyard, sorcerer, where I make everything," he replied, gruffer. "I make everything here, from the cheese I press to the clothes I wear. You still haven't gotten to the fucking point."

"Hurry, Cleon," said Manwe, taking a cup of wine when it was offered. "Before his privilege gets up and walks away."

"I should," shouted the Senate Consul as he rose to his bare feet. His prodigious belly shook as he blustered, red-face and angry.

Cleon thrust a finger in his face. "Sit down. I still haven't forgiven you for those boys."

The point of his nose an inch from the sorcerer's finger, the Senate Consul dropped back to the couch at once. He leaned as far back as he could into the plush purple cushions.

"We are here to save our very lives, Marcus," Cleon said again the Senate Consul's terrified expression. "This does go beyond your privilege, or my power, or his skill." He motioned to Manwe with the same finger he had threatened the Senate Consul. "These rebels would let the dead walk to win this city and likely their own tribes, but imagine letting the emperor know how precarious our situation."

"The dead none have seen," said the Senate Consul, his tone less inflated. "You ask me to betray my emperor...nay, The Gods' Providence, Cleon! All based on rumor and old native fears."

"They aren't rumors," said Manwe, taciturn. "I saw them. I saw the devil that made them. I saw the heroes who allowed him to."

The Senate Consul's addled gaze switched between Manwe and Cleon. "We have sorcerers enough to deal with one two-bit necromancer. We have a legion."

"But we don't have enough life to fight the dead," said Cleon. "There is a reason why necromancers do not attempt to raise corpses like this—it gets out of hand very quickly, and if this Calla has already done his darkness, then we could already be too late."

"What would you have me do, Cleon?" The Senate Consul shrugged and held up his hands. "If I alert Gypus they will send an army and we will be swallowed. There will be a new government that will be no better than the last one."

"Then perhaps you should have thought about creating a better one beforehand," said Manwe.

"One that considers savage terrorists like you, who rapes this city's daughters and slays it lords? Who robs, ravages, and rebels?" The Senate Consul shook his head, his round face drenched in a drunkard's sheen.

"Gypus or the dead, there will be many new things when this is all said and done. What matters the most here is diverting the disaster, or at least minimizing it." Cleon turned his back on both of them and stepped to the fire, his wine cup by his mouth. "You two need to discuss a third option."

Silent for most of the discussion, Manwe swirled the cup in his hands, feeling the force of the liquid stirring. He stared hard at his lover, wondering if he and the sorcerer would even have a future after this conversation. An old itch to grab his knife and rip it across the Senate Consul's fat throat bothered him, at war with the revolution that always had his mind. Instead, he took a long draw of alcohol, letting the grape's fermented blood burn his throat.

"You don't want Gypus here, and I don't want Gypians like the ones I have had all my life," Manwe addressed Tolivius' governor. "But I've seen things today that are easily forgotten when troubled with the way of nations. Perhaps the line is blurred by the white walls when the sun hits them, or the laughter of the children your sons breed into my people's daughters. We've both been here, Gypian and Juutan, for a long time now."

Glancing at Manwe, the Senate Consul sat quietly for long moments, his eyes or mouth failing to reveal his thoughts. He rose again from the couch and reclaimed his jug of wine. He took a hard slug from its mouth before offering it to Manwe.

Manwe let him fill his cup.

"'Beauty before death,' as we say in Gypus." The Senate Consul vexed on his words. "A lot of people often think that means finding grandeur in the face of what comes, but I know better. The goal of achieving everlasting fame or fortune or worth means nothing next to what is allowed to continue."

Manwe settled farther back in his chair. "Maybe the beauty of the life you cultivate is what matters in the face of the inevitable."

"Yes," said the Senate Consul with a smile. "I love my city. I love her white walls, her little markets, her hills. I love being left alone. This place is better for me than Gypus was, but I would rather not end up dead for it all. Third option, fine, but what does Tolivius get?"

Manwe froze at the question. "You get to live."

"No, sneak-thief, you will have to give me more than that."

Manwe felt his entire world shift beneath his seat. Born a poor man in the countryside as a whelp whose father had withered under the lash and a mother who had endured servitude for the sake of a son who never fit in, he wondered what he was doing here making decisions for so many.

"There would be less rebellion if..." He paused, taking a hard gulp of wine. "Things will have to change drastically."

The Senate Consul sighed. "Demands?"

"Slavery is abolished tonight."

"You're mad." The Senate Consul shook his head at Manwe. "You'd shift away an entire workforce unused to freedom. Have you considered that maybe a good number of these slaves, Gypian or Juutan alike, may not be fit for the world you'd make?"

"Pay them reparations for their bonds. They will be more amenable to cooperation."

"Reparations," the Senate Consul boomed, nearly spilling his jug in protest. He shook the clay at Cleon. "You'd bring anarchists down on my head!"

"Manwe, dear, you have to be more civil. It is hard for these rich honks," said the sorcerer, unamused at the governor's protestation.

Manwe sat taller. "Slavery must be abolished. I cannot walk out of this room if it is not."

Cleon gave the Senate Consul a pleading look. The fat lord, reddened against his exertion, plopped back down on his couch and threw back his vice. Guzzling wine, he heaved when he finished. "Gods preserve me...graduated emancipation within five years."

"One," said Manwe. "And if not reparations then a labor schedule where they are paid for their work. Fairly."

"And who will I demand follow this ludicrousness?" The Senate Consul groaned.

"Lord," said Cleon, "it is a perfectly reasonable offer. One year should be enough if you offer the Merchants' Rows tax relief and let them control their own streets."

"They'll work their way into the symposiums, in time," grumbled the Senate Consul. "Next you'll have them vote at the writ calls."

"And in three years you must allow tribal leaders and vodunis into the Philosophers Courts," added Manwe. "Plus pardons for rebels willing to surrender."

"I cannot simply take such policy to the Philosophers' Courts and say, 'This is the way it will be.'" The Senate Consul gaped in search of a deeper breath, belching a wine stink. "And they will not like local commerce having more control than they do. It affects their pockets."

"There are no markets to manage when we're all dead," Cleon pointed out.

"And what does Tolivius get for all of this liberalism?" the Senate Consul demanded.

Manwe finished his wine and set the cup on the floor as he stood. "Simple. You will be alive afterward to negotiate terms."

⁂

"THIS HAS BEEN AN ODD DAY," MANWE REMARKED AS THEY LEFT THE Senate Consul's office chamber, his mouth sour from the wine.

Cleon spoke when they reached the manor's main level. "In times of struggle, Chaos is the only thing to be counted on. But now that is done..." The sorcerer snapped his fingers, a small spark leaping from when the pads sheared together. A loud sigh issued through the halls as if dozens of voices collectively let out a long held breath.

"What did you do now?" asked Manwe, concerned any time his lover worked his power.

"Oh, nothing serious." Cleon winked at him as they traversed the stairs. "Just all those glamours and enchantments are gone. The servants will question why we are here, the guards will subdue and maybe kill us...all good fun."

"You didn't," said Manwe, stopping directly in the foyer's center.

"Oh, I did," Cleon answered, jutting one of his hips out to the side playfully. "Now, here's a part I didn't tell you—the sugar drink your larcenous ilk crave is ready to be moved somewhere in this house. Where I don't know, but there's the fun of it all."

Suddenly the manor was not simply a manor to Manwe, but hostile territory, a place where his shadow could mean his death. His knees bent, he readied himself to spring away at the first sign of someone's presence other than Cleon's. "We don't know where the loot is, which guards are on duty, how many servants there are, the location of both lord and lady…"

"Manwe, Manwe," Cleon whispered under his breath, drawing his finger down the center of his face. A trail of black smoke followed the path of his nail. He faded from sight like some intrigued apparition who had decided they had seen enough.

Cleon's voice echoed in the foyer. "Are you this city's greatest thief or not?"

⸺⊳⸺

MANWE DASHED ACROSS THE FLOOR TO ONE OF THE SHADOWY CORNERS OF the foyer, finding one of the deepening parts as the sun started for the horizon. Mouth shut and knife drawn, he backed behind a large piece of pottery, its sides depicting a relief of a red centaur wielding a spear against some old Gypian hero in black armor. He checked the ways into the room, fighting to find his breath and a moment of calm.

Minutes passed before he left his corner. Creeping down one of the halls, Manwe recalled the last time he had visited the manor when he had lifted The Savannah's Tears from the Senate Consul's wife, a scandalous lady named Nelo. In the darkened halls he found small alcoves and places to hide as he cased rooms along the passages, none of them holding more than slaves. He listened to their small conversation, ears open for clues to his prize.

Down one of the passages the hall forked in three directions. Standing in the center of the junction, Manwe listened for the patter of bare feet or sandals, his hand on his knife.

A sudden realization caught him: he had been here before.

He looked toward a closed chamber and remembered a heist from another time, when he had searched for a treasure he had already stolen and for the love that had vanished with it.

An intuition born of hard times nagged at him, but Manwe took the path toward that room and hoped that the door did not have a lock—he had not brought his tools. To his surprise, the door opened with a gentle turn of the handle.

Set in a neat stack beyond the doorway, two crates of sugar drink lay in the center of the room, next to a small stool where two oil lamps sputtered to offset the darkness. Even more disconcerting to Manwe were the two green glass bottles that rested on the top crate. He repeated the same words he uttered the last time he found himself in a room like this one, speaking them with a heavy sigh.

"This is clearly a trap."

"Isn't everything?" called a woman's voice, its tenor strong and silken.

Manwe turned in the doorway of the room to view the lady who stood in the hall. Standing the center of the three-way intersection, she posed like a fine statue stitched in gaudy sequins, the sheer material of her himation clung tight to the subtle curves of a body both beautiful in form but aged from years of overindulgence.

Lady Nelo blinked her olive eyes, her thin lips set in an unimpressed line.

Naked save for his loincloth, a sly smile crossed Manwe's lips when he remembered the last time he had seen her at work, the center of a drunken orgy—the same orgy where he had stolen The Savannah's Tears right off her neck.

"Lady," he said, bowing his head slightly. "It seems you've caught me."

"The only time a cat is caught is when you have it by the tail," she said, dry. "So, young man, you've returned to steal more. And with that bugger sorcerer somewhere in these shadows I have no doubt."

Manwe opened his hands and shrugged. "I must do what I must do. I'm sure you've heard that reason many times."

Nelo reached up and adjusted the silk over her bust. "And I'm sure your reason here is quite laudable by your standards, and perhaps my husband's, given how easily swayed he is." Folding her hands over her stomach, she studied him. "So, Panther, is it liquor now? No more jewels?"

"Everything goes to a just cause," Manwe said. "Your husband understands that now, I think."

"That boy lover understands little beyond what he is told. He's not one for going out and getting his hands dirty."

"And you are?"

"What woman isn't?" She flashed a violent grin. "I know criminals, be they in the government or the streets I arose from. There was once a time I was not so gilded."

"A pretty knife is still a knife," Manwe replied. Posted in the doorway of the treasure room, he leaned against the frame. "You'll have to let me pass, though. I know very well how to handle a knife, even when it is not in my hand."

"Do you?" Her cheeks bunched with laugh lines as her grin grew. "And where would that knife plunge if I let you go? Into my back? Into the backs of those who you claim oppress you?"

"Into those who would want you dead."

That cocksure smile Manwe had seen on the faces of lords, ladies, slavers, and enemies contracted. Nelo's stare hardened. "And who would that be?"

Manwe opened his hands again. "Not me."

Nelo tilted her head in contemplation, her rigid stance broken by the slight movement. She glanced to the ground, her mouth screwed with troubled thought before she stepped forward. "My husband might be cowed easily, but I'm not, thief. You will have to give better reasons."

Manwe nodded at the boxes stacked behind him. "There is no excuse beyond what it will go to—and that is the freedom of the savannah."

"Again, for whom?" she questioned.

"For the living," he answered. "Not the dead my friends would raise."

Nelo's eyes flared in confusion at the answer. A fear, sincere and considered, puckered lips as second passed on in a contemplative silence. Her attention shifted for a moment before it settled again on Manwe.

"Do what you must and begone from my house. Both of you," Nelo said, turning away. "Do you hear me, Cleon?"

As if summoned by name, the sorcerer's black shape rose from the tile floor like an apparition, taking on depth. Resplendent in his crimson robe, he placed both hands on his hips in a dominant show of his power.

"Lady Nelo," he said, bowing with a grand flourish. "To think you expect so little of us vagabonds and thieves, it would not do to depart without paying the hostess of the house a fine gift for her kindness."

Nelo glared at Cleon. "I've had enough of you already, sorcerer."

"Then take this as payment for my poor behavior."

Drop by sparkling drop dribbled out of a pocket on the inside of Cleon's robe, each bead blazing as The Savannah's Tears formed a loose line of glory between his pinched finger and thumb. Manwe watched the lady's eyes as the necklace fell down under its weight.

She reached forward. "Give it to me. Give it back."

"Funny how vice works." Cleon tossed the strand of diamonds to Nelo, who caught them like a hungry beggar catching fruit fallen from a farmer's cart. Cradling the necklace in her bejeweled hands, the precious stones set in her rings dimmed when compared to The Savannah's Tears. The luster burned brighter than the coldest stars.

"Yes, funny indeed." A pleasured smile spread across her face once more. "Boys."

Three slaves stepped into the intersection, dark men clad in little more than loincloths and carrying stout staves of ebony. Trembling from head to toe, these broken souls slipped between Manwe, Cleon, and their lady, their eyes to the floor.

"You should be smarter than this, Nelo," said Cleon, his smirk unwavering. He crossed his arms in front of his chest and addressed the slaves. "Do you know who we are, boys? Do you know that she is sending you after a sorcerer of great power?"

"Silence," shouted Nelo, clutching The Savannah's Tears to her chest. "Take care of them! You serve me, not him—"

"Did she tell you who this man is standing behind me?" Cleon asked. "That is Manwe the Panther, the greatest thief in all the lands and a talented murderer."

The slaves' eyes, white and wide in their black faces, shifted in Manwe's direction. He gripped the handle of his knife and set both feet set apart. "They're scared, Cleon," he whispered to his lover's back. "I'll not kill them."

"Then make whatever you do impressive," the sorcerer said aloud. "I believe Lady Nelo needs a demonstration." Without another word, Cleon drew his finger down his face a second time, and as before, he disappeared into the shadows like a wraith.

"You damned trickster," Manwe cursed under his breath when he saw Nelo's smile curl. He drew his knife.

The lady of the house stood tall once more, her confidence imbued in the cocksure posture. "Kill him or I'll have you all whipped," she said simply, half-turning to appraise the necklace again. "The first man to kill him might even win his freedom."

The three slaves charged.

Meeting the first man who entered the short passage between the hall and the treasure chamber, Manwe ducked a clumsy swing of the slave's club and pushed to the side, using his foe's momentum to force him into the wall. Spinning into a deep crouch, he threw his leg out, sweeping the slave off his feet.

Manwe came up and stomped on the first slave's face, mashing his nose into a bloody pulp as the second slave chopped for his shoulder, forcing him to dodge left. He blocked the second slave's reverse swing against the flat of his knife and jabbed the man's floating ribs.

Paused by the sting, the slave screamed when Manwe drove him to the floor with a brutal kick to the back of his right knee. Manwe dispatched the second slave quickly, an elbow into his temple.

He readied the third slave's attack. The stripling froze between him and his lady.

Manwe stalked forward.

The slave fled the hallway, shrieking as Manwe darted forward into a sprint. Nelo fell back against the wall as his shadow fell over her, clutching The Savannah's Tears in one hand as she thrust both of them out to stop his advance.

Manwe raised his knife and brought it down. The blade buried in the ebony wall next to the highborn lady's head with a thunk, eliciting a shrill cry from Nelo as she quivered into a terrified ball.

"I told your husband he had a year to free all the slaves in Tolivius." Seething at the type of person he had spent most of his life learning to despise, he glowered at the wealthy abuser of his people—of all people held beneath the heel of oppression. Manwe yanked the diamonds out of Nelo's hands.

"Tell your husband that he only has six months now," Manwe said as he left her there to sob and weep.

***

"I DON'T HOW I'LL FIX THIS SPAT BETWEEN YOU AND NELO, YOU KNOW." Cleon wiped down one of the bottles of sugar drink with a cotton cloth he had borrowed from the barman. "The Senate Consul won't like it that you stabbed at his wife."

"I stabbed at her, not into her. There's a difference." Manwe watched the door from the table he and the sorcerer shared near the back of Bacchs, an old tavern the Five Fences had established in the western slums of the city. A pillar of the felonious side of his community, Manwe had been there a few times but appreciated its aims as one of the few places that would give man or a woman a decent cup of clean water and a crust of old bread without fuss.

The bottles of sugar water, gleaming dark and green in the light of the small oil lamps and smoky hearth at the other end of the room, were lined between him and Cleon, ready for their party guests when they finally arrived.

"I've had a good day, you know," said Cleon. His brown eyes were a warm caramel.

Manwe glanced his way. "Aye?"

"Aye. A bit of running around, a new robe, some good-natured robbery with a very handsome thief...what more could I ask for?"

He grinned at the compliment. "You certainly caused trouble."

"I had a partner who was more than willing to handle his share."

Manwe's smile grew at the ridiculous answer, a quirk he found endearing. Burglary, intrusion, and intimidation were easy things, but to face those he spurned, the people who had once relied on his skills only to see them thrown away for the sake of revolution, made him wonder at the reception he would receive.

The moody thought dampened the humor Cleon had brought him.

"Oh, what now, Panther?" asked the sorcerer. "You went from smiling back to glum in an instant."

Before he could reply, the battered door of Bacchs swung inward with a bang.

A group of five led by Legbas scuttled out of the night and into the dimly-lit bar, following as they checked the dark corners of the room for occupants beyond the Manwe, Cleon, and the elderly bartender who snoozed at the counter. The five who followed were immediately recognizable to Manwe as the Five Fences, a collection of four men and one woman who lived lavishly off the percentages they took from all thieves who pilfered Tolivius.

The closest man who followed behind Legbas was Sophicus, who nodded to Manwe when they caught sight of each other.

"Who's he?" Legbas asked Manwe when his group reached the table. "Ain't never seen him before."

"He's with me," said Manwe. "As sorcerers go, he's fine."

"A sorcerer?" one of the Five Fences asked, a squat woman with red beads around her fat neck. Older in her years than the rest of those who made their money hawking the wares of criminals, she took a half-step back. "You brought someone with juju, Panther?"

"Is this where I start wiggling my fingers and sparks fly, Manwe?" Cleon asked from his side of the booth, waving his hands in a mock gesture. "Should I show them a trick with shadows?"

"He's fine," Manwe told Anzi, the woman who had addressed him. He glared the sorcerer. "I promise he'll behave."

"So say you," teased Cleon.

Sophicus broke forward to lay a smooth hand on a bottle of sugar drink. Tall and a handsome face covered in a dark brown beard, he looked to Manwe as he lifted the vintage. "These for us, Panther?"

"One for the each of you, plus a few to split up," replied Manwe. He motioned for the Five Fences to take their bottles. "Go on, find a place to sit and drink."

"But we're not here to drink," Sophicus said. He held up the bottle against the small oil lamp on the table and grinned at the brown liquid within. "But looser tongues are usually more honest. We'll come to you in a bit." He looked back at his fellow fences. "Come get your bottles, you dogs."

The Five Fences retreated to one of the tables in the barroom, taking with them one extra bottle not left out for them. Cleon moved to say something before Manwe silenced him with a small signal, his attention focused on Legbas, who had remained.

The old conman held one of the sugar drink bottles in his gnarled old hand, a sly smile on his lips. "You impress, Panther, even when you go off the page a little bit. The fact that those five didn't put up a big fuss coming here is a good sign."

"Aye, god," said Manwe. He looked to the door. "Are the city vodunis still coming?"

"They better," said Legbas. He opened the fold of his shabby robe to reveal a bunch of cannabis tied together by a small white string. "Can't smoke this all myself, you know."

"I might help you with that, old man," said Cleon. He pushed out his chair and dusted the front of his new robe. "I'm not much for drinking anyway."

Before Legbas and Cleon wandered away from the table and out into the night to smoke their holy herbs, Manwe called, "Legbas."

The old man turned back. "Yes, god?"

"The Songbird," said Manwe. "Is she coming?"

"Who knows, Panther," replied the old conman. "I left her a few notes. If she shows she shows, if not..."

"I understand," said Manwe, waving him and Cleon to go on their way.

Manwe sat there at his table in silence, observing the Five Fences as they drank the liquor he had stolen and caroused, whispering secrets to each other that only those who partook in the illegal trades shared. For long minutes, maybe an hour, the five of them carried on until Sophicus rose from his chair, red-faced as he came back to Manwe's table.

"Mind if I...?" Sophicus asked, holding up his near-empty bottle.

Manwe nodded toward a place on the other side of the table, the spot where Cleon had rested. "Feel free to take another bottle. I brought plenty."

Sophicus lowered into his seat and threw back the sugar drink in one last shot. He wiped his wet mouth with his hairy forearm. "Before you got into the business with those spear-chuckers."

"Careful, Sophicus," Manwe said. He lifted his eyes to the fence. "Those are my people."

"No, we are your people," he replied. "The streets were your home before the hills were, no matter if you arose from them or not."

Manwe scratched his woolen beard, picking out a gnat that had gotten too close to the skin of his cheek. "I didn't come here to debate politics, Sophicus. It's not why I had Legbas call you."

"Legbas didn't fucking call me, Panther," Sophicus said. He grabbed another bottle and pulled out a small dagger to trim off the wax seal. "I've been waiting for this day."

"Have you?"

"Yes, I have," he continued, his tone taking on an air of annoyance. "Revolutions, activism, organization—they work for criminals but never for good men. You're a good man, Manwe, and you finally learned the folly of it."

"I rebelled for my people." Manwe gripped the edge of the round table between him and the fence. "I fought so that Juutan children didn't have to whore themselves in the streets, or live in chains at the beck and call of some abusive petty lord who valued status over flesh and blood."

"And now you're fucking a Gypian sorcerer and meeting with those same lords you drew your knife against."

Manwe almost lurched out of his chair; his fingers dug into the cracked wood.

Sophicus grinned at his reaction. "What? You think you're the only one who has friends or loose tongues? I always knew about Toba," he said, motioning to the other fences at the nearby table. "We all did."

"Then why did you never say anything? Why did you do nothing when Leomachus took him?" Manwe struggled to level his voice. "Why didn't any of you care?"

"Because he earned it. The rules for criminals have always been clear on that," said Sophicus. "The hard thing you revolutionaries never seem to grasp is that you make the beds you lie in." Freeing the bottle of its cork with his teeth, he took a hard draw of the fiery liquor. He made a sour face. "Will you fucking drink with me, Panther? You make me fucking nervous when you're this serious."

Paused on his adversary's words, Manwe took the bottle and sipped. The brown drink bit his tongue with raw sugar, sweet but harsh. It rolled down his throat to form a knot in the center of his stomach. He coughed. "You demean me for having the courage to do what you and the rest of our ilk should have been doing all along."

"How do you think that?" asked Sophicus, retrieving the bottle to drink again.

"We're criminals." Manwe loosened his grip on the table's edge and took a deep breath. "We do not steal, smuggle, or murder because we were born to it—no, not for a moment. We're criminals because we were forced to the bottom by those who did the exact same things we did, but they started out with the money we never had. We give them permission to do it, we work with them, but when it comes time to pay for the deed they are the last to take responsibility. They never give back. It is an unearned privilege and nothing else."

Sophicus stared hard. The two remained quiet, letting the chatter from the other table thread the silence with laughter and idle conversation.

"Then why did you stop fighting them?" Sophicus asked when the quiet went for too long.

"Because I'd rather live in a corrupt world filled with thieves, lords, and liars than one filled the dead and the damned." Manwe retrieved the bottle from Sophicus and swallowed more of its fire. "I thought Toba's brother would lead us right, or at least would be better than he turned out to be. He threw in with a voduni who is ready to raise the dead to destroy Tolivius, and—"

"One moment," Sophicus interrupted. "Toba's brother is a leader of the rebels?

Manwe nodded. "He was a good man."

"And this voduni wants to raze this city to the ground with the undead?"

He nodded a second time.

Sophicus glanced all around the barroom, his mouth agape as his brow knit in troubled thought. He opened and closed the hand he had placed on the table between himself and Manwe, at which point the latter handed over the bottle of sugar drink. Sophicus took four hard gulps before he slammed it down on the table.

"I have to tell you, Panther," he said, "I came here tonight because I was sure you were finally going to fess up to the foolishness you involved yourself in."

"There's more," Manwe said, grabbing a new bottle. This time he used his own knife to whittle away the wax. "Gypus is ready to march their great armies upon us, especially after what happened to the Latian I slew. You, the rebels, lords, the entire city. The mad voduni Kosey follows wants them here. He would turn the dead created by what is coming into something to take out everyone who is not him."

Sophicus snatched the bottle as soon as the cork was free. He held the green glass when he raised it to his lips, his bright eyes hard on Manwe. He sipped a small amount of the liquor. "What's your plan?"

Manwe shrugged. "I will stop them."

Sophicus made a rude sound in his throat. "What, you and that sorcerer you brought?"

"That sorcerer helped me make a deal with the powerful of Gypus," Manwe informed him. "Our hope was that those in the dark would be ready to help as well."

The fence eyed him before scratching the brown scruff on his cheeks. He looked to his four friends at the other table and sighed. "You keep getting me in trouble, Panther."

"Does that mean you'll help?"

"There's always honor amongst thieves," said Sophicus. "Especially when it could cost us our hides."

⁂

Manwe exited Bacchs a few minutes after Sophicus left, armed with a bottle of sugar drink and his knife. Outside the balmy air clung to his lithe muscular form, refreshment from the smokiness of the bar. Thick storm clouds obscured the night sky, and over the howling of stray dogs and broken smatters of shouting and noise, a far-off rumble echoed to warn of the coming rain.

Manwe spotted a cluster of folk off the right. They stood, engulfed in white smoke, in the mouth of one of the many alleys along the backstreet. Shaking the bottle in his hand to ease the nervousness, he approached the miasma of chronic and entered, his eyes immediately irritated by a hazy irritation.

Within the fog of sweet-smelling weed, he found Cleon and Legbas, standing side by side as they conversed with two men and two women garbed in a variety of animal hides and bedecked in scores of beaded bracelets and necklaces. Their dusky faces lined and smudged with white ritual paint, they listened as Cleon waxed on snatches of a subject that Manwe tried hard to recognize.

"I implore you to understand, my good folk," said the sorcerer, "that Gypian or Juutan, anyone worth their morality, must believe that life is life and death is death and these two forces are both bound and separated by their sacredness. To violate these two things by spell or song is to muddy the edge between what your gods created and mine hold true. Surely we can all agree?"

The folk with the painted faces, the city's most powerful vodunis, murmured agreement as they toked on the burning bush. All four of them, along with Legbas and Cleon, noticed Manwe when he approached.

"And here's our man, gods," said Legbas as he opened the circle for the thief to join.

Manwe stepped into the space allowed, eyes to the ground as he offered his bottle of sugar drink to whomever would take it. "Thank you for coming, vodunis. It is more than kind that you would grant me even a moment of your attention."

One of these mystics, a woman of middle age and crowned in a headdress made of horns and feathers, took the offered liquor. She smiled, her teeth dyed red. "Ah, the new fire we keep hearing about while we talk about fires we keep hearing about," she said, sly and silken.

"Voduna Erzuli has been asking many questions since she arrived," Cleon related to Manwe as she drank deep. "I've done my best to answer, but perhaps you could enlighten them a bit more than I can."

"I'll try," Manwe replied.

"Big difference between trying and doing," said another of the vodunis, a diminutive man who stood at shoulder height with the rest of his brethren and with two white lines of paint smeared under his eyes. His fuzzy hair crusted with salt, he held his joint between hands worn smooth by a fisherman's callouses. "You either catch the fish or you don't."

"Oh just go and ask your question, Agwe," chided Legbas. "Get to it."

"All right, all right, god," Voduni Agwe said, his bare brow furrowed. "All I need to know is this, Panther: did you see Calla raise the things you said he raised?"

Manwe retook the bottle of sugar drink when Erzuli offered it back and gulped down a healthy swallow. "I did," he got out after a few coughs of the burn. "I saw him stand ankle deep in the coals as he ensorcelled his pot of pitch." He shuddered as another memory forced another draw of sugar drink. "I saw the faces within that pot—fangs and all."

The third of their number, a brawny fellow with a series of hard scars scattered across his chest, spoke. "I'm Voduni Ogun, Panther. If what you say is true, I know this ritual."

"You would," murmured Voduni Agwe.

The hulking priest glared at his short accomplice. "Either way, such darkness can only be found in dark places. Where he learned it is not near as unsettling that he did it, and if he did commit such evil, we must rise against Calla."

"To rise against him would bring about a schism between the city and the plains," said the fourth and final member of the city vodunis, a slender woman who dressed more like a man and had painted images of gods on her arms and face. Armed with a short Gypian sword, she stood as rigid as Voduni Ogun, one hand resting on the hilt of her weapon. "We must be sure."

"So what would you have your brethren do, Voduna Freda?" asked Legbas.

Manwe looked at the voduna for her answer. She averted her eyes from his gaze, her face set to the black clouds beyond the cloud they had created.

"We'd have to think about," said Voduna Erzuli said.

"Then let's get to deeper thinking." Cleon nodded for Manwe to depart as he took fresh joint from the pocket of his brilliant red robe. "We've got all night."

Manwe wandered from the smoke. Red-eyed and exhausted from the last few days, he slinked down the street in his daze, wondering what ill design fate had in store next.

The answer came with a whisper. "Panther."

Standing in the mouth of one of Tolivius' slum alleys, Folami the Songbird emerged from the deep oppression of the night's shadows, clad in a slip of black cotton and simple leather sandals. Iron knives gleamed from the holsters on her belt. Her black hair, braided in coarse dreadlocks, sprouted from her scalp in the natural crown of a queen too regal for jewels.

"You came," Manwe said.

"I heard what happened," she said. "I've heard other things as well."

He checked the bottle and saw that only a few more sips remained. "I'm sure you have."

Folami tilted her head to the side, her full lips curved downward. "Who is this man before me?" She stepped from the alley, letting the muddy light of the few torches ensconced nearby gleam in the oiled knots of her hair. "This is not the man who would rob a lord with less than a shred of luck and wit alone. This is not the man who paid me kindness when I rightfully had lost the game we played."

"Maybe I'm not that man anymore." Manwe started to bring the bottle to his lips.

Iron flashed in the darkness. The glass bottle shattered in Manwe's hand before he could move from the small blade's trajectory, his drunkenness destroying his reflexes.

"Maybe if you stop wallowing, you can be, Panther," she said, resolute against his baleful gaze like a goddess undeterred by an expression he knew she had spent her life having to accept without response. "There is enough going in this city to give you purpose if you stopped being so blind."

His glare turned to confusion. "What do you mean?"

Folami turned back to the alley she had arisen from. "Come and see."

A HOT RAIN FELL UPON NIGHTTIME TOLIVIUS AS MANWE AND FOLAMI sprinted through the allies and cross-streets of its urban decay, their pounding feet silent against the tat-tating of the showers upon the soupy roads and tin roofs. His heart pumping, Manwe almost smiled as he chased after the Songbird, at the edge of a laugh and sob as his drink-addled brain cleared with every beat in his chest. Thunder boomed and lightning flashed in the great black vault above, a divine drummer who's beat only the gods knew.

This was how it should be, he thought, as he tried to keep pace with his competitor, his equal. They raced to the other end of the western market district, the same place where Manwe had met Legbas earlier that day. Folami, as nimble and light as her namesake, leapt to the low edge of a nearby roof, pulling herself up. He followed her path, his hands finding the same holds she grabbed on her way to where there would be no shield from the storm.

The run went on, harder and more frantic than it had on the ground. At every roof's edge, Manwe's breath caught when he flew after the Songbird, landing only a few inches behind her as she jumped to and fro, crisscrossing the broken paths they traversed. She came to a sudden stop a moment later, crouched down on a small parapet overlooking a wide alley sandwiched between the building they stood upon and the city's great wall.

Below, in the muddy row, dozens of young boys and men gathered around a small square platform. Upon it stood a muscled youth draped in a patchwork of iron and hide armor, armed with a short spear in one hand and a collection of dried, severed heads attached by hooks to a rope.

"I know him," Manwe said to Folami, his voice low against the rumble of the thundering skies. "He's one of Voduni Calla's men."

"He's been coming to the city every night for the last week to this very alley," she said. A droplet of water fell off her wide nose. "He pays Legbas' toughs behind the old man's back to gather street urchins and broken souls who will come for stolen hardtack. More leave with him at the end of his show."

Manwe scanned the crowd below and the roofs around them. "Follow me. I want to hear what he says."

Leading the way, Manwe skirted across the roofs once again, leaping from one edge to the next as he and Folami crossed atop the hovels. Finding a spot where they could drop to the street below, they weaved through gutters and alleyways until they neared the junction where Voduni Calla's man had set up his stage. Beneath the broken rhythm of the rending skies and the patter of the rains, his voice carried upon the city's stinking air.

"Hearken to the beat of your Juutan hearts, you truest of men," cried the armored speaker. "For though you live in the squalor of the invader's shadow, the light of Anyanwu nears to wash away the filth of the long centuries." He lifted his collection of shrunken heads, misshapen by the moisture they had collected. "You have heard the victorious roars of the rebellion out in the hills, like lions on the hunt, while the jackals of the olive lords who oppress you hide within flimsy halls, neither willing nor able to meet us on the honorable field!"

The youths clustered before the stage paid little fanfare to this speech, their hands on their hungry bellies while the older men, tired souls too unlucky to find work in a city of slaves, stared forlornly at the severed heads with lifeless gazes.

"Are these the only ones Calla's man gathers?" Manwe asked Folami from their hiding spot in the shadows. "There are not the people who should be made to war—not when they already have so little."

"There's the rub, Panther," said Folami. "It's never the powerful who actually march out to the battlefield."

The answer struck Manwe, and returning his attention to the crowd, the events of the day crashed in. These were the people he had been warring against, never noticing that they, too, were victims of a war of circumstance, victims of a society that thrived off subjugation and a society too lost to remember what it lost in the first place.

"Everlasting glory, everlasting life is the prize for those who would bleed for their folk—for their land." Calla's man thrust his spear into the rain. "And power that your masters will never give you."

Manwe knew what lay behind that veiled promise as another scene entered his mind's eye. Pitch-covered, the burnt flesh of the slain rebels filled his nose as they shuffled towards him with groping hands, their eyes rolled to white as they came forward, forward, ever forward. He drew his iron blade.

"Ready?" he asked Folami, glancing to her for any hint of hesitance.

She drew one of her smaller daggers. "If you're the Panther I know, will it matter?" she asked with a dangerous grin.

They exited the alley into the cross-street, headed for Calla's man and his stage. The toughs noticed the Panther and the Songbird first, pulling their small shivs out as they advanced to meet them. The crowd shifted their attention from their host, a hushed awe coming over them when they remembered Manwe, the hope in their eyes spoke that they had not forgotten.

Folami flicked out one her small daggers first, bringing the closest tough down when it buried in his bare kneecap. Meeting the wounded fighter on his march toward the stage, Manwe leveled him to the ground with an elbow to the jaw. The other man, younger and more agile than his fellow, grunted in surprise as he charged, thrusting forward with a hard stab at Manwe's abdomen.

Manwe evaded the blow with an easy tilt to the side, letting the thug's momentum carry him forward until he tripped. Rolling head over feet, the thug leapt and rose, red with embarrassment as he faced off with Manwe a second time.

"Just go home, boy," said Folami. "It isn't worth it."

"Fuck you," the thug cried. Turning to attack Folami, he slashed wide. She caught his arm before the rough iron blade could score her neck. Spinning him about in a wide swing, she sent the thug back to Manwe in a heap of flailing limbs.

Manwe brought the thug over his hip and tossed him onto his head. The last thug's head cracked with ground with a rattling thud.

"Heretics!" Calla's man pointed his short spear at Manwe. "Look, you forgotten and enslaved," he cried with the thunder, the tip of his black iron weapon gleaming dull in a flash of lightning. "Look upon those who have fell from the grace of revolution! Look upon a hero who lost to the vices of servitude!"

Standing before many witnesses, Manwe let his knife hang at his side as he stared back at the hopeless and the lost. To kill this man, this mouthpiece of a greater evil, would mean nothing to them. He looked over his shoulder at Folami.

Her black eyes gleamed like obsidian, sharp in a goddess's way. The Songbird stared questions into him, a chaos of opportunity, risk, and reward if one dared survive.

Manwe reset his concentration on the zealot. "Tell them what paradise costs them." He brandished his knife at the armored man.

Calla's man leapt down from his perch. His held his spear in both hands, the honed muscles on his forearms knotted. A wiry body lay beneath his scrapes of armor, scraps Manwe was sure he had earned. "The way to paradise is in the heat of the sun."

"You mean burned in tar, dead but never done." A hush at Manwe's words elicited a cruel smile from him, his gate steady as he and his foe circled. He saw how Calla's man moved. His were the steps of a fearless man, and fearless men were stupid, lazy with their power. So much of it gave the feel of a show.

Manwe did not give shows. "Your master seeks to imprison not just the sacredness of our past, but corrupt the future. You would have these poor and weary, tired yet hearty, carry on in an unnatural state, never allowed into the earth to find heaven or rebirth."

The crowd murmured. No man, no woman, no person of Juut would forfeit their souls in such a way. Calla's man roared in defiance as he charged. The two combatants stabbed for the hearts and minds of the future. An iron blade sliced a throat, a spray of wine-red blood. A body thudded face first into the muddy crags of a broken street.

Manwe the Panther walked onward, ready to rebel for justice. He stopped before the awed masses. "Go home," he told them. "Let the free and the damned fight from now on. Just stay alive to enjoy what treasures we leave in the ruins."

MANWE WALKED THE STREET OF WHERE BACCHS STOOD, DRENCHED FROM the warm rain. He found Cleon on a stool beneath the tavern's tattered awning, wrapped warmly in his red robes as if cocooned under a mountain of cloth. The sly enchantment, illusion or not, surprised Manwe when he considered how intense the sorcerer seemed. His piercing gaze, a pair of burning agates, lifted to meet his.

"You seem better," observed Cleon. His reddened eyes blinked lazily, bloody after hours of inhalation of a guardian spirit. Love filled them then, relieved and tired. "You look better."

Manwe stepped under the awning. "The Songbird will join us. We'll hear from Sophicus soon if you haven't already gotten word."

Cleon shrugged in his mound of red. "Where we go from here, it may not matter."

"Why?"

"The vodunis of the city suspect that Voduni Calla's power lay beneath the world." The sorcerer's grin bore little comfort. "Interestingly enough, both your people and mine have similar ideas of the underworld—full of true magic and deeper secrets. Of darkness and necromancy."

"Be clear, Cleon," said Manwe. "What did the vodunis tell you?"

"They said you would know better." Cleon the Sanguine gleamed like a ruby in the night, his robes reflecting the grandeur of the stars, the mysteries of the universe. "Tell me, Panther, what was it like to climb down into The Maw?"

THE END

THIEF OF NATIONS

DESIGN IN MALICE

Called "The Maw" by the Gypians long after they had conquered the savannah, Manwe stood at the edge of this hole in the earth, solemn against the solid darkness of its depths.

No matter at what angle the sun sat in the sky, it never lightened, its shadow ever-present to whomever gazed upon it as a hard reminder of what it was: this opening was the entrance to another world, a world that had harsher costs than the one above it. Manwe the Panther had gone once into the underworld and learned that truth the hard way.

Now he readied to go again.

The two people flanking him checked their packs for a second time, making sure they had brought enough food to last however long they needed to be down there. Cleon the Sanguine, an embodiment of Gypian sorcery wrapped in crimson, cinched tight the belt around his lithe waist. A copper wand hung from a holster sewn with multiple compartments. They shared a smile before Manwe glanced to Folami.

The thief known as the Songbird slipped the last of her spare daggers and throwing darts into the bandolier built into her leather chest plate, though he knew she did not have enough for what lay beneath. She made up for the eventuality with a wicked fighter's knife strapped across her armor, a shaped layer of hardened hide tied to a powerful form with strong leather thongs.

Manwe felt naked next to them. He would enter The Maw like he had the first time—armed with his iron knife, clad in his loincloth and sandals, and his hands wrapped in strips of undyed canvas. His pack hung light on his wide shoulders, stuffed with little more than food and a blanket to keep away the shadows' constant chill in those moments where he felt safe enough to sleep—moments that would be few and far between.

"Ready?" Cleon asked.

Folami nodded in the affirmative. "Let's get to it."

Manwe understood the lack of muster to her voice. The three walked down the grassy knoll toward The Maw, unraveling the length of rope he had cut long to lower them to the bottom. After they pounded a stake in the earth, they fixed their line between worlds, forsaking the last opportunity to turn away.

"Now," Cleon said as he took hold of the line, "the city vodunis said that most of their kind usually go east to the channels, but it is also known that the necromancers using these passages go to the west, or the 'warrens' of the underworld. I suggest we avoid those and go eastward first to search out what information we can among the vodunis that sit in meditation. They might be able to assist us and save us a trip the other way."

"You hope, at least," Manwe replied.

"Come up with a better plan, Panther," said his lover. Cleon leapt of the earth's edge, down into the deep. His voice echoed as he fell. "And we'll follow that one!"

One by one, the three slipped away from the world of light and life. Manwe's feet touched the cold ground when he landed last, a chill that ran a shiver up his spine as he considered the last time he had been here, searching out his dead lover and fence, Toba, who had been cast down into gloom for a robbery gone wrong.

Cleon drew his copper wand. Tapping it in the palm of his bare hand, he summoned a small speck of light, an immortal spark that shone close to light his handsome features. He craned his head back to take in the central vault where they landed. "My, my, Panther," said the sorcerer, gaping at its immensity, "you could get lost down here."

Folami crouched down as she searched for the nearest walls. She had already drawn a pair of darts into her hand. "I imagine many have."

Manwe started eastward, aware enough still of which direction he faced. "Let's go this way. There was a series of ledges that made getting to the lower channels easier."

Folami and Cleon fell in behind him.

As promised he led them to a series of wide-set ledges, rock layered upon rock, and used these natural steps to pick their way farther east. For a time, they contended only with the noises they made—an errant pat of the sandal here, a displacement of crumbling stone there, and their breathing. When they met the bottom of the cavern floor, he turned them to the south, to where the tunnels opened.

"These are the channels you mentioned," Manwe told them. He let Cleon turn his magical light on the openings in the cave's wall, five voluminous doorways into the hell he had longed to forget. He spotted the fourth passage from the left—Toba's body remained somewhere in that hollow hell where the cannibals lived.

Folami broke ahead of them. "Which one, Panther?"

"Farthest one on the right," he said. "The air in that one smells different."

Cleon clucked at him. "Manwe..."

"I'm guessing," he admitted, "the rules don't work the same down here when it comes to the channels. I wandered into that one blind." He pointed to the fourth passage from the left.

Folami sighed at the answer.

"It is felicity, then, that I remember a story from my childhood of an easterly wind." Cleon flicked his wand out at the channels as he walked forward. "Do you know the tales of the easterly wind, Panther? What of you, Songbird?"

Manwe glanced to Folami and shared her confused expression.

"Oh, well, time for a story," Cleon said with a bit of self-satisfied glee. "Once upon a time there was a great sorceress in Barintha named Dadera, a sailor by trade. One night she and her crew were trapped in a storm far to the north, not far from the continent of Talav, mind you..."

Manwe interrupted. "Is there a reason for this story?"

Cleon cleared his throat in annoyance. "When trapped in this storm, she and her crew at their wit's end, a single word came to Dadera, a word that summoned something very peculiar that showed her the way eastward, toward Talav's nearest coast."

"And that was?" asked Folami.

The sorcerer's grin widened at the question. "Glaros."

The end of Cleon's wand spat gouts of blue sparks and from them formed a seagull coated in black feathers with a red beak. The manifestation flapped a few times to pick up speed and altitude, glowing as it ascended to the great ceiling of the cavern. Stone that had not seen light since time immemorial revealed veins of mineral and raw gem, a rainbow of majestic purples, blues, and crimsons. The gull flew in a great wheel before returning on a course toward the entrance to the channels. Swooping low into a gentle glide, the bird entered the second opening from the right.

"And our path is set," said Cleon, pleased with himself. Returning his wand to his belt, he marched with a spring in his step.

"I bet you this isn't the last time he's going to do that," Folami muttered as she followed.

Manwe cracked a grim smile, glad for some humor. The opening of the passage to the east loomed like the mouth of some buried god, the threshold between the place where the last light died and the sun never touched, a passage that only the chosen—or the mad—would take. Resolved, the three entered nothingness.

Left to a perfect pitch of black, only the red haze of Cleon's magical sprite led them along the passage, its wings fluttering for short bursts as it swooped around corners and forks.

"How could anyone ever walk this?" asked Folami, her voice lonesome and bare.

"Those in search for power do powerful things," Cleon answered. "I've heard of things my kind have done for secrets. This seems like a fair approach to them."

The stone beneath Manwe's feet, smooth and unbroken, tracked onward without blemish. The only thing he knew was that it was cold, and the longer he marched, the more it bit past the thin leather soles of his sandals, until the nerves numbed.

Time ceased. Cleon's light, bobbing in place above the red sorcerer's shoulder, ruled alone in the straits of the underworld. Manwe followed that flash of red for hours, he thought, pawing walls and corners every time it made a sudden deviation from the everlasting dark that seemed to go on forever.

Until Cleon stopped.

Manwe felt Folami's hand on his back. "What's wrong?" she whispered, the words echoing.

The sorcerer shushed them.

In the perfect stillness of the pitched realm, Manwe heard the patter of feet. He drew his knife, holding it down at his side in preparation to stab. He heard

Cleon's breath ahead of him, a few inches to the left. The sorcerer moved, his robes swishing. Folami stopped.

Everyone stood still.

The footsteps not belonging to them, a smattering of more than three or four pairs, closed in with each passing second until Manwe struggled to keep his blade at its neutral position. He remembered the kind of things that lived down in these depths.

What if they attacked first? What if he missed his thrust and stabbed Cleon? What if his lover died before he ever knew what happened?

Blind, bound, and burdened by the shadow, Manwe stepped forward as light blossomed from the tip of Cleon's wand. The flash slowly rose toward the ceiling in a soft ring of white, lighting the sharp stalactites in columns of green emerald.

Standing before Cleon formed a shape, clear enough that Manwe knew him to be a man. The stranger's black eyes follow the ascending ring of illumination. Naked, pale, his flat face opened as he raised his stone ax in challenge, his fat lips parted to reveal teeth filed into wedges.

Manwe thrust at underworlder the moment Cleon's spell ended.

Hot blood coated Manwe's hands as he drove his knife into the chest of the underworlder again and again. His victim died with a great struggle, scratching at him until he stilled, wet arms splayed wide.

The noise of Cleon's baleful magic conquered everything, booming with the flashes the sorcerer cast with every word he spoke. Somewhere in the strobing explosions, Manwe watched two of the Songbird's throwing daggers tumble past his face, burying themselves in the throat of a charging enemy. Life moved in still shots of revelation, blackness, terror, blackness, death, blackness. Manwe danced around the figures as they appeared before him, their razor mouths gaping. Throats opened in drizzling lines.

Wine ran in the galaxy of Cleon's starry summons.

Manwe wrenched back the head of an underworlder and plunged his knife into the man's jugular. The body flopped to the hard stone, kicking in the pain as life spurted from his neck.

Manwe turned, teeth bared at the dark world, ready for whatever monster came next. A hush came when a final body smacked the floor, a stale breath from the battle's heat that exhaled before a brooding silence asserted itself.

Cleon mumbled, and a slow, burning ball of azure light formed. Casting the underground vault blue, the light shimmered in the wall's mineral veins in hues of salmon and purple. The powdered forms of the dead underworlders blended well with the gray beneath their feet, their stone and wooden weapons broken.

Cleon had remained on his spot in the center of the vault, untouched and not a hair out of place. Folami crouched by the wall, the front of her leather armor glistening blood. Her fighting knife trembled in her hand. Manwe surprised himself by how far he had gotten from them. Three bodies lay face down in their pools, stabbed and sliced to death by his quick work.

The sorcerer's light cast the gore a purple-red to match the augmented hue of his robe. "What are these things, Panther?" he asked with honest curiosity. He stood over one of the bodies, glowing eyes fixed on the wedge-like teeth in the dead man's mouth. "Is this what men become if they stay down here too long?"

"I've fought with these… things before," Manwe replied. "They are a cruel sort, bred for feasting on the flesh of their own."

"Maybe not," Cleon contended. "Vodunis can be 'men or women, not-men and not-women,' as they would say. What if these are the descendants who came down here and were forgotten, unable to become the holy things they had set out to be?"

"Then the worm-god Lacroi has charmed mortals into a horrid fate," Manwe said, disturbed by his lover's musing at what he knew to be beasts—the same beasts who had taken Toba first and would not hesitate to take Cleon either. Beneath the weir-light, he spied ahead, letting the dim channels be revealed. For some reason, he thought he saw a flicker of something farther along, and not the gleam or shine of transcendental rock, but a light, an impossible star in a void.

"Look on," said Folami. "Do you see it, Manwe?"

Cleon turned in the direction they gazed, a beacon of red in a blue world. "Perhaps our journey is closer to completion than realized. Hurry!"

Without a moment's rest, they continued, leaving behind the dead to do whatever the dead do in a lightless world. The farther they traveled toward this beckoning glow, the more shape and size returned. The tunnels, now easy to see and simple to navigate by sight alone, smoothed as if someone had taken the time to give them their luster. Before they could wonder at these feats of masonry, they were halted, staked to the ground when the saw what lay onward.

The darkness had faded to the splendor of an illuminated city.

A pair of staggered towers, like the fangs of a ridge-lion, grew from the unseen ceiling of a vault beyond a size Manwe had ever reckoned in a place often narrow and tight. Windows had been cut in the side of the rippling stone, and in a few places, torches sputtered in halls and on flights of stairs that riddled the descending structures like an upside-down anthill. A strange green light emanated from the obsidian metropolis built beneath these massive stalactites, a collection of shanties piled atop shanties holding up old stone structures, a necropolis that had built up instead of out. The viridian glamour seemed to streak the granite and swirl the metamorphic dark when Manwe realized something quite clear about their discovery.

This was a city of ghosts—and it was abandoned.

THE THREE TRAVELERS FOUND A ROAD CUT WITHIN THE STONE, A LIGHTED highway that led to the first tower. Their path ended at a broken wooden door, its faces cracked by a great inward blow. Flecks of a weird scale smeared the damaged edges.

Cleon held his shimmering wand forth to shine on the portal. "Interesting."

Manwe picked at one of the scales, its thin sheet brittle between his fingers. "This is dry. Whatever passed through here did so long ago."

"Perhaps none of Tolivius' vodunis know about it," Folami conjectured. She entered the tower first, sneaking beneath the fallen furniture heaped past the entrance. "Coming?"

It was not long before they came upon the first bodies. As they combed through the subterranean tower, they discovered rooms filled with corpses, finely dressed men and women with pleasant faces that were painted white, red, and yellow. Their bodies torn open, entrails hanging from crude hooks hammered into the walls. The old smell of their rot pervaded the keep. Not an insect or animal had disturbed them.

On one of the many flights down to the base of the stalactite towers, Folami stopped in the threshold between the next stairwell and a room that must have served as some meditation cell. The soft light of a brazier set in the wall flickered, its flame a bright lime color.

She looked down the lighted steps and slung off the pack she carried to rummage through it. "The stairwell is clear."

Manwe took the corner of the room facing both the doorway to the stairs and the hall they had entered from, resigned to sleep upright so he could watch from his easy vantage when it was his turn to guard them. "What happened here, Cleon?" he asked his lover. "The city vodunis told us to go east to find their kind as if someone would be here to meet us. All we've found is death."

"I bet Folami's first guess was the right one: news below the earth moves slower than it does above." Cleon drew in the air with a bare finger, leaving starry strands pinned to nothing. "Those men we ran into in the channel might have been scavengers, picking the last loot of this place."

"Then coming here was a waste," said Folami.

"Bear hope, little bird." Cleon rolled out his blanket for the night. "Tomorrow is a fresh day and hopefully there will be fresh signs to follow. For now, I'll be glad for a bit of light that I don't have to make," he said, his voice long and forlorn.

Exhaustion claimed the three of them as they settled the hard ground, surrendering to the dangerous notion of sleep.

On the first watch, Manwe could not count the hours since they descended into the underworld. Had it been a day? Or days? What if they had died in the battle, and now they were spirits, wondering the places beneath until the Mother called for them to live again and make up for their sins?

What if it had been weeks since they last saw the sun?

Letting the ache in his feet eat at his consciousness, he fought with his eyes to stay open. Rainbow-smeared walls wriggled as they cleaved from each other, threes upon sixes upon nines before it crashed into stark focus. Manwe's mind played tricks, sneaky little things that he tried to ignore:

The cold hard lips of dying Toba, his last bit of affection for the man he had failed to save.

A centaur charged a canyon.

Somewhere, in the distance, lords and ladies bred before a strand of glittering diamonds.

When the rainbow smears settled, Manwe stood beneath his old jackalberry tree, its boughs thickened by summer's warmth. Grass tufted the hard soil, emerald pillows that only appeared for a short but wonderful time during the rainy season when sunshine and lightning bolts mixed in startling displays.

Toba's fingers laced with his, but it wasn't Toba who held Manwe's hand.

It was Cleon. Seated on the branch they shared, the sorcerer gave Manwe the kindest smile any Gypian had ever deigned to give him, the kind shared between people who simply saw each other for themselves.

At the back of his mind came a familiar drumming, bone-on-bone knocking to a quick beat. Wedge-toothed devils chewed on pink intestines.

The sorcerer's handsome face slackened as the sun arched over the savannah, and as the orange disk headed for the earth, Cleon's face withered and decayed, a dead skin mark that clung to the bones, mottled and black. A moan of torment echoed from the emaciated body. Time carried on, eroding at things material until... Souls passed on, to live and arise, never left below the dirt.

Cleon's soul could not break the dirt.

Manwe woke with a start, bolting upright from the ground. On his feet, he searched the dimly-lit chamber where the three of them slept, his knife at the ready. No nightmares attacked.

"Panther," Cleon whispered.

Manwe turned in the sorcerer's direction, his knife raised for harm.

Cleon stared back at him, his golden eyes swirling in black sand deserts, tornadoes of shifting embers. The rich fabric of his red robes glowed faintly, like a bright fruit struck by night's little light.

The sorcerer did not flinch. "It's only a nightmare, Panther."

Manwe sniffled, embarrassed. His knife fell from its place, hidden from sight like the fell thing it was. He palmed some tears from his eyes. "Isn't everything down here?"

Cleon's eyes shifted a second time toward the lime brazier. "Aye, but little things can make it suitable."

"Suitable?" Manwe scoffed at the idea and the brazier. "How can this be suitable? This is not a place for living folk."

"That is why the great vodunis come down here," Cleon said. "Perhaps in this place between all places they find a different sort of sorcery, something more innate to our kind."

Assured that they were alone, Manwe relaxed his vigil. He returned to the corner he had fallen asleep in. He glanced to where Folami slumbered, her head buried beneath the pair of small blankets she had brought with her. Curious to if she listened or not, another wave of tired invaded Manwe. He slouched into his place. "Then what does that say about the sorceries we see up above?"

"It says that we are further than we think yet feebler than we can imagine," Cleon replied, his expression thoughtful. "It makes sense that to learn to raise the dead one would go to a place where the dead supposedly go. We are at a nexus between life and death, where one walks those threshold places, where the rules that govern the world above may not hold in the world below. The dead might be the least we deal with."

Manwe regarded his lover in that moment, curious about what horrors waited beyond the next set of stairs.

***

MANWE REACHED THE BOTTOM LANDING TO A NEW HALL, THIS ONE LONGER than the last a floor above. He signaled for Folami to follow, who, in turn, let Cleon know to bring up the rear. The three had risen an hour before, ate a cold breakfast of nuts and sun-dried fruit, and set to combing the halls of the tower, this time heartened by the lack of corpses that had choked the upper levels. Allowed a fresh breath of clean air, the trio meandered through the rooms, taking their time to examine the few things they could spot with Cleon's weir-light.

"They must have lived simply down here," Manwe whispered while he observed a broken oil lamp he had picked up along their route. "They all had their little lights."

"And if the power of a voduni is as it says it is," Cleon followed, "then whatever power snuffed them all out must have been ferocious."

"Have either of you dared to look at the ground?" Folami asked. "I feel like we've been walking on shells."

"Odd…" Cleon directed his weir-light to the floor. The ground sparkled with the luster of pearl and malachite-hued lavender, robin's egg, and daffodil petals. Smeared on their path, a drying husk carpeted the floor.

Folami dared the question. "What if that ferocious power is a ferocious beast?"

Manwe's two accomplices stood perfectly still. Cleon's light sputtered out, leaving them in the shadow-less dark again.

"What say you, sorcerer?" Folami asked. "What are we doing here at this point?"

"Searching," said Cleon, his voice filled with light amusement. "For a clue."

"A clue." Manwe screwed his face, blind to anything around him. "What kind of clue can you find in a dead city?"

"The kind that is required in understanding how a powerful enemy wishes to raise the dead," Cleon responded, as if the idea were the simplest thing in the world.

Manwe looked to where he thought Folami stood, imagining the sour expression on her face.

"Look," said Cleon, taking up the fresh silence, "let's keep going until we have to make camp again. If we don't find a way out of this tower, we can work our way back to the channel. From there, we can return to the surface, having wasted our time finding something to use against Voduni Calla, or we can go down some other way and hope, against the odds of these underworlders and gods-know-what else lives here, that we find what we are searching for."

Folami signaled her surrender first in the dark, her sigh heavy. "If we run into this beast, I'm throwing the sorcerer at it first."

They traced the trail of sloughed scale, though the only sign they knew of its presence was the odd crunching beneath their feet, a sound that fed the terror crawling Manwe's back the longer he walked.

MANWE FOUND THAT TERROR AT THE BOTTOM OF THE STALACTITE TOWER.

The approach had started as the day had, trapped in the absolute absence of light save for the spells Cleon sometimes conjured. The rooms they passed, the wreckage of what had been once-fine apartments, were appropriately furnished to allow wholesome comforts—a soft bed, a solid bench, and places to gather around what light there was. Manwe spotted reflective mirrors knocked out of alignment, a sure sign that who lived there did so with impressive technological achievement.

For a city beneath the earth that was clearly ancient, these small things bore solid testaments to something man had done in a place where man was not supposed to be. Beautiful columns carved from the rock, decorative only, accented what Cleon guessed to be temple halls, chambers for quiet contemplation and learning of what lay beneath the material of humanity.

Perhaps, Manwe admitted to himself, these halls were the places holy ones should go, the darkness where they stripped senses for the sharpening of the mind. Before the beast, he guessed—before the beast and the underworlders picked their civilization clean, leaving behind the desolation he now mired in.

Were the underworlders not like the Gypians if the westerners had simply been more honest? Or what if the underworlders were stronger than the westerners? What if only the sun kept them from doing what all conquerors were born to do?

Manwe was the first to spot the light in the hall. Faint and aubergine, it lit the place where the wall met the floor in a broken strip, its third quarter bent at an obtuse angle. "Look," he said, desperate. The hope of light called too loudly.

Renewed by the sheer idea of something other than darkness, the trio charged through the rooms without the stealth they had maintained. They reached the lighted hallway cast purple by the ensconced flames burning in a pair of stone holders.

At the end of the passage opened a way to a wide bridge in the open air, connecting the first tower with the second.

And someone stood upon it.

Peering toward them, he held his loaded sling at the ready. A slight man with dark skin powdered to a coarse ivory, he stood vigilant, his focus exuded in his poise. Behind him rose the doorway to the next tower, its entrance barricade by pile of broken furniture.

"He doesn't look like an underworlder," Manwe said. "He knows we're coming."

"There's no scale on the bridge," noted Folami, crouched behind him. Cleon waited behind her, his gaze set on Manwe. The sorcerer had folded his arms together, deep in thought.

"What is it, Cleon?" Manwe asked.

"Folami is right." The sorcerer examined to the flat stone floor. "Look around. There is not a speck of it, even in here."

"Which means the beast didn't make it this far down the tower," Folami concluded. Her obsidian eyes widened. "That means it left before we came or we sneaked right past it."

"If that is the case…" Manwe stepped out into the hall, making sure his knife was hidden behind his back. The powdered peltast froze when he walked under the purple torches and out into the cool air of the underground. His hands out at his sides and open, he presented himself to the native, showing no sign of threat.

"Do you speak?" he called.

"Of course I speak," the peltast said in a smooth, low tone. "Who are you? How did you get here?"

"My name is Manwe. The vodunis on the surface told us that the vodunis beneath could help us. We face a grim evil in the world the sun touches."

"You come at a horrid time." The peltast looked past him into the purple tunnel. "Who else is with you?"

"Two others," revealed Manwe, seeing no point in a lie. The way went forward or back, and he dreaded what they might find if they went back. "We came from the channels that lead to The Maw."

"We know of the door." The peltast loosened his hold on his weapon. He stared hard at Manwe with a deep curiosity. Manwe noticed his attention wane for only a moment as Folami and Cleon made their sojourn down the magenta passage. "Did you see it? Is it gone?"

"Is what gone?" Manwe asked.

"The Koebeeng," he said. "The Dead Man brought it here when the Witch People invaded. The beast forced us into the Tower of the Elegba when it took the Tower of Lacroi, where we thought it had nested."

Cleon approached Manwe's side with Folami in tow, his red robes fluttering in the slight breeze flowing through the great cavern. "Why the barricade then, my friend?"

"It is to stop the Witch People," answered the peltast.

"And who are they—"

The bridge rocked when a force struck underneath its wide stone platform. Both Manwe and Folami took a knee, a more stable position, while Cleon, without a moment of hesitation, whipped out his wand on his way to the edge. The peltast ran to stop him when a second impact rumbled, this time with a flash of strange light. Rocking to the side to save his balance and stay away from the edge, he reached out toward Cleon.

The dead city below launched another volley of strange black orbs that seemed to float up toward the ceiling of the cave. Illuminated in a light that was *not* light, Manwe was the first to notice a shifting line on the face of the nearest cave wall. A tail slipped from sight, hidden by shadow.

The Tower of Lacroi shuddered suddenly, as if a great weight had entered so violently Manwe wandered how it all did not fall away. A hard scraping sound grew in its wake.

The sound panicked the peltast. "We must flee!"

Manwe stood frozen as the tower shuddered, ignoring Cleon when his lover yanked on his arm to pull him to the other side. Folami sprinted to the other end of the bridge, letting the peltast lead her through the odd angles of the barricade.

"We have to leave," Cleon shouted as more black lights slammed into the towers. "Panther!"

"I have to see it," Manwe said, hollow. "I need to look it in the eye."

"I've no time for your heroics! We must evade if—"

The tremendous bellow of the Koebeeng silenced him. At the end of the purple tunnel where the darkness fought at the edge of torch light, six luminescent eyes radiated azure. Bright enough to reveal the beast's horrid face terrible visage, fangs longer than a man's forearm protruded from a tall, wedge-like head, the flats scarred by the bleeding cuts the stone had made where it passed. Strange whiskers along its bloody lips writhed like maggots.

Cleon raised his wand and fired.

MANWE LEANED BACK AGAINST THE STONE DOOR, HIS EYES TO THE BLUE lamp hanging above them. The bowl filled by the cerulean flame swung and shuddered each time the Koebeeng's hammer face crashed the other side, filling him with dread that it would spill, burning them alive.

"I don't know what came over me." Cleon braced beside him in the pause between the cryptid's strikes. He pushed his thumbs on the length of his wand, bending the copper ever so slightly. He looked at Manwe, honest surprise in his eyes. "I didn't even think."

"I know." He clenched his hands into fist as the Koebeeng drove hard into the door. He grunted in frustration and thrust his elbow back, nearly shouting at the bone sting. "I should have listened when you told me to run."

"Oh, my dear Manwe," said Cleon, "what would ever happen in the world if you listened to me?"

The question elicited laughter, a sound at odds with the pounding of the fell beast outside. Slowly but surely Manwe's hand slid to the sorcerer's, fingers playing until they rested, intertwined in a surprising moment of peace. Theirs remained together until the attack stopped. The Koebeeng slithered across the bridge, rising up into the Tower of Lacroi, and fell silent.

Sore from the monstrous assault, the pair rose from their places and stretched their tired backs. The next chamber of the Tower of Elegba's lowest level lay a short distance, ending in another hallway lit by a second blue lamp hung from the ceiling.

Folami waited in the corner with a cadre of the peltast's companions, young vodunis who had come beneath the earth. They stood ready, peering around corners with slings and spears in their grasps. Easing when Manwe and Cleon cornered the hall, the entire mass met them.

"Do you two need help?" the Songbird asked, concern on her dark face.

"It must be able to carve off chunks of the wedge on its face," mused the peltast, disconnected from the conversation. "It couldn't fit past the other tower's door the last time."

"What happened here?" Manwe asked.

The peltast cast his eyes to the ground, avoiding the question. "I am Voduni Anansi. By what names would you take? Why have you traveled to this realm beneath?"

"We seek the wisdom of your brethren," said Cleon, his robe tomato red, a curious enchantment in the azure light. "One who came from beneath wars against life above. We seek to know what you can tell us about Voduni Calla, a cursed shaman who raises dead from the earth."

Anansi's eyes lifted. "Who are you to know of a Dead Man in the sunlit world?"

"A dead man," Cleon replied, pleased with the unbidden revelation. "What an apt name."

"It is true," said Manwe. "The revolution to free the savannah of the Gypians sullied itself to bloody evils. Even now ruin marches upon us, a meeting of forces that will bring nothing but hell."

"And so you thought to seek an answer to a Dead Man's power." Anansi traced his powdered fingers in his brown palm, his eyes far off for a moment. "And the rise of the Witch People is recent compared to even that. Perhaps we are upon the crack of an age again." He looked to both Manwe and Cleon, his hard, black eyes focused on both of them, as if appraising the pair before he turned to study Folami. She seemed to flinch beneath his stare, a slight movement betraying her disturbance.

"These Witch People," Manwe said, "I've seen their kind before—what are they?"

"Some people go the wrong way. Some of them get lost in the darkness. They find others, huddle around black fires, breed with their cousins, and feast upon each other if the hunger takes them. They are us evolved in the depths of the earth, young man, and they are filled with a void where the soul would be. They are often the thralls of those you would seek to defeat."

"And from where do these necromancers draw their power?" Cleon asked, drawing a glare from Voduni Anansi. The dreaming gaze of the underworlder sharpened to hard steel, which the red-robed sorcerer met with a mocking respect.

Folami scoffed. "Kings and queens," she whispered.

The two mystics broke their glowering.

"Does your Dead Man wear anything of note, or carry an item featuring a stone?" Anansi asked.

"His staff is simple wood, burned and carved by a lunatic hand. But it features no stone," said Manwe. He measured the interplay between Voduni Anansi and Folami. The two exchanged furtive glances, a surprising transmission that he never expected out of the Songbird for the many years he knew her. Leaving the thought behind to focus, he noticed Anansi's people moving in the next hall. Their bodies as nude and powdered as their host, Manwe let silence take him as they neared.

Anansi ushered them through the bottom floor of the Tower of Elegba, to the first of many staircases where they climbed upward. Unlike the dead, barren chambers of Lacroi, decorated rooms gleamed bright, cast iridescent by the weir-lights summoned from the mouths of children, the youngest adherents of the old ways of the Juutans.

Through timeless halls of gentle dimness, they came to a large sitting room, its round walls encircling a platform piled with seashell pillows and stuffed cushions beaded in suns. The glittering spheres dazzled beneath the mixed lamps that shone orange and purple. Anansi bid Manwe and his companions to sit, an offer they took without a word of protest. Hard floors, lost in harsh darkness, melted away as they lounged in gentle comfort.

Fighting the need for sleep, Manwe focused on the form of the sorcerer lying upon a nearby hill of black pillows. A bright crimson splotch, Cleon's eyes drifted across the space between himself and Anansi. The voduni rested upright, his back supported by a cushion to help achieve his meditative posture. Tension exchanged between the magic-users, a type Manwe could not decode through their shining eyes and passive faces.

"He wears the skull of a vulture on his chest," Manwe murmured, straightening on the dais. "I have never seen him without it."

"I imagine this stone is the equivalent of a phylactery, a vessel that most necromancers attempt at making—though few rarely succeed," said Cleon.

"True enough, Gypian," said Voduni Anansi. He untied the stout thongs of his sling from his body, which fell open upon his great pillow to give him four more thin arms, as if he were some weird spider. "One would need a stone of fine distinction, pure in quality and structure to perform the direst of witchcraft."

"Witchcraft?" asked Folami. Nested in a pile of old camp blankets and a few large bags filled with down, she watched both the voduni and Cleon as much as Manwe did, her darts spread across her covered lap as she mimed a restive look.

"What his kind does." Anansi nodded in Cleon's direction. "Those who fancy themselves 'sorcerers'."

"Taken from a man who cuts the throats of chickens and moans for spirits," Cleon said with a laugh. "I'd never deign to raise the dead..." He almost glanced in Manwe's direction. "Even if the loss devastated me."

Anansi eased his bearing, breathing his annoyance through his broad nose. He scratched at his side, digging fingernails into his ribs. "Our people use stones as well to gather spirits to us, and for all the spirits of power and will they muster, they are meant for clairvoyance of the inner, nothing more."

Cleon's mirth widened his grin. "These stones amplify magic."

Anansi's firm baritone regained its edge. "Aye, sorcerer. For good or for ill."

"But what does that have to do with defeating Voduni Calla?" asked Manwe. "If he does have a stone that empowers him, it is in the vulture skull he wears. What do we need to counter its foulness?"

"If it was easy enough, you would simply crush it," said Anansi. "But with this power to raise the dead, it will require more to neutralize... a countering spell mirroring his own, but fueled with a different sort of magic."

"Your spirits of knowledge and assistance may help with that," guessed Folami.

"We will need to find a way down to the crystal caverns at the bottom of the city," Anansi proposed. "The vault has been conquered by the Witch People and their great monster. This time of foulness, as above and so below, speaks volumes of tales that few hear, though they resound throughout the earth. The march down will be treacherous unless one has a keener mind for a plan."

"How long of a march?" Manwe asked, hesitant of re-embracing the gloom. Even in the false weir-light, he was glad for it, whether it was illusion or not.

"Five days if one marches without foul." Anansi flashed a silver smile. "And the way is rife."

"And we do not have five days," added Folami. She looked at Manwe, no longer tired. "It looks as if we have to plan a heist, Panther."

THEY SLEPT FOR HOURS, UNCONSCIOUS OF TIME AND SPACE, SAVE THE WARPED realms of their dreams. When they awoke, they tracked back to the stone slab door, bring with them a crew of younger, stronger men to carry the cables of rope Anansi produced from the Tower of Elegba's upper storerooms.

"We used to hang a spider tapestry with this rope," he whispered to Manwe as he ordered his youths to secure it to the stone rings on at their end of the bridge. "It will do more than enough to hold you on the way down."

The grand vault of the underground city was silent, an echoing twilight grand in its coloration. Striations of blue and purple rock rippled in the source-less light, and down below, the dead city sprouted like a thorn bush—black, prickly, and flowered with guttering fires throughout.

The hush held as Anansi signaled his young crew to continue lowering the cable toward the city below. The rope hung near one of the city's high towers when its fall ended, an old turret supported by the many platforms erected around its wall.

Manwe stared down at the point where Cleon would levitate them, bewildered when he considered that the rope passed through a nether between the ebbing, flicking lights of the city and the stalactite towers.

"We're ready," Anansi whispered, his words dancing off nearby surfaces and into distant crevices.

Folami lowered herself onto the rope first without a moment of doubt to its security, hands and feet wrapped in stands of cotton and silk torn from the vodunis' silk pillows. Sliding down the length, she started the long descent to the tower.

His hands already wrapped, Manwe readied to go next.

Cleon approached. "Now not too fast, Panther. I need to be able to see you to perform my enchantment, and if I can't, then you're on the hook."

"A bad choice of words," Manwe mouthed silently, making a nervous smile.

Cleon gave Manwe's hands an affectionate squeeze. "Don't go doing anything you'll regret. I can only save you so many times, Panther."

Manwe eased himself off the bridge, his weight suddenly in his hands and feet as he tried to stop the immediate slide. Controlled, he allowed Folami decide the room she needed, letting her sink further into the space between the towers and the city. A few times he lost her, only the noise of her sandals scraping against the taut line to let him know she was there. Foot by foot, minute by minute, they went on, each strain taken in complete silence. The slight breeze in the cave, birthed from some unseen place, chilled bare flesh coated in nervous sweat.

The apex of the city's tallest tower closed, a welcome relief when Manwe caught sight of it again.

Black lights flared from the city, spiraling upward with fury as the bolts of magic tore through roofs and supports. They raced past the three companions on the rope, striking the Tower of Elegba's bottom. The cavern complex shuddered at once. Boulders the size of rhinos dislodged from the ceiling.

Manwe hugged the rope as the blast slithered down the line. Cleon fell from his place as the coarse fibers writhed like serpents. Panicked by his lover's fall, he thought to reach out when he noticed the sorcerer gliding toward the tower, his robes gathered in his hands. Shouting above the next volley of malefic magic cast from the city, Cleon flew towards the turret and crashed on the floor where he lay still.

More black lights launched. Tremors forced Manwe and Folami into a swing, and swaying back and forth, Manwe tried to angle in the direction of the turret.

Folami shrieked when the Koebeeng shot up from the darkness, its fanged mouth snapping at her legs. Manwe let one hand free and drew his knife, ready to sacrifice himself to buy her more time. The nightmare face dropped back into the abyss with a thud, crushing whatever it had landed on.

"We have to reach the turret," Manwe cried above the next volley of black lights. "Swing!"

Folami kicked her feet in the direction of the turret, which Manwe mimicked. Cave dust rained on their shoulders as they gathered momentum to carry her close to the tower's edge. Leaping at the end of the next swing, she let go, missing an ascending black light by mere feet. Smacking the edge of a parapet hard, her legs hung freely in the air as she clung to its side.

Free of her weight, the rope wriggled as Manwe fought to recover his balance, turning in the void when he saw the Koebeeng hurtling toward him. Bringing his feet up in time to push off the beast's face, Manwe screamed in terror as the monster's flight knocked him wide of his desired course.

The fiber of the cable dug painfully into his palms. Manwe cried out a second time as he let go.

His fall ended short.

Held aloft in the air, Manwe struggled in the unnatural hold of forces beyond his perception, flailing his arms and legs until a familiar voice called.

Amplified beyond the chaos the subterranean battle between the resolute Tower of Elegba and the conquered city below, the booming words rose high above the explosions of Witch People's black lights. "Stay still, Panther," Cleon shouted, his hands curled into claws as bright yellow light pulsed from his fingers. The sorcerer, one foot on the turret's fence, stood in defiance of the hell breaking out around him. Blood matching his robes trickled down the front of his face, leaving him masked in crimson as he held his bare hands up, fighting to maintain his spell.

A black light whizzed up, its rude light showing that Folami knelt behind Cleon, crouched over a third person Manwe did not recognize. When it struck the ceiling, it dislodged a second large stone that traveled in a spill of dust. Manwe jostled without volition, his head inches away from its path. He felt a sudden jerk, and suddenly he was free again, flying through the air without the power of Cleon to guide him. He opened his eyes in time to see Cleon flying to meet him, arms out.

The world disappeared in flares of red. Held in strong, thin arms, Manwe let his body go limp as he and sorcerer bombed the center of the turret with a bone-rattling impact.

He awoke to a sapphire light, as deep as a berry but shining with an otherness. On his side, Manwe blinked at the strange rock stuck in the ground, troubled by its blue shine. His thigh and shoulder ached from the hard earth, but wiggling fingers and toes, he took it as a good sign everything at least worked how it should. Sitting up, he felt the fiber of a carpet beneath his hands, the warmth of oil lamps on his skin. Near the small door to the hut, Cleon nestled in a shadow, watching the haunted city outside the small window cut from the wattle wall. To Manwe's right, in another alcove like the one he sat in, Folami rested beside the sleeping form of a young girl, arms hugging her knees as she stared off into nothing. Blood dyed the bandages tied to the girl's exposed shoulder.

"Where are we?" Manwe asked, breaking the quiet. The windows to the world beyond their walls revealed shacks built atop shacks, a maze of small alleys and lanes only one or two could fit through at a time.

"We made it to the bottom of the spire," Cleon whispered. "You hit your head when you landed. I carried you until Folami found this place."

"Who's she?" Manwe motioned at the sleeping teenager beside the Songbird. "I saw her before. Right before I blacked out."

"One of Anansi's, apparently," said Folami. "There was a hatch on the floor of the turret. She came out of it to help us get away from the battle."

"How did she get wounded?" Manwe asked.

Folami grimaced at the question. "I mistook her for one of the Witch People. One of my darts is buried in her shoulder."

"Is she the only one?"

Folami gave a sullen nod.

Manwe rubbed his eyes with his fingers, massaging away the last dregs of unconsciousness before he crawled toward Folami and the girl. Squatted beside the Songbird, he checked the girl's face first, peering through the darkness to discern her features. Satisfied by the normal slope of her forehead, the darkness of her skin beneath the chalk-like powder, he investigated the bandaged wound on her shoulder. Lengths of dirty wool wrapped around the shank of an iron dart, soaked to deep rust.

"All right," he said to Folami, "moving her will do more harm until we can redress the wound with something cleaner. There had to be healers in this city before the Witch People came."

"So, we're going outside," Folami concluded.

"No, Manwe's going outside," Cleon said. "Wounded or not, we're not here to save her—we need to find one of these stones Anansi told us about and get it back to him before it's too late up above. What happens on the surface of the world matters more than some little fool the voduni failed to rein in."

The sorcerer's blunt answer drew a glare from Folami, but Manwe could not fault his lover's logic—the longer they stayed beneath the earth, the less likely they were to stop the disaster above it. Reaching behind him to discover by some miracle he had retained his knife, he crawled toward the door. "Anansi said the crystal caverns are at the bottom of the city. I just need to be pointed in the right direction."

MANWE LET CLEON'S WEIR-LIGHT LEAD AS HE WANDERED THE CATWALKS of the abandoned city, the red point ruddy so it did not draw attention. The silence of the rickety buildings, wood and rope and nails, towered like the skeletons of forgotten behemoths. He could spy the towers above him through the mess of roofs and ladders, the two massive stalactites from where he had descended gigantic from this vantage point.

The boards of the walkways creaked under every footfall, whether it was Manwe's or something else, the noises louder in the silence no matter how near or far they originated. The foreboding darkness seemed liquid to his eyes, having adjusted after...

He did not know how long he had been underground. The disturbing fact failed to deter Manwe's pace, but the specter remained as he scaled down ladders to the deeper catacombs. Had Toba lost track of time? Had he even known where he was, suffering the tortures the Witch People put him through? Had there been anything else other than pain and the pitch of this underworld?

The lower levels of the vodunis' city transformed from buildings made of wood to those of dark, solid stone carved by chisel and hammer. Smooth lanes led to blind alleys of abandoned homes ransacked in the recent invasion. Manwe passed these homes in silence, thankful at least for the quiet of where his feet now tread.

Stairs were replaced by long, sloping ramps that led to the bottom of the vault, upon which had been built a great dome of bones. A weird light escaped between the gaps in the mortal slopes of the wall, lime and bright, which fluttered like a dying heart. Pieces of the barrier had been blasted away, leaving the blackened edges sharp. This was where the black lights had been launched, Manwe surmised. He reached up, hesitant, and closed a bare black hand around the red light Cleon had summoned for him. Slight warmth, an odd buzz, and the spell died with nary an effort.

For the first time, he was glad for the shadows. Bent in a deep crouch, Manwe drew his knife and ran for the dome, his attention keen to any movement. A chorus reached his ears before too long, a droning chant he recognized as the dread song of the Witch People. An awful beat, bone rapped on bone in uneven percussion, almost halted his charge. Memory rose from his mind without warning, of blood and sorceries, wedge teeth gnawing on guts hung from the ceiling as cultists danced.

Gritting his teeth, Manwe let his rage rise with the terror. These were the bastards of the earth who had taken his Toba, the bastards that had given power to the malignancy that was Voduni Calla, a Dead Man—and the bastards that had destroyed his revolution. He leapt upon the wall, crawling hand and foot for the apex. The songs hummed in the bones until his hands hurt. He stopped midway up, near one of the holes where the black lights had blown through the ancient skeletons.

Packed into a shallow pit, dozens of Witch People danced in broken circles, their bare feet leaking as they tramped on a field made of bright green crystals. Smeared red by the cuts they had made, the sharp formations throbbed with the beat the drummers created, bashing the tops of human skulls with crusted femurs they had stripped of flesh but left raw and gross.

The scene, far too reminiscent of one Manwe witnessed above on the savannah, played out in its macabre manner, surrounding a pair of figures at the center of the chaos. Seated on a pile of dingy furs, a man sat with his legs crossed, his eyes wide with madness as he took in the ritual around him. Mumbling through gore-stained lips, he turned his head right and left in small jerks. Hands stained with blood, he suddenly thrust out an arm, its length opened and oozing from a series of shallow slices.

His aide, a young girl dressed in rags, shrieked in response. Manwe watched her closely as she ran into crowd of dancers, noticing how her features matched those of the Dead Man that had ordered her charge—perhaps his daughter? She dragged one of the dancers to the center and drew a sharpened piece of bone from the mottled hide tied around her waist. The chosen dancer stood in perfect stillness as the girl plunged her bone knife into his abdomen, ripping and gouging until he slumped to the glowing floor.

Father and daughter set to work ripping open his rib cage to expose to the steaming organs, and from the horrid chasm, the Dead Man extracted his follower's still-beating heart. Holding it up, he shouted a series of unintelligible words, slurred and coarse. The life flowing out of the severed arteries dripped onto the crystalline ground, staining the green lights in runny spots of black.

The entire cavern vault rumbled when the crystals flared, causing the ritual dancers beneath to fall to their gouged knees. Shaken by the quake, Manwe clung to the dome of bones as a scraping, drumming sound vibrated the air, so close and so powerful he almost lost his bowels when he looked down in time to see the smooth length of the Koebeeng slither through the natural spaces of the skeletal structure. Massive, terrifying, the dread cryptid moved like shadow changing the light, its hard flesh unharmed by the points jutting out of the floor. It came to a stop before the Dead Man and his daughter, its six blue eyes focused on the dark heart the former displayed.

His mouth cut open by his fear, Manwe marveled at the sensation coursing his entire body, putting every nerve on end when he considered what he saw before him. The power, the evil, the sheer... he could not find the words to describe what he felt, too swept up in a terrified awe. He continued to the dome's peak, watching below as the Witch People prostrated, crying in celebration of their summoning. When he reached the top, Manwe found a hole in the crooked ceiling, large enough to slip into a drop that would land him directly behind the Dead Man.

He paused. Manwe knew what would happen when he broke the Dead Man's connection to the Koebeeng. He knew he would not survive, set directly before the beast, unless he knew exactly where to move the moment the spell broke.

With one last look to the Dead Man, his daughter, and the Koebeeng, Manwe freed his iron knife and leapt into the hole.

Landing on the rocky floor beneath the dome, Manwe cut open the throat of the Dead Man's daughter. Blood dotted his face as the shaman turned to watch his child fall to the ground, her hands held to the hissing wound. The heart fell from the Dead Man's hands as he sunk to his knees and cradled her draining form, letting out a wail of sorrow that did not fit his inhuman appearance.

Manwe turned for the nearest wall of the shallow pit, bending down while he went to wriggle loose crystals from the hard soil. A few of the Witch People not stunned by his sudden appearance made to converge on him when they were halted by a piercing roar.

The Koebeeng awakened.

The monster darted at the kneeling Dead Man, who wept bitter tears as he and his girl were swallowed whole. Turning upon the other adherents, it reared like an adder, fangs dripping gore. Manwe found a loose stone near the wall's edge, and stabbing his knife into the dirt, wrenched it free. Cutting his hand as he took it up, he jumped as high as he could, grabbing hold of the top ledge with his free hand. Nearly screaming, he hauled himself up as the Koebeeng writhed and devoured, claiming life in each passing moment.

Manwe crawled into the gapes in the bones, weaving his way past the dome before the Koebeeng burst out the top of the structure, collapsing inward. Running headlong, he dodged the skeletal shards where they fell, refusing to look back at thing chasing him. He heard the rumble of the beast growing close again.

A red flair shot from the higher levels of the city, a streak that halted the grinding noise of the Koebeeng. Another rose, then another, and before long, a line shaped itself in a clear path headed eastward. Recognizing Cleon's sorcery, Manwe went in the direction of the first shot, guessing at his lover's trick.

For the first and last time, he looked over his shoulder.

The Koebeeng had halted its chase, entranced by the streaming flares before it broke off its pursuit and headed east.

Manwe sat upon the way connecting the Towers of Elegba and Lacroi, looking on the unlit city as he thumbed the hard edge of his iron knife. His mood matched the sullen dark of the wooden crown that formed the highest reaches of the metropolis, its points stabbing up at him as if to reclaim one that had escaped. Blood crusted the thin line of his weapon, the only remnant of a deed he struggled to banish from his mind.

"I'd know that troubled brow anywhere."

He glanced up to his left, unsurprised to see Folami standing over his shoulder. The front of her leather armor was scuffed and stained. Her eyes went down to the city as well, a slight frown on her full mocha lips.

"It's been a time, Songbird," he said, wearily returning his focus. "A long time."

Folami sat down beside him, her feet dangling over the edge. "I cannot image how you came down here the first place, especially if all you found were those... things..."

"People," he replied, correcting her. "There were people down there."

"How can you say that?" she asked. "They were the ones that took Toba."

"No, a lord took Toba." His cheeks tight, he closed his eyes. He could feel his dead love's weight in his arms, a weight that grew when the last breath left. "But I took a little girl today. Or yesterday." Manwe stroked the coarse beard on his cheeks. "Whenever it was, she was a daughter. She was lost, like the rest of them. And I murdered her."

Folami said nothing. Side by side, the two thieves continued their vigil until she spoke again. "Why?" she asked. "Why did you kill her?"

"Because I knew that if I wanted to break the Dead Man's concentration, I had to hurt him." Quick to the point, he shook his head. "I can't stop it, Folami. I can't stop myself when I know there is weakness. I saw that Dead Man pull the heart from the body of his fellow, hold it aloft like some trophy, and all I wanted was to hurt him the most."

"Because of Toba?"

"Because of Calla." Manwe swallowed his bitterness. "All I saw was him, taking away the thing I had fought so hard to make real."

Folami hummed knowingly. "Your revolution."

"Yes. That damned revolution." He scratched the dried blood on his iron with a thumbnail, clearing a small line in the burnt red. "I lost Toba, and the centaur, and Kosey. I can't let go of that anger."

"The centaur?" she asked, confused.

"It doesn't matter," he said.

Folami bent slightly to make sure he looked back. "We lose people, Manwe. For whatever reason, we just do. Sometimes it is by an accident, other times by a mistake, but very rarely do we choose why things happen. You chose to kill that girl because it broke her father's spell on the monster. Tell me, would she have survived if you had killed her father instead?"

"No."

"The maybe what you did was a mercy. Maybe." Folami scooted back from the ledge and stood, dusting the back of her muscular thighs. "None of us will ever know the scope of what we do. The only thing we can hope is that whatever we do is good, and we will rise from it."

Wordless, Manwe contemplated this idea before the arrival of Voduni Anansi, who came with the young girl that Folami had injured during their sojourn into the subterranean city. Her wounds bound in red cloth Cleon had ripped from his own robes, she hunched slightly in pain.

"I'm glad to see you well," Folami told the girl, who smiled meekly from her place behind Voduni Anansi.

"Nsha has been forbidden to speak for a day," Anansi replied quickly, casting his charge a glare. "Going off on adventures, plotting with her sisters an escape... traveling to a conquered city! Considering all she did was bleed a little, she should be happy I'm not revealing the rest of her mischief. Women these days."

Folami did not hide her anger at the voduni and the young girl, her once-apparent appreciation of the handsome man diminishing with every word he spoke. "Women indeed, voduni."

"How goes your work on the stone?" Manwe asked before any more passed between his friend and the mystic. "Does Cleon still toil?"

"If you wish to call his brilliance such," Anansi said, withered by Folami's reaction. "For a man who has indulged in witchcraft, he is unusually adept at the work of the spirit."

"Careful, voduni. You might accidentally start telling wondrous tales about me." From the darkened doorway of the Tower of Elegba emerged Cleon, his mended robe a ruby in the everlasting gloom of the cavern. Blue bolts of light leaked between his fingers.

Manwe approached, squinting against the foreign light. "Is that it? Is this what we need?"

The sorcerer closed his fist around the stone, its glow boundless. "It is just a rock, Manwe. Not a miracle."

THE END

FRONTLINES

At first Manwe thought it was simply a wisp of gray cloud on the horizon, a bit of the sky lost in the great blues of the savannah.

And then the cloud grew—taller, thicker, a ribbon of dust that stretched back to where the sun would sink in half a day's time. Droves of birds, thousands upon thousands, moved in chaotic dances on the warm winds.

"That must be them," he said. "How many do you think Gypus sent?"

Standing beside Manwe at the top of the small slope looking westward, Cleon shimmered in the unhindered light of the late morning. His hood cast back, his brown hair fell around his perfect cheeks in a shaggy mop, parted so his golden eyes could take in the world. "Thirty thousand at least if they want Tolivius. Maybe more. It will depend on how seriously the emperor and his Philosophers' Court took the rebellion and how much they know."

His gaze to the yellow hills and bramble plains, Manwe let his focus wander on his beloved fields and ponds. Far off, to his right, a second line of dust kicked into the air as herds of wildebeests charged glades of squat dry trees. Did they know what was coming? The weight of all bore down until Cleon took his hand, the sorcerer's fingers laced with his.

"How are your eyes?" he asked.

Manwe looked down at their joining, glad for a moment that the man who had once been his enemy had become more. "I went into the underworld before, so I knew to what to expect. What about yours?"

"Oh, Panther." Cleon grinned wide and sighed deep. "I'd rather blind myself with the sun's face than to miss another moment in your shadow. I'm glad we're here."

"Even now, with your masters on the doorstep?"

He squeezed Manwe's hand. "Even now."

They left their spot, marching over a gentle hill and down to where a line of chariots waited for them with a half-dozen horsemen ready to ride. At the head of this group stood a small man in a sweat-stained tunic and thick pelt made from the hide of a cheetah. Wiping his thinning pate with an old cloth taken from one of his servants, he eyed the sun with contempt.

"They are on the way?" this man asked Cleon when he and Manwe drew near.

"Yes, Marcus," said the sorcerer. "They aren't being quiet about it either. You should see the birds soon."

"It is troubling they have not sent a representative ahead." The Senate Consul of Tolivius grunted his displeasure, wiping his forehead a second time. He looked over his shoulder to the men on the horses, a cadre of thieves led by Sophicus, one of the Five Fences that ruled his city's criminal element. "Tell me, Panther, why are your ilk here? Do they have an army hidden somewhere? What great secret that gives them right to our troubles?"

"Only what they have taken from you. They care about their city as much as its government does," Manwe replied sternly. "And they are ready to help defend that city to the last against what comes. Is that a problem, Senate Consul?"

Marcus hemmed some words, his face flushed.

"Come, Marcus," Cleon said, motioning him to the chariots. "We've much to prepare before our overlords arrive."

"Schemers, the pair of you." Marcus started for his chariot. "Damned awful thieves."

Manwe and Cleon shared a final smile as the latter followed. Left by himself, he went to where Sophicus lined his horsemen, rough brigands and mercenaries who accepted coin in exchange for their loyalty. A handsome man atop his chestnut mare, the fence offered a slight nod.

"Mine have moved their families and businesses out of the city, Manwe," Sophicus informed, reins loose in a hand. "Before too long we will have to ready those for the battle."

Scratching his bottom where his tan loincloth failed to cover, Manwe grabbed the hilt of the knife tucked behind his back, a habit he indulged. "Any word of the rebellion or their whereabouts?"

"None yet, though I have my little eyes and ears perked," the fence said. Sitting taller in the saddle, he glanced at the clearing where they had posted, calm amidst buzzing insects and the constant breeze. "They will show sooner than later, however. I doubt those fanatics would turn down the chance to show off the mad priest's power."

"Perhaps Folami will have more information when we meet later," Manwe replied. "I sent her to convene with the city vodunis with the magic stone we brought out of The Maw. Perhaps they will have divined for us."

"None of my business, Panther. I'm just here to do what is needed when you need me." Sophicus turned his horse and signaled to his men, whistling the call to retreat for the city. "Magic stones, dead men rising, an imperial invasion... the trouble you keep getting me into."

"At least we're busy."

The fence laughed heartedly at that, squeezing his hips against his mount's flanks to urge her forward. Alone again, Manwe started after the dust, walking gently as he allowed a moment of peace denied this last year.

The dappled shadows cast by the trees on the red clay, the way the breeze edged through the branches and pass the thorn thickets. This savannah was where he could be alive, away from the world and the politics. Relief found him in tranquility, and for hours he continued, passing glittering ponds where gazelle sipped at the edges. They paid Manwe no mind as he walked by, mindful of those that meant no harm and the predators that always stalked the glens.

Then those gazelle broke their drinking, faces pointed at the south-southeast. Manwe took notice, stopping to listen for whatever clue they caught.

Then he felt it.

The ground shook, sending the gazelle to open ground. Exposed in the bare clearings, Manwe knew a great horde approached, thousands of marching feet thundering. Without a horse or easy shelter, he looked up at one of the towering trees above and charged for the nearest trunk.

Calloused hands and feet found cracks and ridges in the bark to press into, letting Manwe climb to the uppermost branches to hide from the army. Black warriors wearing scrap armor carried spears and rawhide shields as they ran, their bodies covered in a thick layer of dust. Dogs ran with them, vicious hounds with tawny fur that barked as they loped after their masters. Horsemen came next, a few dozen equipped with swords as long as their legs.

Manwe recognized the rebel forces of Juut immediately, young men he once stood beside in battles to free their homes from Gypian dominance, before they turned to the darkest witchcraft. His assumption was confirmed when the last group passed under him, a line of old battered chariots that groaned when they clattered over rocks hidden in the red dirt.

In the largest cart leading the line, two men rode in regalia unmatched by those they rallied. The driver, an upright warrior of black muscle and sinew, whipped the reins in his hands against the flanks of the two horses, lathered in a sweat from the savannah's oppressive heat. The man behind him, old and leathered, cackled while he thrust the amulet he had torn from his hollow neck into the air, a vulture's skull that glowed green from its sockets. Behind them another wagon followed, carrying on its bed an iron cauldron of stinking tar.

Kosey, the great hero of the rebellion, and Voduni Calla, his malevolent priest, rode to war.

Their numbers too few to win, Manwe understood their plan the second he saw the stone in the voduni's hand, the cauldron, utterly horrified at what he knew would come next.

BY THE TIME MANWE REACHED THE BATTLEFIELD, THE FIRST GHOULS HAD risen, Gypians and Juutans in torn armor that stumbled forward, leaking scorched blood from the final wounds they had taken.

Manwe knew Voduni Calla's work when he saw its results. Set upon a ridge overlooking the melee from afar, he watched the cloud of dust created by the constant movement of a few hundred versus thousands spiraled into a tornado. Green light flashed in the debris

The Gypians fought well with their phalanx, rebuffing the Juutans who threw themselves into the fight, breaking spears and iron swords against the bronze-faced shields before they were skewered in the faces. Dozens died at a time, felling two or three before they met ends. Every time a body fell, an emerald flare would light the dust, and somewhere hot tar crept behind the Juutan line, finding corpses.

One ghoul became three, three swelled to twenty, and soon the Gypians found themselves at war with their own comrades, undead that remembered the ideas of defend, attack, defend, and attack again.

Running hard, Manwe backtracked the path he had taken to follow Kosey and Calla's army, cutting down the hill and into a long ravine that took him northeast, toward Tolivius' white-walled metropolis. The cacophony of the battle, the screams of dying men and clashing iron, chased for long, long miles before it faded in the distance.

The sun had set by the time Manwe reached the southern gates, where he was met by the local guards donned in breastplates and polished helms.

One of these men stopped him before he crossed into the stone tunnel. "Halt," the guard shouted, holding out at hand at Manwe. "Who comes running toward this city?"

Manwe dodged past him with a quick step. "The dead, you fool."

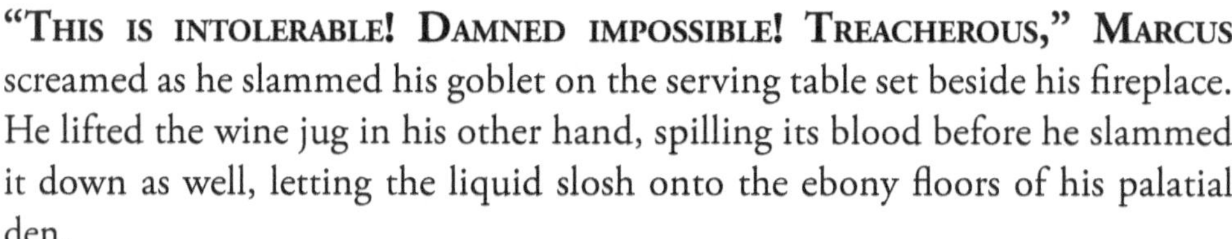

"**THIS IS INTOLERABLE! DAMNED IMPOSSIBLE! TREACHEROUS,**" **MARCUS** screamed as he slammed his goblet on the serving table set beside his fireplace. He lifted the wine jug in his other hand, spilling its blood before he slammed it down as well, letting the liquid slosh onto the ebony floors of his palatial den.

"It was a bold stroke, milord," said Sophicus, seated on the couch before the marble hearth. Still dusty from his ride, he rubbed his eyes, the dirt-stained fingers doing little to remove the grime. Knowing the futility of it, he grunted, choosing instead to wipe his palm on his stained tunic. "Nobody could have expected them to swing down from the northwest. Even my spies were late to report it by the time battle commenced."

"Forgive me if I don't take well to the efficiency of thieves, mongrel," the Senate Consul replied. He downed his cup in a single draw. "I had the finest scouts in this city's guard seeking out the rebels."

"Were they any better?" Sophicus asked.

The questioned muted the official.

Manwe turned from the window overlooking the Senate Consul's sprawling gardens, his black arms folded on his chest. He paced to the center of the floor. "It matters little now. Voduni Calla can defeat any army Gypus might send at him, and no matter how much we batter him, he will win. His sorcery ensures that."

"So, what are we to do?" asked Sophicus. "We cannot face his horde head-on. We will only add to it."

Cleon finally spoke, seated behind the Senate Consul's desk as if it were his own. Upright in the rich seat gilded in platinum, cushioned in the finest cowhide pillows, he leaned forward with both hands on the desk. "Our course is clear, my lords both high and low. If you are to defeat sorcery, you must first defeat the sorcerer."

"Did you truly wait to speak only to state the obvious?" Manwe asked his love.

Cleon smirked at him. "I believe there is a saying about how words are easier than actions, but if the hard part is to be done, we must form a sound strategy."

The statement quieted the room again, a long pause.

Manwe looked back out the window to gardens that stretched back many centuries to when the Gypians had first settled—he would say invaded—bringing their culture, philosophy, and dominance to the land he loved more than anything. Studying the manicured lawns, a sinking feeling drilled into his stomach, a sadness birthed from the success of the revolution he had yearned for all his life.

And yet this revolution, which he would have let destroy all western things, was about to destroy his people as well.

But only if he failed.

"Then we know our first step," he said. "We must kill the voduni. How do we do it?"

"If no army can be sent against him, then we are forced to work outside honorable means." Marcus sighed at the cup in his hands. "We all may disagree with each other, but I hope that we all agree that the citizens of this city should be spared that fate."

For the first time, Manwe saw something redemptive in Tolivius' lead politician. "What are you willing to give, Senate Consul?"

Marcus glanced his way. "The guard in this city is small by the standard of a Gypian army, but if I can get a proper sense of where the rebel's undead will approach, I can properly man those walls."

"I can help figure out some of that," Sophicus volunteered. "At least in terms of the approach."

"Isn't it fantastic when people work together?" Cleon said in a high tone, slapping the desk. "Now, as to our necromanc—" He was interrupted by a great pounding at the office door, a hurried fist beating the hardwood. Marcus opened the portal, and in marched a trio of guards, their faces dripping inside their iron helms.

"My lord..." heaved the point man, "they have come! The Imperial army has come!"

THE STREETS OF TOLIVIUS ROILED IN THE CHAOS, FIRE SMOKING THE cobblestone streets as the lost ran in no direction at all, seeking places from the doom they always feared while those with something, even a pittance of a life, sought pitchforks, clubs, and simple weapons.

The taste of burnt shit and cinders on the air joined the song Manwe had once wished to hear as he ran through alleys toward the western gates of the city. Cleon followed close behind, a bolt of dark red in the muddying, flicking light. This was the chaos he had dreamed—and now, at the end, the nightmare he despised.

"No dallying, Panther," said Cleon. "We must get there before Marcus and the rest do."

"Why?" Manwe asked between gasps, his knees aching as his feet slapped the stones beneath.

"Just follow and you'll see."

There at the western gates, the panicked citizens of Tolivius set against the incoming Gypians limping in through the entry tunnel. Dirty, bloodstained, and broken, these few hundred were unprepared for the torrent of abuse. Rocks, clods, and bottles flew at them, which bounced off dented shields raised by the final will they had left. The city guard, their swords drawn, forced their way into the scene, desperate to make sure more blood did not spill.

Halted at the edge of an alley's mouth, Cleon put his arm out in front of Manwe. "Let's wait here and see what happens. No need to run into the middle of a fight."

Manwe stayed in the deep shadow of the narrow alley. "There're very few left, Cleon. Calla broke them."

The sorcerer said nothing as they watched Tolivius' reinforcements come with the Senate Consul, leading a cadre of men heavily armed to deal with the rabble that had gathered. Cowed by the sudden appearance of fresh fighting men, the frightened citizens quickly faded, knowing better than to challenge their organized might.

"Perhaps it is time we split ways, Panther," Cleon said. "Go and find Folami and see what she is up to with the city vodunis."

"What are you going to do?" Manwe asked as his lover broke away, leaving the alley to approach the Gypians.

Cleon smiled back. "I'm going to go be me."

***

THE CITY'S VODUNIS CROWDED A TABLE, THEIR FACES CAST DARK BY THE glowing blue stone set in the center. The white paint on their faces shone bright in contrast to the natural tones of their skin, hues that ranged from wet sand to deep ebony. Whispers passed between them as they studied the magic stone Manwe, Folami, and Cleon had brought from the world beneath their own.

"What do they think?" Manwe asked as he stood beside Folami in the other room, watching the holy folk examine their prize.

The thief shrugged her bare shoulders. "They've been in there since Cleon gave it to them. I think they doubted that a Gypian helped make a blessed thing that only our people knew how to create. Sometimes I think they are just dumbfounded."

"Mortal are what they are in the face of the real." Manwe, his hands on his hips, leaned forward to ease the ache in his feet and back. "Do they at least know how to use it?"

"It's confusing, but from what they have told me, a sorcerer harnesses the rock as a focus for their magic instead of their body, which would drain from the transfer of power if it was not there to save them." Her cheeks hollow, Folami frowned at the scene before them. "Did you ever think our lives would be like this, Panther? Allying with age-old enemies, setting ourselves against an evil born from our own?"

"Like walking into a lightless hell where only the mad would dwell?"

She cracked a tired grin. "What are the streets like?"

"Chaos." Manwe rocked on the balls of his feet. "Gypian or Juutan, the poor know what comes. They know no one will care what happens to them."

"And so you will have your revolution." Folami's grin dimmed, her mouth returned to a small line. "I'm sorry. I shouldn't take humor from it."

Quiet to her words, Manwe squinted against the azure light of the stone, remembering how he had stolen it from the deepest depths of a subterranean city conquered by the same evil that had taken his first love, the fence Toba.

He remembered the young girl he had murdered to win it.

"If these days aren't jokes now, I fear to see when they are," he said, deep and low. "Voduni Calla will lay waste to the guilty and innocent alike and all they will have is the ruin of a world where nothing, good or ill, shall ever rise again. If that is revolution, then I would find it as laughable as you did."

"How long do we have?"

Manwe pressed his lips together until the feeling left. "I'd rather not guess."

One of the vodunis broke away from the circle in the next room. A tall, muscular man dressed in scraps of old rawhide and chain armor, he greeted Manwe and Folami with a firm nod of acknowledgment.

"What do the kindred think, Voduni Ogun?" Manwe asked. "Was our sojourn to the underworld worthwhile?"

"Very much so, thief." A scarred man, Voduni Ogun folded his hands before him. "The power of the stone is immense, pure... the kind of thing one would need to combat Calla's evil. The ghouls should shy from it, but he won't."

Manwe's shoulders drooped, accepting the truth for what it was. "So, whoever faces him will have to get close. Close enough to kill."

"Yes." Turning halfway to where his brothers and sisters revered what may have been their only chance at salvation, every fiber tensed as Voduni Ogun stared—not at the light, or the stone, or even the room, but something past it. "A mere soldier could brave the course to him, but I suspect a sorcerer would fare better with it."

"We have one of those," Folami remarked.

The tall voduni glanced back at her with a kind expression. "That we do."

Manwe refocused on the blue stone, eyes set on its glowing glory. "We will have to find a way to let the innocent escape the city before the dead are upon us. Can the city vodunis help with that?"

"We are already in preparation with the Five Fences." The voduni smiled, an out-of-place thing for a man who seemed nothing if not stoic. "You two should be commended. For the longest time, the choices were war or subjugation, never compromise. If the Senate Consul is a man of his word and ends slavery after all this is over, then there will be a new age, Panther. An age you, Folami, and that lovely sorcerer birthed."

"Then to the death with the old one first," Manwe said, trying his best to sound appreciative. "Let us go, then."

Final agreements made, the plans for their roles set, the city vodunis exited the abandoned shop with Folami in tow, headed off to gather the people they would march out of Tolivius. Where they would go, how they would treat each other—such worries meant little to Manwe when he was left behind with the stone.

Walking to the table it rested on, he vexed, his face bathed in the odd cold its azure light shed. He whispered to no one, or someone, be they there or beyond his small prayer. A sigh that could have become a whimper of sadness, he palmed the stone to snuff its illumination.

***

ONWARD THE DEAD MARCHED, BURNT, DECAYED, SHUFFLING AS THEY CROSSED the fields of Tolivius' southern farmsteads cutting down any living things they came across. The few survivors of Kosey's living army, a few dozen teenage boys and girls that had survived the battle with the Gypus' imperial force, slaughtered those they found hidden in barns—no matter if they were Juutan or Gypian, free or enslaved.

All innocents were enemies under the order of Voduni Calla.

The first calls came in the middle of the clouded night, when the gods wove thick curtains of storms to hide the stars. Manwe wondered at his people's own gods and their ways as he stood on the city's white walls, long the symbol of the Juutan oppression. His hands and arms wrapped in old canvas up to the elbow, his feet covered in a pair of war sandals plucked from an emptied armory, he watched them come, line after line.

This was not what Toba had wanted. This was not what he had wanted.

All people free, Juutan or not, left to love and be left alone. For others to be treated with the dignity they were born with from the Mother's womb. That was what he had dreamed of.

Not this. Not evil.

And yet he had made this so, he realized when the horde cleared the farmsteads and crowded the packed dirt highway leading to the southern gates. Every home robbed, every jewel stolen, he had helped this awful thing come to be—first out of patriotism, and then vengeance. Vengeance of the kind Voduni Calla carried in his heart to infect those Manwe had called comrades.

Were any of them still alive, ravenous and wild in Kosey's band of lucky few, or were they somewhere in the mass of the desecrated? Was Karlee, the young boy who had been so brave at Aemon's Fort?

Manwe did not know, thumbing his knife's edge while studying the formations the Gypians sent to defend their gates while its citizens fled north. Freed or enslaved, brown or tan, lawful or lawless, they went together, made equal by the doom that had come to claim them.

Tears filled his vision when he heard the barks of the commanders in the tunnel below him. He might never see Folami again, thinking on how he had never told her how much of an equal he thought her to be, or inform Sophicus about how right the fence had been about revolutions.

He didn't say goodbye to Magera, the priestess of the Goddess of Love and his truest friend.

Where was she?

The smell of dead ghoul flesh, roasted by the pitch their fell master had covered them in, reached his nose first. Their moans, broken noise that found no harmonies, rose in cacophonic chorus from hell. Tens of thousands spread in a disheveled line, left to a lone order.

Destroy, he heard the dead sing.

Destroy.

"Silver for your mind, Panther?"

Startled, Manwe sprang, his knife bared for a fight.

Cleon—handsome, ethereal Cleon—stood on the parapet they shared, that knowing smile plastered on his beguiling mouth. The sorcerer had sheathed himself in a leather cuirass and soft leather gloves. The red cloth of his robe shimmered in the dull gloom of the night's endless shadow, just a small hint of his magic at play.

Calmed, Manwe reset his vigil, hoping to spy out where their wicked enemy might be. "Calla will have to be found quickly. We may number a thousand, but his forces number more. It is important that he dies quickly and that we destroy his stone."

"Oh, that will happen."

"Only if we put in the work."

Cleon chuckled. "I've always liked that about you, Manwe. In fact, I love you for it."

"What do you mean?" he asked.

"The focus. The willingness to do what you think is right, no matter the outcome. It is something not many have."

Manwe darkened at the compliment. "Would that less had it."

Cleon touched Manwe's face, a light sensation as he drew him around so that they looked into each other's eyes. The sorcerer smiled widely at him, containing a happiness the latter could not match. Faces closed, lips met, and for a brief second, even Manwe could find no reason to fear.

Until the scene bubbled and hazed.

Lightness bled into his every nerve of his body. Manwe's knees gave away. Swooping in a red blur, Cleon caught him in his arms, a place of warmth that threatened to pull down the dark into the place of dreams and sleep.

"Cleon... what have you..." Manwe fought make words.

"Oh, Panther." The sorcerer cooed like the mischievous lover he was, proud at the sweetness he had accomplished. Manwe felt the sorcerer slip a hand into his loincloth and extract the blue stone he had placed within, its weight wrapped in a small wad of cloth. "Did you really think I'd make it so easy?"

CLEON STRUTTED TOWARD THE GATES, WHISTLING A MERRY TUNE HIS MOTHER had taught him when they lived in Gypus' dark streets. Oh, those years... pickpocketing during the day for bits of bread and gruel, hiding from sight when her callers would come for their few minutes of pleasure at night. It had been a hard life before he found his talents at spells and spying, after he was discovered by...

No, too much. He did not want to tell that story.

Oh, he looked marvelous. He had picked the breastplate out of the Senate Consul's personal armory, leaving Marcus to curse about the iron armor he'd have to lug to the gates. Say what he would, Cleon at least respected the little shit for having a fine sense of quality. The softness of the harness, the rich brown of the crafted leather—oh, he did look marvelous. The armor matched well with the red.

Under the torn skies he tarried, noticing how the smoke from the ruined fields outside the walls had overrun Tolivius' skies, a portent he thought appropriate for what waited on ahead. A hot breeze eddied like snakes in the alleys, leaving the coming night steamy. On high, he spotted an eagle, its tawny span far from where they usually flew. Another omen, he guessed, sent from the gods of Gypus.

"You're probably wondering why this matters," he said to the predator as he made for Tolivius' southern gate. "See, looking good is the difference between being remembered for ten years and being remembered for a thousand. Stories work like this: you have a hero, which is my Manwe, and you have a villain, which was me before the real villain—a fascist, no less—appeared and ruined what was going to be a very saucy tale. The sex we could have had... I personally blame the people who said nothing during this entire tragedy. Audiences love a good speech about how they are going to make things better, but nobody wants to get their hands bloody over what they did wrong. Manwe did, and that's why I respect—"

Cleon stopped in his tracks and touched his lips with a finger. "No, it is why I love him. I may not agree with his views, but nothing is sexier than a man of conviction, which is lacking in most of you gods with your white towers built of sand, or you victims who decry *every microscopic thing* with no regard that people are suffering, enduring, surviving, and moving on to actually help make the world a better place for others like them. You, the 'elite', with your feckless selves and your undeniably broken kids."

The eagle cried back at him.

"Have you met me?" he asked, booming with amusement. The march for the gates continued. "Now look at Manwe again: blacker than black, queerer than queer, wearing nothing but a loincloth and carrying a knife, and not a pretty one at that. For the heavenly dull-wits like you, he is a representation of heroic purity, the kind of thing myths are made of. Minimalistic, rugged, and willing to do everything needing to be done, even it means he gives life and limb for others. I find it foolish when I consider you lot, yet he is so terribly inspiring."

Turning at the corner of a rundown street he was sure had been beautiful once, the soles of his hobnailed sandals—the finest to be found and sent from Gypus' most revered cobbler, by the way—clacked on the gray stones. "Now, I'm not a hero. I'm a spy and provocateur, skulking in the shadows or gallivanting at parties in the best fashions. I use my power for my whims and my whims alone. Some of you petty little boys and girls will say something about lawfulness and evil. Spare me. I'm me, not your categories. You'd be lucky with your bum-lives to be even near as glorious as I have made myself. Praise-be to god complexes."

He spotted the mass of volunteer soldiers lined up before the tunnel, an ancient channel made of dingy white stone with two great elephant statues on either side, gaudy accoutrements that threw back to when the conquerors appropriated the conquered as a method of subjugation. These fighters would die tonight, brave but forgotten.

And so might Cleon.

"So why am I doing this, if this is a foolish end with a foolish hope that you undeserving may sup on its miracles?" He halted for a moment to check his robes for the tools he had brought.

There was his copper wand, a few potions that did interesting things he'd not reveal at the moment, some old nails that would come in handy, and a hammer—a plain hammer, made for smashing rocks apart. He'd need that. "Well, the answer is complicated, as love always is. I can't let Manwe throw his life away for people who will never appreciate it, and second... well, heroes have a way of making us better queens."

The battle, probably the first that ever mattered to the sorcerer, waited beyond the tunnel.

"If you would excuse me," Cleon said dismissively, "I have to go be better than the insensitive prick that I clearly am. For love, life, and the fight for freedom, I guess."

CLEON WAVED HIS WAND TO THE SIDE, DRAWING THE FIRE HE CONJURED LIKE a great ribbon. It licked alight any of the ghouls near enough to be ignited by its heat. A stupid thing, he thought, that Voduni Calla would revive the dead with such a flammable substance, a clear miscalculation among many that the wicked priest had made.

The length of red copper in his right hand, the blue stone in his left, he focused his power through its many facets and chambers instead of the more delicate instrument of his body. Impressed with the bauble, he marveled at its ability to manifest even the most complex of desires, a focus he had researched into distinctly, as all sorcerers at some point do, during his time under the tutelage of Gypus' greatest sorcerers.

His flaming tongue dissipated. Bringing the tip of his wand to the stone as charred ghouls fell, dead and destroyed, he swirled it around the edges of its cut corners, summoning forth another conflagration, this time a curved bar of fire that held itself solid beyond the line of burnt corpses. The barrier served its function, causing the oncoming tide of ghouls to slow their approach.

Arrows and stones flew down from the wall behind him, downing undead struck in the head while turning others into hobbling pincushions, horrifying sights Cleon thought amusing given the hellish comedy of the world. Over fifty thousand attacked, only to be decimated by his great power. It had been enough to convince Marcus and his volunteer militia to retreat to the city, preparing a way for the peltasts and archers posted on the parapets.

"They're not doing much," Cleon said, scanning the field for what came next. "But sometimes you need to let people feel like they are important to the task. The Panther is much better at that than I am. I don't need to organize a city, after all."

One of the ghouls made it past the firewall, its bones revealed through the popping blisters that exploded yellow pus. Arms raised, it came at Cleon, leaving chunks of flesh behind with every step it took. The knees boiled, bones blackened, both legs broke before it reached Cleon. Writhing for a few seconds in one last attempt to reach the sorcerer, the ghoul stilled.

"Perhaps I gave this voduni too much credit," he said in sing-song, daring whatever god listened.

The creeping dead ceased their constant march, locked in place where they stopped. A green flare from the farmlands, a fan large enough that it set the smoke of the destruction and magic to a ruddy green, appeared in the distance. Booms shattered the air, distortions that twisted reality in glasslike cracks. The explosions grew closer, closer, until it sounded as if a giant marched upon the city.

"Oh, come now, you dramatic sows," Cleon chastised with a wry smile. "He's just showing off. Watch this."

Without thought, he tapped his wand on the azure crystal he held, drawing a bit of its power. A small point of blue held itself to the copper tip until he pointed it at the smoking clouds above. A burst of light, blinding the world, flashed and subsided instantly. Rain fell from heaven, drops of gold that caught the debris in the air, banishing it in a period of minutes as all fires were snuffed out. For those who watched from the wall, the brief respite offered more. They cheered when the shower ended, alive and loud, seeing the starry sky and the beautiful face of the moon in a time when they had never expected to see it again. Songs, of Juut and of Gypus, choired in the heights, their faces washed clean of grime.

Cleon paid them no attention.

No, instead the sorcerer focused on what his exorcism of evil had revealed, a haunting figure dressed in robes darker than his walnut flesh, with the fabric cut and stitched in places so his shoulders lay bare. With that skin barred, the mass of scars made by a slaver's whip displayed themselves, pale and gnarled. A gaudy vulture's skull, strung with leather, hung around his neck. Green magic pulsed from its hollow eyes. The voduni came bearing a short staff, a knife tucked in the yellow sash binding his robe shut, and behind him rested a trio of hens in a wooden cage.

"You and your chickens," Cleon said. "I guess you will be blowing fire next and rolling your eyes into the back of your head. Maybe a little dance and shuffle as well, right?"

Voduni Calla, his eyes sunken, stared unblinking.

Cleon stared back, his cocksure grin widening. The two men, experts in the arts arcane, stood like statues on the field they had chosen, a sloping hill posted in scores of ghouls that neither moved, or sounded, or saw.

"I remember you," Voduni Calla said. "You were there."

"Excuse me?"

"When they took me to Gypus. When they caught me for escaping for trying to free my wife—you were there."

Cleon's smile waned. "You'll have to forgive me, dear, but we've never met. I've met many loathsome individuals in my time, and I would have remembered you."

"I wasn't me then," the voduni replied. "I was just a slave tied to a block. You were there when they whipped me. You were there when they gave me these." Calla lifted his arms slightly, bringing attention to the wounds on his shoulders.

The red-robed sorcerer shrugged. "Maybe? I saw a lot of prisoners whipped, not only Juutans. Pays not to run away, I guess."

"You're a slaver."

"Guilty."

"You're a traitorous Gypian."

"By birth and culture," agreed Cleon.

"Then why did the god of this story, if it lasts, deign to make you the hero instead of me?"

Cleon burst out in laughter. "Because I never set out to desecrate the dead, you twit, or convinced innocents to drown themselves in pitch. You can cry out your title as a freedom fighter but you are nothing, if anything, but a terrorist who hides behind perceived holiness."

"There are no innocents," Calla shouted. "Just those who suffer and those who make others suffer! I decided long ago to be neither, to master myself and bring my people forth!"

Cleon gave a mocking wave at the dead. "What grand works you've made."

Roaring hatred, Calla stepped forward and thrust his staff at Cleon. The ghouls attacked, falling over each other to get at the sorcerer, who raised his wand and cast it like a stick against a drum, sending small red sparks that engulfed the corpses in shrouds of flame.

When the smoke cleared, Cleon went forth, letting his wand lead him as he manifested a wall of electrified air, a shield he hoped would alert him to any attacks the voduni summoned. Instead, he discovered Calla on his knees, having cast aside his staff to draw his knife. A beheaded chicken in one hand, he scrawled his bloody blade in the dirt and threw his arms out, eyes rolled back as he chanted grim words.

The ground shook beneath Cleon's feet. "Oh, damn." The earth exploded, sending him flying into the air.

Wheeling in a freefall, he ignored the searing agony in his legs, knowing by the fact he could wiggle his toes that the damage would heal. Seeing the earth rise up to catch him, he pulled at the edges of his robe and released its hidden enchantment, a flying spell he had only used a few times since procuring the garment.

Too late to halt his descent, it halved the impact when he struck the ground, rolling into the oozing legs of a ghoul that swiped down at him with its black nails. Dodging the slash, Cleon pressed his blue stone against the reanimation, satisfied when the body disintegrated into a fine dust. He reached into a compartment in his belt and drew out of the iron nails he had brought with him.

Calla slaughtered his second hen, smearing the blood across his chest and on the skull of his vulture pendant. Growling, he took up his staff and charged, holding it up like a club.

Drawing a small amount of his stone's power, Cleon whispered at the enchanted nails in his palm. They zipped from his hand, flying at the charging voduni. The iron pierced the wretch's shoulder, knee, chest, as the last one bounced off the vulture skull, unable to break past its protective blood charm.

Undeterred by his wounds, Calla swung at Cleon's skull.

Cleon dodged, his feet constantly moving as he drew out one of the glass vials in his belt. Removing the cork with his thumb, he slashed upward, splashing the green liquid in Calla's face. The voduni yelped like wounded animal, wriggling to the soil as he struggled to control his flailing body.

"I'm surprised you fell for that one," Cleon said, allowing himself to catch his breath. "Most people don't let other people throw Nestor's Poison in their face unless they're unaware or idiots… so never mind. You should be feeling your spine turn into jelly. That's the blessing. You won't feel the mess fry your mind by the time the poison reaches it."

Calla, on his side and curled into a ball, gibbered nonsense in response, lost in a torturous stupor. Grabbing at the vulture skull, he held tight to the bone-cage of his green stone, its light pulsing in rapid beats until finally, he stilled along with it.

Cleon sighed at the sight of his defeated foe, somewhat surprised. "I thought that would have gone on a bit longer. You didn't even get to use your last chicken."

Drawing the rock hammer from his belt and putting his stone away, he approached the body. As he did so, he noticed the way the vulture's skull had changed, its calcified material now thick, mottled, and gray. Cleon checked the sullen, lifeless face of his foe, noticing how his poison had blackened the veins around his eyes and lips, leaving him looking like he wore one of those macabre masks actors used in Gypus when dark tragedies were all the rage. Satisfied, he took hold of the bird-skull.

Calla woke, his poisoned hand gripping Cleon by the neck. His knife appeared in his other hand. "Not everything goes the gods' way," he hissed as he stabbed the sorcerer in the side.

MANWE WOKE TO A FOREBODING SILENCE, A LACK OF NOISE SO ACUTE THAT he wondered if he had found himself back in the underworld, beneath the earth where darkness pervaded. The air was warm, clinging to the flesh of his chest, arms, and legs like oil. Sitting up, he held his head, confused by its lightness when he expected pain.

Then he smelled the world.

Rotten like the sweet-sick of fungus, death choked him until he coughed, unable to bear the disgust working up his throat. Standing, he leaned against the broken edge of Tolivius' scorched wall, arms braced as he tried to stop the vomit. Heaving, he shut his eyes, focusing on a calm he often relied on in the moments he needed it. When he reopened them, he looked out upon the fields outside the city.

They were gone.

Fields burnt to crust, no birds flew the brightening skies as the sun rose in the east, and no animals threw dust in their chase to find water, food, or safety upon the savannah. No one traveled upon the road to the city.

He gaped, unable to accept what lay before him. Without thought, his hands went to his mouth, his eyes filling with tears.

What had become of Cleon? Or Folami? Or Sophicus?

Where was the victory so many had marched to make?

This hated city, this bastion of imperialism and racism and lies and oppression had become a great tombstone, an effigy to something that had been and now was gone.

Where was Manwe's terrible city?

Where was his home?

Those questions disappeared when the dead sang.

Manwe froze in panic, dropping a few inches as his knees bent without thought. Broken in harmony, thousands—no, more—lifted torn voices to the morning, a bellow beyond beauty or ugliness. Inching to the other side of the wall, he spied over the edge.

The encroaching sun spread its white wave on the shore of a great sea of broken buildings and dirt. Dark plumes of smoke wafted from a hundred different points, each feeding the great cloud that stretched northward. Beyond the cinders and massed in the streets, the alleys, the multitude of the bloated milled among the emaciated ones, neither seeking nor finding whatever their master willed of them. Lost in the wreckage, the ghouls moaned for deaths denied.

Life had lost.

Above the sound of the cruel wind, the haunting music of the ghouls, Manwe picked out a third noise in the din—laughter. Running the wall, he searched for its source, desperate for something, anything to signal the presence of life. He regretted his search the second he found its source.

Brighter than the coming sun, the green power of Voduni Calla's stone scored the heavens as the mad priest stood atop one of the city's higher roofs, his cackle reverberating far and wide to all those that fell under it.

Too far to see his enemy's face, Manwe knew well enough that he did not have to—the bastard's glee was enough to hammer home the truth. Tolivius was a graveyard now, and left by himself, he remained its last ghost.

Something sparked in the corner of his eye, something small and bright in a window of the city's old temple district. He recognized the tower from which this bit of light sprang.

The Temple of the Goddess of Love.

The first battle for the souls of the savannah had been lost, but that flame, that knowledge steeled Manwe for an inkling an idea, a hope he fanned until it grew into an everlasting flame to match.

His revolution had not been lost. Not yet.

THE END

RUN THE JEWELS

MANWE SKIDDED SHARPLY AT THE JUNCTION WHERE THE ALLEYS INTERSECTED, the hobnails of his sandals scratching the stone flagstones as he tried to make the left turn into the next narrow lane. The six ghouls behind him, dripping black tar, chased him with the hands grasping in his direction. His knife free, he stabbed the closest one in the eye, the orb popping with a wet sound. Undeterred, the undead thing simply gaped, reaching to claim him before he escaped.

Arms pumping, Manwe ran hard down the alleyway, looking ahead at the low roof of the abandoned shed at its end. The ghouls shuffled behind, crowding each other between the close walls.

He leapt, hands grabbing onto the edge of the wicker roof as he hauled himself up. Sticking his knife into the thick, twisted band of his hide loincloth, he regained his footing and jumped a second time, one foot flat against the plaster to push him higher. He grabbed the next ledge and pulled himself out of view of his pursuers.

Above the street, Manwe waited for a few minutes, flat on his back before he rose. He walked a few feet and collapsed, rolling onto his back again. His heart beat hard while sweat dripped in his eyes, stinging worse than the bright white sun he faced. The smoke from Tolivius' ruined buildings had long died hours before, allowing the cinders to wash away with the wind. Now all that remained was blue, pure and clean and mocking.

Manwe sucked air, heaving past the dead stink on the wind. He sat up, wiping his eyes clean of dust and debris with long black fingers. Exhaustion weighted in heartache paused the need to rise, but rise he did, taking the time to examine the surroundings.

Tolivius' roofs, whether they were shingled or built of wood, smoked in the daylight, billowing black as the dying embers ate away at the last of their edges. Somewhere Manwe could pick out the cries of the few living lieutenants Voduni Calla left alive to share the spoils of his victory, young men and women who had confused bloodthirst with patriotism. These clusters, no more than a few dozen, roamed the streets in search of those who had failed to abandon their homes and shops, ending their lives with merciless spear-thrusts or at the edge of their iron swords.

Manwe huffed, finally able to take a calm breath. Off to the northeast rose the spires of the city's temples where he had spotted a small bit of light from the Temple of the Goddess of Love's high precipices. He went forward, fixed on this destination.

Head down, bent forward, he sprinted across the roofs, crossing the gaps from one building to the next. The thrill of the danger, the chance he might not judge the distance right, should have stirred some happiness in his thief's heart. Yet the alleys beneath passed without thought, the ghoul-choked streets became mere background, a thoughtless trek, he let his mind sink inside until nothing existed. Through ash and across many blocks he crossed, the miles melting away in this state of meditation and movement, minutes passing by as Manwe embodied his namesake.

From the southern quarters of the city where he began, the incline rose, the hill upon which Tolivius had been built like the world itself—those with less on the bottom, subject to both man and nature, and those at the top, emboldened by their proximity to the heavens. The buildings came at him in weird approaches and angles, forcing him to climb at points, work around them at others. The entire time he remained off the streets where ghouls lumbered in gross masses.

An hour later, Manwe ascended to the temple quarter, surprised to find it free of both ghouls and Calla's reavers. Climbing down the side of an outlying building outside of the main square where the Gypians had built their holy sites long ago, he marveled at the beauty of a place he had visited since the days his mother had brought him to listen to the debates in the Philosophers' Court, one of the many meeting places Tolivius' great minds met to examine the world they lived in. He passed the small clay alcove his mother used to instruct him to remain in while she went about selling her loafs of bread, many that were taken from her without payment or consideration for the plain and simple reason that the color of her skin did not match those who made up most of the audience.

He remembered those days well, and the anger, the shame, but most of all, he remembered what she had told him: "Keep listening, Manwe. One day you'll hear something different and see it, too."

Now he heard nothing as he walked the red-brick path set in the pavestones, a perfect rectangle that allowed its travelers to pass by each house of worship, tall buildings built of pale stone. The Gypians had constructed them of varying heights, signifying each god's importance in society. Some, like the house of Adias, lord of the skies and king of the gods, stabbed for the sky in a smooth tube of silver-shod granite. Others, like Mercas, the god of traders, took up a small spot in a corner where his offering bowl rested, heavy with coins and small charms given by those who did business in the city.

Manwe had never given the Gypians much thought in comparison to the Mother or her spirits that resided above and below her face, but he always considered the mysterious Goddess of Love worthy of some veneration. Her house had been the place where he first met Toba, the fence who had owned his heart, and also the place where he and Cleon found succor from the travails of the world. A structure of pink-white stone marbled in dizzying designs, its white doors were barred like the rest, the sacrificial fires within snuffed.

Manwe slipped into the alley separating The Temple of the Goddess of Love and the house of fleet-footed Illo, a Gypian wind deity that served Adias as his messenger. Down the cobblestoned path lay a case of steps leading to a familiar door set in the foundation of the goddess' temple.

He stopped in front of this portal, looking at it for a few moments while the memories swept in. Not a man to indulge in sentiment, he knocked on the door, knowing no one would answer.

The slot slid open.

A woman spoke. "What is the goddess' secret?"

Manwe wept at the question, filled with joy.

As a priestess of the Goddess of Love, Magera always cut a stunning figure no matter what room she entered, though her typical garb had changed. Gone were the revealing blue silk that had girded breast and loin and the golden chains that had held them up, replaced in a simple himation folded with brown wool. Resting a wooden tray of heaped with food and a jug of sour wine on her hip, she came gently to where Manwe lay, nestled in a corner of the alter room. Only a few oil lamps of dozens remained lit, disregarded by their owner in the wake of the last few days.

"This is all that I have left," Magera said as she knelt beside Manwe's litter, placing the tray between them. She gave him a wavering smile in the short light. "A good fare, if I say so."

His legs covered in a blanket he had taken from the private chambers of the temple's bordello, Manwe sank to the pillows of the bed he had made for himself, resting for the first time in... he did not know. All he cared for in that moment was that he was in a place he considered home, which remained as it had been, with a person he considered as close to him as a sister.

And yet he could not let go of the world outside the door. "Why are you still here, Magera? Why didn't you escape?"

She plucked a purple sausage from the platter. "Eat, Manwe. Regain your strength."

"Priestess."

"I stayed for the same reason you did." Blond hair shimmering in the lamplight, she chewed a small bit of meat. "This temple is my home. The goddess would never forgive me if I abandoned it, and I will never."

"If Kosey and Calla's reavers had decided to knock down the door..."

"Then I would have died in defense of my faith." She looked hard at him. "As you would die for what is right."

Manwe knew better than to argue. He glanced to the plate of food and picked at a piece of sliced bread, eating crusty bits of it with some old goat cheese. The tangy bitterness almost made him smile, the sensation of taste an escape he reveled. His stomach growled in appreciation, and enlivened, he started for the dried salted pork and the sweet grapes, each bite fueling a strength flushing into his fingers, toes, until his gut ached, stuffed with a sudden infusion of joy long missed.

"Are you the only one left in the city?" Magera asked as they ate.

"I don't know." Manwe filled a cup she had laid out for him, spilling a little wine from the pitcher. "I know Calla roams, as does Kosey. Celebrating their spoil, I imagine."

"I'm sure they will be quite fulfilled," she said dryly.

Manwe grunted in dark agreement. "For as long as it lasts. I'm not done for today."

"What do you mean?"

"I need to find Cleon." He blinked past the sleep in his eyes, keeping his mind centered on the sorcerer. "Alive or dead, I have to know. I need to stop Calla as well."

"How?" Magera refreshed her small clay cup, the red trickle falling in a glistening line from the pitcher's mouth. "Save for the temple quarter, the city is overrun with the dead. What is left to gain?"

"Justice," said Manwe. He looked to one of the oil lamps, its warmth matching the anger in his face. "I'm under no illusion, Magera—I know I have lost. But I am not defeated, and as long as there is breath in my body, I will not surrender."

The priestess stared back, her full lips a flat line before they formed into a sad grin. She sipped from her cup.

Manwe peered at her through the dimness. "Must I ask?"

"You've always been so adamant, Manwe, so willing to run into death's waiting arms for no other reason than you believe there to be a prize to be taken. It would be almost heroic if you weren't such a brazen thief about it."

He laughed aloud. "At this point, it may be all I have."

Their shared mirth was interrupted when a loud boom shook the earth, knocking dust from the crevices of the bordello's stone ceiling. Quick to rise from his bed, Manwe plucked his knife from the ground beside it and hurried to the door. Magera followed behind, carrying no arms but as brave as any warrior.

Outside the sun had set behind the plains to the west. More smoke gathered in the sky, clouds of hot ash that glowed red from the blazes that fed them. Standing in their little alley between the temples, Manwe and Magera watched in terrified wonder as a stone landed in the center of the square, obliterating the raised verandas of the Philosophers' Court. Manwe turned his body to shield her, pressing them both into one of the nearby walls when a second stone dropped from the sky, smashing Mercas' shrine into bits.

"We're under siege," Manwe coughed through the dust and falling shrapnel. "The city is under siege!"

MIDNIGHT HAD COME AND GONE BY THE TIME THE INITIAL BOMBARDMENT ended, leaving the city silent once more in the stale warmth of the renewed fires. The entire southern quarters of the city lay flattened or covered in the rubble of what were once homes, businesses, and artisans' corners.

Manwe emerged from the Temple of the Goddess of Love, the one building that had been miraculously spared of the Gypians' stones. Securing his knife in the band of his loincloth, he pawed the canvas wrappings around his wrists and hands, feeling the lengths and edges of the lock picks he always kept there. The feel of them brought some sense of certainty to the madness he planned to create.

"Will you return?" Magera asked from the doorway, her hourglass outline cut by the re-lit lamps.

"When the sun rises, perhaps," he said, bending down to tighten the leather thongs of his worn sandals. "Other than that, I don't know. If I can I will, after I find Cleon. If not..."

"Let us pretend things will turn out better."

Manwe nodded and started off over the rubble, headed northward to where the stones had not yet fallen. Near the midway point up to the next level of the city, a terrace of streets and housing before the famous Merchants' Row, a high mound of broken walls had fallen atop of each other like a pile of boards. Climbing to the top of the ruin, he wheeled in place, allowing a moment of careful study of what the Gypians had made of Tolivius.

As he expected, the southern quarter had been demolished, and even past the fire and carnage he could make out the Gypian camps to the southeast, a surprise force none had expected in the wake of the first loss the west had suffered against Kosey's Juutans and Voduni Calla's undead. Guessing when this second army had arrived was pointless, so Manwe set his attention to what mattered. From his place in the central temple districts, large swaths of the western, northern, and eastern city stood, plenty of territory for the dead to gather and the reavers to reorganize.

He knew what lay in a rebel's heart. For Manwe, no victory would have been sweeter than to have pillaged Merchants' Row, sacking manor after palatial manor. Skirting past broken buildings and crushed roads, he kept his ears perked as he reached the broken line where the destruction ended, not far from the still-pristine avenues of the wealthy.

He heard laughter in the abandoned streets. Carrying on as if the entire world was theirs, the reavers burst out of the gates of one high-gilt manor Manwe passed, loaded with armfuls of treasure, cloth, and spoil. Many of them had gone unwashed over the last few days, mired head to toe in blood and dirt, but for all the physical signs of war Manwe expected, they seemed listless, miming joy as they pillaged. Dumping their gains on the grass where the finer things were sometimes broken, sometimes ruined, they re-entered the house, not content in what they had taken. Manwe watched them through the gapes in the manor's iron fence. He counted seven from the first second he laid eyes on his prey. Two fighters more came out later, making it nine.

Sneaking along the fence, he turned into the open gateway and darted for the first line of manicured bushes inside the perimeter. Manwe worked his way around the lawn and gardens, on the lookout for an entrance before he spotted an open balcony at the northwestern corner of the house.

He sprinted across the grass. Like a great jungle cat, he sprang onto the wall, his arms wrapped around a corner column. He shimmied up its length and found finger holds in the pale facade, enough to climb higher toward the balcony. Moments later, he dragged himself over the fence, landing on the tiled platform in a crouched position. The two doors to the chamber beyond had been shut, locked by a simple latch inside the gap. Using his knife, Manwe levered it open and entered.

The bedroom had been torn apart, the feathers of a fine mattress spread about like the snow Manwe had heard of on his dusty savannah, but never seen, though he surmised that it looked much the same. The walls were streaked with sword-slashes, spear-holes, marks left behind by the reavers who had come, looted, and then ransacked for no reason other than the opportunity to do so.

The door had been left open, and through its crack seeped a small bit of orange light.

Soft-stepping to the door, Manwe looked through, spying an empty hall but not the origin of the rosy light. Opening it a bit more, he slid through the space he created and stopped, his ears keyed for any human sound. To his right, down the passage, a fire still out of sight painted the walls red. A shadow crawled across the floor, the singular shape of a man.

Manwe skirted to the threshold.

In the next room sat a lone figure facing the small blaze. His spear and hide shield on the ground beside him, a sack of loot lay against the wall near a window that overlooked Tolivius' smoking ruins to the south. Shoulders sagged, the reaver hung his head.

Silent, Manwe crawled behind his target. Rearing up, he grabbed the man's head with his left while pressing his knife into the right side of his neck. "Shout and I will kill you."

The captured reaver shuddered. "…Manwe?"

That voice, too high for a man's, made Manwe pause. Moving around his hostage, he looked upon the illuminated face and gasped. "Kaarle?"

Tears ran black paths on the young rebel's face, which scrunched as he froze in Manwe's clutches. "Are you a spirit come to claim me? Has the Mother sent you to collect the debt of my evils?"

Manwe's knife clattered on the floor when he took his friend in his arms. He shushed him, eyes to the hallway from where he had first entered. Fixed on how exposed he made himself, he patted Kaarle on the back of his woolen hair, speaking in low, soothing tones. "Where is the voduni, Kaarle? Where can I find him?"

"Voduni Calla?" Kaarle sniffled his despair.

"Tell me, boy. If you ever want to make right what you've done, you'll tell me now."

"He went north, to where the lords he once served lived. Kosey is with him." Speaking in a slow, hollow tone, Kaarle did not take his wet eyes from the fire, too haggard to break his listless gaze. "They told us to do whatever we wanted. They didn't care if we ran, or stayed, or lived, or..." He clenched them shut.

Manwe released his embrace. "Do you really wish to make amends, little brother?"

Kaarle looked his way. "Yes," he said without hesitation. "More than anything, yes."

"Then run." He bore the seriousness of his order in his eyes and voice, a forceful bass that inflected every word. "Run south, to the Gypians. They may imprison you, they may kill you, but run to them. Tell them that the dread priest that raised the dead lies in the north of the city. Tell them to rain their artillery there at dawn." Manwe paused at the next order, blinking his doubt before he steeled himself. "Tell the Gypians to level it."

"Where will you be?" Kaarle asked, his full lips parted in confusion. "What will you be, Manwe?"

"It doesn't—"

"There!" Standing in the hall's threshold, a reaver pointed out the pair with his spear to his six brothers and sisters, who crowded the passage.

Manwe yanked Kaarle to his feet by the back of his neck, pushing him toward the window of the room. "Go!" He charged without checking to see which way the boy ran, letting his knife lead him to the enemy before the seven reavers flowed from the hall.

Manwe met the first attacker, dodging past his spear thrust with a flourish that brought his knife to the man's throat. The artery severed, blood fanned in a gory mess. Turning in time to deflect a sword blow with the spine of his blade, Manwe skipped to the left to let a third reaver run into the second man. Tangled together, they were helpless as he jabbed at their faces, leaving them blinded.

The final four, momentarily startled by Manwe's viciousness, attacked in concert, prodding at him to create room to defend their wounded comrades. Slashing wildly, Manwe wheeled backward, avoiding the longer reach. He screamed when one of the barbs entered his side, a shallow puncture that upset his balance enough to send him careening into a wall.

His knife pinned at his side, Manwe threw himself back hard, causing two of the spear-wielders to miss what would have been mortal blows. The iron heads buried into the smooth plaster. Manwe sneered at them, the pain of his wound radiating as he pounced on one of the reavers that failed to dislodge her spear from the wall. Snapping his forearm down on the shaft in the woman's hands, he broke off the head and backhanded her. Reeling, she crashed into the two fighters who had joined her attack, a disruption that allowed him space to pull the broken piece free. He swung out, the sharpened head of the spear tearing a reaver's chest apart. Following up with his knife, he penetrated the lioness he had disarmed in the heart, lodging his blade in her ribs.

The last of the trio swung his sword. Manwe brought up his broken spear in both hands to catch the edge on small section of wooden pole afforded to him. The blow tore it from his hands, but he lunged, tackling the swordsman to the ground where he battered him until the man stilled.

Quiet took the room. Hot blood smeared the floor, puddles that streaked where two of the reavers writhed, caught in the agony a sharp knife had made of their faces.

His side wet, Manwe pawed the cold spot to the right of his stomach, wincing each time his sticky fingers touched its raw borders. A flesh wound at best, he ignored the fire it made when he breathed, looking instead for the body of the woman where he sheathed his knife. He yanked it free with a gross sound, like a fruit being squeezed.

On both knees, Manwe brought himself to his right foot first, then the left, before he pushed to a standing position. Guts turned at sudden movement, making him grip the nearest wall for support. He looked up when his stomach calmed, glad to see Kaarle had escaped.

Fulfilled by that fact, he focused on his final two victims, eager finish what he started.

BLOOD SPOTTED THE STONE IN HIS WAKE.

What had started as a small drizzle ebbed to a dried crust, a jagged set of tributaries for a shallow river of crimson, now flaking away from his black skin in shreds. The pain, dull and warm, stung where it once burned, allowing Manwe the ability to walk upright. Somewhere near the edge of Merchants' Row and the rolling hills where the lords of Tolivius built their great houses, he pilfered a healer's shop, helping himself to clean bandages and a concoction of herbs he stuffed into the hole with wheezing grunts. It was enough to do the work needed.

The smoke off the south dissipated during his trek into the uplands, revealing an ocean of bright, cold lights that seemed to go on forever and ever. The sight of these stars summoned a small sense of peace, a final respite before the cruelty of fate hammered him like a piece of ore struck between the bludgeon and its anvil.

Manwe wondered as he wandered the paved streets, drifting by abandoned mansions that not long ago would have drawn his attention, targets of wealth and promise. He gave all that wealth, all those jewels, those coins, those prizes—he had given them away for something he believed.

All people, light or dark, man, woman, or in-between—they deserved the freedom of the earth, the great Mother from where life sprang like a joyous child, innocent in temperament before it discovered the dangers of itself.

Why had he done what he had done?

For love?

He had loved Toba, his passions, the need for a freedom. Such an idea that had been unthinkable until it was whispered beneath the sheets of their bed, a conspiracy that inflamed a patriotism he never expected to find.

Manwe wished he was back at his jackalberry tree, among the groves of umber thorns, the glistening pools of clean water that fed the herds of buffalo, zebras, even the lions and jackals.

Back where things had been simple. Steal here, eat there, sleep wherever. Live and let live.

The smell found him first—the sick of death and dying. It glommed the humid air of the post-midnight world. His left hand unconsciously went to his wound, worried the disease carried by the wind might somehow seep, spreading a sickness. A sound came next, a low, droning note that persisted, louder and louder when, finally, he ascended for crest of the next rise and spotted something odd.

A line of ghouls stood in the middle of the pavement, their sagging arms spread out to the sides and their heads cast back.

Rotten maws opened to reveal their broken and tar-stained teeth as they faced south. Some wore the cracked armor they had died in, or some simply posted, pale, naked, and bloated. Clothed or not, whole or battered by whatever end they had suffered, the ghouls sang in harmony, a dread unison Manwe had never considered them capable of.

He approached, slow at first, his knife held before him. When he neared the top of the hill, he halted again, this time startled by the appearance of a second line, then a third! Inching closer to this silent, unmoving wall, Manwe soon saw a sight both wondrous in symmetry and terrifying when he considered the sheer force of will needed to have made it.

Multitudes.

The word seemed so small, feeble for what Manwe wanted, but it fit for the rows upon rows upon rows of dead that dotted the northern hills, all of them holding their arms out to hug the sky. Monuments to the ruin he once wanted himself, Manwe understood the point of Voduni Calla's display as he came right to the edge of this dare, this flagrant show of defiance in the face of the Gypian Empire's artillery. In grids set upon the grass green, the sidewalks, the lawns of stately dwellings that once housed his tormentors, he laid his last line, a warning that no matter how many times the catapult battered his numbers, he would make more.

Manwe brushed his blade against the back of a ghoul's open hand, expecting it to lash out. The dead thing, once a Juutan, simply continued to gape at the starry sky, caught in whatever twisted nightmare his master imbued.

Ducking past the arm and slipping in the spaces between this slave and the ghoul in front of him, Manwe picked his way through the lines, holding his breath when he could to forestall his stomach's need to loosen its content. The journey, slow and arduous, placed him on the other side of the hill's crest minutes later. He found a spot where the wind did not seep sickness, ending his dip under the arm of a slain child that had posed issues traversing.

In the shallow valley below, where the few heads of government had claimed, lay an empty street—save for two figures. They stood in the center of the lane, facing southward. From his place from the south, southeast, Manwe knew them—Kosey and Voduni Calla surveyed their last battlefield, the place they thought the latter's magic would win the day. No dead crowded with them, leaving them exposed, unguarded, and unaware of anything other than the field before them.

Manwe smiled at the situation. His former friend and dire enemy were perfect marks.

CROUCHED BEHIND THE GATES OF THE SENATE CONSUL'S MANOR, MANWE unbound the bandages around his torso, snorting as the mass of cloth he had padded over the stab wound peeled away. Satisfied at the lack of severe pain he expected when the stinking air hit it, he started to redress in the night shadows while Voduni Calla ranted on.

"Look upon the damned, Kosey," cawed the fell priest. "Fools are the Gypians! Imperialism has made them fat and lazy. Instead of facing us on the field of battle, as any true man of Juut would, they hide behind their war machines, relying on sciences instead of faith, trickery instead of honor!"

"Yes, voduni," replied Kosey, his words drawn in exhaustion.

"Let the sun come, boy! We shall show them the power of our people."

"Yes, voduni."

Manwe grunted in dark humor as he listened to Toba's brother scrape for a madman's approval. Tying off the knot to his wrappings, he peeked past the gates, checking to make sure neither man detected his presence. Their scarred backs, bathed umber in the blue light of the stars above, they kept their vigil pointed toward Tolivius' steaming remains. Pressing to the support block of the gate's arch, Manwe shut his eyes and concentrated on his breath and the buzz running up his spine.

At the end of it all, the fate of the savannah rested his simple thievery.

Manwe looked at Calla's back again, focused on the skeletal bastard's thin neck. The strand of leather that held his vulture skull pendant, the bone-house for the stone that enabled his vile necromancy, sat in a heavy knot just above the first visible vertebrae. Had his victim been an innocent, Manwe would have taken care to remove the jewelry without harm—a consideration he need not pay this time. He thumbed the edge of his knife, waiting for the perfect moment.

Time progressed in silent foreboding, weighed by a direness that dimmed the molten hunger that devoured the city below. The wind changed then, and upon its current traveled a new smell. Not the same rot Manwe had grown so used to, but an acrid scent. Was it ripped from the lines of undead that plagued the gentle slopes, or born of destruction that came with the death of any city? Confused by this sudden infusion into the warm fall night, it gave him pause.

Voduni Calla spoke again. "Does it boil, Kosey?"

"It does, voduni."

"Good. It will be over soon, champion. You will finally reap your reward."

"I hope so," Kosey replied.

"Go and get the pot," Calla said gently. "Be careful not to burn yourself."

Kosey, muscle and sinew, lumbered out of sight, leaving the voduni alone.

Manwe began his approach, the grass beneath his feet muffling his steps. Iron-eyed, jaw firmed, he gave a quick glance to where Kosey walked. The warrior's shadow stretched long to the west, as behind the three of them the edge of night warmed, the red light of dawn welling like blood.

The seconds slowed until finally Manwe stepped onto the white pavement, his knife raised to strike at the man who had blighted the freedom Toba gave his life for. Voduni Calla cried out, the iron blade flaying apart the nape of his neck. Manwe swung his free hand around, moving his enemy off-balance enough to catch the vulture skull as it slid down the front of his dingy black robes.

Manwe almost laughed aloud as he darted away. The voduni screamed after him, his pained cry transformed to one of shocked outrage. Running hard down the flat street, he met the turn in the road with a hard skid. Legions of undead shuffled up the rise, their grotesque states hindering their speed, which was quickly made up by their overwhelming numbers.

Seeing the descent choked with ghouls, as well as the hills immediately to his left and right, Manwe retreated for a moment before he ran square into Kosey's broad chest. He stumbled back from the fallen rebel leader, who carried at his side a small iron bucket of simmering tar.

The two former friends stared hard at each other for a brief moment, exchanging relief and hatred for what fate had cast as their roles.

"Die, Panther," Kosey shouted, driving in to spill the bucket on Manwe, who dodged to the side of the black goo. Spinning into a wide wheeling kick, Manwe swung his heel into the back of Kosey's head, knocking him face first into the burning puddle he made on the sidewalk.

Screaming as he smacked its center, Kosey flopped over involuntarily, his agony a high note as the substance boiled flesh from muscle and bone.

Too horrified to look at his former friend's deserved death, Manwe returned to his previous path, only to meet Voduni Calla. The voduni wove his hands in an intricate pattern, mumbling words beneath the wind as the world brightened around them.

Suddenly free from the bonds of gravity, Manwe flew to the side, cast like a stone by some invisible force. Smashed into the fence of the Senate Consul's home, he fell to the ground in a bruised, bleeding mess.

"It has... been... long since I willed the spirit without the stone," Voduni Calla said, panting to regain his breath. He drew his dagger from its place on his thin belt. "To know one's limits in light of afforded limitlessness is... refreshing."

Manwe had lost his knife. Unable to focus, his vision blurred when he posted up on his arms, coughing a glob of blood when he tried for a breath. The vulture skull had remained in his hand. Sunlight flowed over the street, deepening the voduni's shadow as it fell over him. Day arrived, and satisfied with how things had gone, he let himself collapse on his side.

"Beg me, thief," Voduni Calla goaded, his poisoned face cut by the shadows of the sun. His eyes, the bloodshot and dotted black, glowed. "Beg me to make you a ghoul. It will be kinder than other the other things I will do."

Manwe spat blood at his nemesis' feet. "Just hold on."

Calla kicked him hard in the chest, driving the wind from his body. Breathless, Manwe wheezed in attempt to laugh, hugging the vulture skull to his chest. The pathetic sound drove the voduni into a deeper rage, and he kicked him again, and again, and again, until he hobbled away, having broken his toes. He limped back over, shoving Manwe onto his back so he could mount him. He forced his dagger under his chin, the edge hot against the black scruff over the apple of his throat.

Manwe laughed at him.

"Why are you laughing, fool?" Voduni Calla pressed the blade in. "You're about to die."

Manwe grabbed the voduni by the back of his head, pulling him down until their noses touched. "We're going to die together."

His foe tried to pull away when the first stone cast by the Gypians dropped a few feet from where they lay. Dust blossomed with the shattering of pavement. Before Voduni Calla could react to the sudden explosion, Manwe tossed the vulture's skull—and the stone—into the crater the impact had created. Another boulder landed on the same spot, and the sunny world pitched to darkness as the magic released, blowing away Manwe's consciousness in an instant.

***

FOR ALL THE INVASIONS, THE REBELLIONS, THE CREATION OF GOOD THINGS and the destruction of the bad, Manwe knew life never made sense.

Only nature did.

The bosom of Mother Earth could be cruel or caring, but no matter what she gave to the things born of her flesh, all thieves knew that she would claim her dues in the end. She would eat his body, wear at his bones, returning the child to her womb while his spirit sank to the underworld to be judged worthy or deficient. The cost of the latter meant he might live again—another life, another strife to endure.

So when he opened his eyes to the broken streets of Tolivius, whole and unharmed, the confusion that followed settled hard. Leaning against the broken column that once served as the gatepost for the Senate Consul's manor, a question formed as he woke. "How?"

"Magic."

Cleon rested beside him, clad in his red robes that dazzled in midday. His face freshly shaved, he seemed no worse for wear than the time the two lovers had last seen each other.

Overcome with emotion, Manwe scrunched his face as the tears rolled. His hands came up without warning, the meat of his palms grinding into the sockets as sobs racked his body.

Cleon scooted closer and drew Manwe into his embrace. They sat there for long, long minutes, exposed to the gentle eddies of a cloudless blue sky clean of smoke, the stench of the dead, or any sign that their world had ended there. Calm found Manwe, and wheezing past the snot in his nostrils, he glanced out at what remained of Tolivius.

On the gentle hills lay a rug of rubble, and beneath that, the soil had blackened with the blood of the ghouls. The great manors lay in tattered bits, mounds of debris dotting the places where the mighty and powerful of the west had ruled the savannah with such certainty for so long.

And now they were gone.

The revolution was over.

"I never wanted it to be like this," he said, his mouth trembling. "I never wanted so many to suffer, to die. I just wanted my people free."

"And now they are, Panther," said Cleon. "They are free from of Gypus, of Tolivius, and of evil. At least for now."

Manwe rose, hips pressed against the gatepost. "Where are the Gypians? I thought they would want to retake the city after their victory."

"Oh, no." Cleon got to his feet and brushed off the back of his ruby coat. A small smile turned his lips up, and his brown eyes sparkled as he lifted his gaze to the sky. "Too many lost, too few to gain. They took what survivors they had and headed westward. I can only imagine how the emperor is going to react when he hears that nothing was won."

"And the Juutans?"

"To the spiced winds, Manwe, as they have always gone."

He nodded. He pawed the back of his loincloth's band, wondering where his knife had gone. Catching sight of the rubble again, he sniffed sadly at the realization that it was probably gone with Calla, Kosey, and everything else. "I tried looking for you. I thought you had fallen."

"I did. Or at least I did for a moment. Magera was incredibly sore that I did not come and find you after I dragged myself to—"

"Magera!" Manwe broke away, sprinting south to clear the hill. Cleon followed behind as they picked across the fragmented roads. When they met the bottom of the descent, they came to an outlook that the Gypians had built long ago, a stone fencing that survived the westerner's bombardment.

With a view that surveyed the entire breadth of the south, the entirety of the destruction was made clear.

Save for one building.

Where the temple quarter once stood, only a single spire remained, pink marble that glistened like a torch to hope, feeding down into a foundation untouched by what had befallen all else. The Temple of the Goddess of Love shone like a beautiful rose, a testament to the goodness still left in what had been a place bereft of it. The sacrificial fires in its halls burned, billowing white smoke to bless luck and bounty. Out on one of its many precipices, a tiny figure swathed in blue silk waved at them.

Manwe sank to his knees, black arms hung on the stone fence of the overlook, weeping happiness. Cleon secured him from behind in his gentle arms and whispered how much he loved him. Silenced by the emotion he refused to restrict, the thief let his sorcerer say what was needed, knowing that he would reply likewise when able.

The winds whipped the savannah, carrying ancient secrets from scrub and squat trees only the Mother knew. She sang to her children, man and beast alike, who answered in beautiful notes or cacophonies, as they were meant to. The world continued on as it had, different than it was before.

There would always be masters, slaves, lords, and thieves, but as always, there would remain one constant.

Change.

For Manwe, the world had changed, yet for better or worse, love still reigned with the Mother. If fate was kind, it would seed whatever came next.

For Manwe, that had been the revolution Toba had fought for.

THE END

FALSTAFF BOOKS

Want to know what's new
And coming soon from
Falstaff Books?

Try This Free Ebook Sampler
http://bit.ly/falstaffsampler

Follow the link.
Download the file.
Transfer to your e-reader, phone, tablet, watch, computer, whatever.
Enjoy.

ABOUT THE AUTHOR

BORN ON A GRIM GRAY DAY, Jay Requard is an Epic Fantasy and Sword & Sorcery author currently residing in Charlotte, North Carolina. With experience in medieval fencing, grappling, boxing, and kickboxing, his work features hardened heroes set against the greatest odds with little more than hope and the strength of their arms to save themselves. A graduate of the University of North Carolina at Charlotte, his love of the Iron Age, India, Scotland, history, and religion infuse his work with themes of social struggle, redemption, love, and the power of the spirit.

Jay is also Business Manager of Falstaff Books.

In his spare time Jay enjoys lifting, brewing, cooking British and Indian cuisine, and hiking the Blue Ridge Mountains. He is also an avid gamer and has a fluffy cat named Mona.

ALSO BY JAY REQUARD

War Pigs
Reefer Snakes!

www.ingramcontent.com/pod-product-compliance
Lightning Source LLC
Chambersburg PA
CBHW031957180726
48283CB00008B/2462